ONE LAST SIN

by
Randolph Tower
and
Barbara M. Hodges

Coastal Dunes Publishing

Coastal Dunes Publishing
187 Alyssum Circle
Nipomo, CA 93444

Author's Note

This book is a work of fiction. Names and characters are used fictitiously, and any resemblance to actual persons is coincidental.

Acknowledgments

A big thank you to my writing partner Randolph Tower, this is our second book together and it was even sweeter this time around. Santa Maria Word Wizards, I couldn't do this without all of you. My mom, Jean, I wouldn't be a writer without learning early a love for stories and words. A big a-r-o-o-o to Jan Cook and Stuart, who won the right to choose Rainbow the basset hound's sex in the story. And last, but never least, my husband Jeff. Without you it would be much harder to do what I love.

Barbara M. Hodges

I want to thank my writing partner, Barbara M. Hodges, who fills my empty rooms with color and life and makes me look like a real writer. My wife Beverly keeps me on the right path and I owe her much. The Word Wizards of Santa Maria are a great writing group and every writer should have a group like this. The Central Coast of California is a wonderful place and any changes or errors in locations are poetic license and necessary to protect the unwary.

Randolph Tower

ALSO BY BARBARA M. HODGES

The Blue Flame (Book One of the Daradawn series)
The Emerald Dagger (Book two of the Daradawn series)
The Silver Angel (Book three of the Daradawn series)
Magical Stew
Shadow Worlds (Co-written with Darrell Bain)
A Spiral of Echoes (Co-written with Maggie Pucillo)
Ice (Co-written with Randolph Tower)

ALSO BY RANDOLPH TOWER

The Last Dawn of Reckoning
Ice (Co-written with Barbara M. Hodges)

Darcie Devonshire

MORGAN AND I stood on the bluff looking down to where the surf pounded against a two-toned, gray, Buick sedan, wedged between algae-stained boulders. We'd had arrived on the scene thinking the body would already be recovered, and had been surprised to find the deputies and the highway patrol still milled around.

"Shit, they haven't done a damn thing. We could be here all day," I said.

"Cheer up. It won't be all day. The fog'll be rolling back in a couple of hours and that'll put a stop to everything." Morgan grinned.

I glared at him. "That makes me feel so bloody much better."

"Don't go all hyper on me, Devonshire. We wait."

"I don't do wait." I walked over to the young patrolman who'd responded to the anonymous call. "Officer, what's the plan?"

"Called the district office. San Luis Obispo's sending a helicopter rescue team to get the body out. They're already in the air. "

"You sure there is a body?" When he didn't answer, I went on. "When's the tow truck getting here?"

"I don't know if one has been sent for."

"You'll have to winch the car up. You know no one's getting down there."

He frowned. "Like I said, Detective, I don't know."

Morgan arrived beside me. "Darcie, let's sit in the Beamer. I'm freezing my ass off." He grabbed my arm and led me to the car. Inside he handed me coffee. "Drink."

"That shit's cold." I said.

"Drink it anyway."

"How do they even know it's Everett Cummins?" I took a sip of my tepid coffee.

Morgan shrugged. "The Buick's registered to Cummins, but it's possible there could be someone else inside. Hell, there might not be any one in the car at all."

I glared at him. "There damn well better be."

The low thump, thump of a helicopter's blades came to me. "Air

rescue's here." I opened the Beamer's door.

The helicopter circled the Buick twice and then hovered above.

"Good thing the winds not blowing," Morgan said.

A side door in the helicopter opened. A man in a harness stood there. He backed out, hung suspended from a cable. A moment later, he started down.

The man landed on the rocks, slipped as a wave hit not three feet below him.

"Damn. I wouldn't want that job," I said.

The man made his way to the driver's side door and opened it. A minute later, he looked up and shook his head.

"Well, someone's in there," Morgan said. "And they're dead."

"But, is it Everett Cummins?"

The man pulled a limp body halfway out of the Buick and then fastened another harness around its waist. He made an up motion with his hand, and the two of them ascended. At the helicopter's side they were both pulled in and the door closed.

Chapter One
The Crash

SMOKE BELLOWED FROM a remote area of Nojoqui Falls. Traffic on South 101 slowed to stare and in the Danish village of Solvang people stopped on the streets and pointed toward the southwest.

When the Santa Barbara County Fire Department arrived on the scene, flames had already engulfed the grassy clearing. The smell of jet fuel confused the firefighters at first, until the sight of a vertical stabilizer came into view and indentified the cause of the fire -- a crashed Lear jet.

With practiced precision, they surrounded the blaze and began the complicated process of extinguishing a fuel fed fire.

"Must be a private plane," one said as he sprayed fire retardant on a stubborn flame.

The captain took off his helmet, wiped sweat from his face. "It burned quick. There's going to be bodies, but it's too hot to tell how many right now."

"Captain, Captain, over there, some more of it," a firefighter shouted, pointed.

At the clearing's edge, away from the charred grass, another section of the vertical stabilizer rested and a hundred yards beyond it, the burned cockpit.

"Check it out," the captain ordered.

The first firefighter to the cockpit looked into the melted and deformed fiber glass side window and yelled. "There's two bodies." He stepped back from the window, moved to the other side of the twisted metal, then stopped, stunned. Lying on the ground was a man, unharmed as far as he could tell. "Get a medic over here."

A paramedic rushed up and leaned down to check for a pulse. "He's alive." Frowning, he straightened, swept his gaze over the still form. "He doesn't have a mark on him. '

The man moaned as they lifted him onto a stretcher.
"He's coming to."
 The paramedic knelt beside the man. "Sir, are you in pain?"
The man blinked without speaking."
"Are you hurt?"
The man frowned. "Where am I?"
"What's your name, sir?"
For a long moment the man didn't answer, and then his eyes widened. "I don't know. Why the hell don't I know?" He struggled to rise, then shuddered and dropped into unconsciousness again.
"Damn," the paramedic said. "Get this man in the ambulance."

Chapter Two
Gail Crane

I TAPPED THE end of the ball point pen against my front teeth. Day one on the job after vacation and it seemed like it would never draw to a close. I couldn't seem to come to terms with being back in the field office. Maybe the time had come for me to think about an early retirement. I had in almost twenty years with the bureau and there were things I wanted to do, like travel to Germany. Maybe I could put in for undercover again? It'd been awhile since I'd gone under.

I straightened the nameplate on my desk, Special Agent Gail Crane. It still gave me goose bumps to read it. It had been a gift from Mom and Dad on my graduation from the FBI academy and had moved with me to twelve different locations. Next to it was a picture of me with my parents at the same graduation. They stood to each side of me; I looked like a giant between them. Both of my parents came in at maybe 5'6". The height listed on my driver's license said 5'10". I was closer to six feet.

Jeez, I looked like such a nerd. My usual, shoulder-length dark hair was cut in a bob, shorter than I'd ever worn, and I didn't have on a speck of make-up. I wore a gray blazer and slacks with a white shirt. My dad wore almost the same ensemble. My serious dark eyes stared straight into the camera lens.

I shook my head and smiled. I'd had a picture in my mind about how a female FBI agent should look and had strove to fit the image. Well one thing, even dressed that way there was no chance I could be taken for a boy. Even at twelve I'd been curvy and the curves had become more pronounced by the time I was sixteen.

I glanced at the clock, sighed; ten minutes had passed since the last time I'd looked.

In three weeks I would be in wind-scoured Santa Maria, California for twenty-four months. Twenty-four seemed to be my magical number; I'd never remained in one spot longer.

I wonder where I'll go next.

Until now I hadn't cared, but I liked Santa Maria. I even had friends here.

Darcie Carmichael was one of them. She and I planned to have a few drinks and catch up right after work. Darcie was a Santa Maria police detective. It seemed the only female friends I ever acquired were on the job.

She'd gotten all mysterious when we'd talked, and I'd bet my nine-millimeter Glock it had something to do with Morgan Garrett. They'd been partners and lovers when they'd both been with the CIA. That had gone sour, but they'd managed to find each other again and rekindle the flame.

I frowned out the window. There wasn't one ex-lover I'd want to hook up with again, but none of them could be called lovers, more like warm bodies to release some tension.

The desk phone rang and I almost groaned. No. Not now. I stared at it; debating, he wouldn't know I wasn't in the bathroom. On the sixth ring, I gave in. "Hello."

"Gail, we got a strange one," my supervisor, Harry Shindley said. "Santa Barbara Fire Department found this guy beside a wrecked plane."

"So?"

"The others were burned beyond recognition, but he's alive. Hell, he wasn't even hurt, except for the amnesia."

"Let me get this straight. The guy's lying outside the cockpit of a wrecked plan, no injuries, and he's claiming loss of memory?"

"That about covers it. The emergency room doctor called it, wait a minute, I wrote it down, retrograde, possibly anterograde, amnesia. They're not sure at this point. He's being MRI'd, CT'd and EEG'd. He's at Marian Medical Center. I want you to go talk to him."

"Why are we interested?"

"My left palm's itching."

I laughed. "I thought that meant you were coming into money."

"Don't be a wise ass. This whole thing doesn't smell right. Check it out."

Good-bye drink and good-bye Darcie. I stood. "I'm on my way

out the door."

*****

Marian Medical Center is off East Main Street, five minutes from my office.

I found a parking slot for visitors and slid in.

The wind whipped my hair into my eyes and brought the smell of a broccoli harvest in progress as I climbed from my tan sedan.

Opening the double glass doors the generic odors of hospitals; bleach and sickness, hit my nose. After a quick stop at the front desk I found the second floor room easy enough. Entering, I could see our mystery man. He sat in a chair and flipped through a magazine. Judging by the gray in his dark sideburns, I guessed his age to be close to mine, mid to upper forties.

I cleared my throat and he looked up.

"Sir, my name is Gail Crane, FBI." I held up my I.D. "Do you feel like talking?"

His brown eyes locked with mine. "I wish everyone would stop treating me like I'm a basket case."

"Well, you have been through quite an ordeal. I don't want to cause you any distress."

He tossed the magazine on the floor. "Too late for that. It's pretty distressing not to know who you are."

"What can you remember? Let's start there."

"I woke up, stretched out on the ground with a paramedic bending over me asking if I was okay, before that, nothing."

"Sir, did you have anything in your pants pockets?"

"Nothing, but it wouldn't have helped anyway."

"Why do you say that," I asked.

"They aren't mine," he said glancing at the stack of clothes on the chair by the closet.

"How do you know those aren't yours?" I said.

"They don't fit. The shoes are well worn, but the wear patterns in the soles don't match my feet. The shirt's too big, the pants too short, and worst of all the damn underwear rides up. I hate jockey shorts." He stopped for a moment with a bewildered look on his face. "How do I know that?"

"You're saying you don't feel comfortable in those clothes?

He looked at me like I was the one who needed medical care.

11

"They aren't mine."

"You understand I have to take them with me."

"Go ahead. Anything you find won't be about me," he said.

"Maybe, but it's a place to start." I held up my cell phone. "I'd like to take your picture. Any objections?"

"Do whatever you think will help you find out who-the-hell I am."

*****

I stared across the office and out my one window, amazed at what I was hearing. The recording was of Tom Singer, my occasional partner, conducting the crash scene interview with the National Transportation Safety Bureau's agent, Dave Kelicoe.

I turned the recorder up.

"The aircraft was cleared to fly straight out from the airport, which was almost direct to the GVO, that's Gaviota Vortac," Kelicoe said. "It looks as if she was exactly on course. There was a slight flicker in the transponder signal and the airplane started a descent, which, as you can see, ended up here."

"Explain the transponder signal again for me."

"The transponder responds to a signal from a ground station by transmitting a pre-selected coded sequence back to the ground equipment."

"Can you simplify that," Singer asked.

"The aircraft's given a four digit code such as 4545, which they program into the transponder. Whenever the ground station queries the aircraft the transponder answers with its preset code, telling the operator on the ground this is the aircraft they're tracking."

"Did the Lear send out an SOS?"

"No. Since they were in direct radio contact with departure control, any distress call would have been verbal over command radio."

"What about the unidentified man they found next to the cockpit?"

"He couldn't have been on the plane. He was unmarked, no cuts, scratches or burns of any kind. That nose section tumbled several times before it came to rest, and how would he have gotten out?

I heard some papers rustle, then Kelicoe's voice went on.

"The four recovered bodies were burned beyond recognition, but we have no reason to believe they weren't the four that were on

board when the plane took off from Santa Maria Airport."

"You know for sure there were just four?"

"The line boys for Global Air, the fixed base operator that handled the ground servicing of the crashed airplane, said four got on, pilot, co-pilot and two passengers. They didn't know their names. We'll have to get them from the owner, Sam Hughes."

"So this mystery guy just wandered up?"

"I can only tell you what I know for sure. I'll know more once we've reassembled the plane and gone over it."

"Where's that going to happen?"

"Mister Hughes is letting us use his hanger."

"And when?"

"It will take a few days for the plane parts to be moved from the park."

There wasn't anything more. I turned off the tape recorder, settled back in my chair and frowned. How had our mystery man ended up next to that cockpit? Someone had to have put him there? Why? Who was he? I rubbed at my forehead. Amnesia? I'd heard that one before. Was it for real? I knew who could tell me sure. I picked up the phone, punched in a number.

"Hello."

"Marty, it's Agent Gail Crane."

"My God, girl, it's been ages. How do I rate?"

"It's those sea-green eyes of yours."

He chuckled. "What can I do for you Gail?"

I told him about the mystery man. "Is it possible for you to meet with my John Doe tomorrow?"

"Tomorrow?"

"I know it's short notice. Marty, I…"

"No, it's okay. Shellie's got a Red Hat meeting. What time and where is our boy?"

"Marian Medical Center. Time wise, how about ten?"

"Okay, I'll meet you in the lobby."

"Thanks Marty. I owe you one."

Who were the pilot, co-pilot and passengers? I stood, grabbed for my purse. I had to get out to Global Air, and talk to those line boys, now, while their minds were still clear.

****

My cell phone rang just as I turned onto the approach road to the

Santa Maria Airport I pulled to the side and stopped. It was Tom Singer. "Gail, where are you?"

"The Santa Maria Airport."

"Have you talked to the mystery man?"

"Yes, but he wasn't much help."

"What did he say," Singer asked.

"He says he doesn't remember anything before he woke at the crash site."

"Is he telling the truth?"

"Come on Tom, how do I know? He seemed to be in genuine distress; of course he could be a good actor and lying through his teeth. I've got a call into Doctor Fields; he's agreed to meet with me tomorrow morning."

"So what are you doing at the airport?"

"I'm going to talk to the line boys while their memories are still fresh and find out the identities of the four dead people."

"Good idea. Are you coming back to the office?"

"I plan to, unless something comes up here."

I'd flown from the terminal before so I knew there were no private offices inside; Global Air had to be in one of the other out buildings. A mile down the access road I came to a closed gate. After I pushed a button, a male voice said, "Sam Hughes. What can I do for you?"

"Gail Crane, FBI. I'd like to speak with you about the plane crash at Nojoqui Falls."

"Sure thing."

The gate clicked and whirred as it slid to the side.

The hangar entrance was a regular door built into a larger sliding door, both opened into a gleaming, grey painted floor and walls. The hangar smelled like jet fuel, grease and Pine-Sol. Fluorescent lights made it look daylight bright inside. Yellow stripes defined a walkway.

"Over here."

I looked toward the voice. In an office to the side of the hangar floor, two young guys waited with an older man who moved to meet me halfway.

"Sam Hughes, the manager of Global Air. You have some ID?"

I showed him my credentials. "I'd like to talk to the line boys who were here when the Lear departed."

14

"Yes Ma'am." He waved the two boys forward. "This is Juan and Rick. They serviced the Lear and were standing by when it left."

The two young men looked to be college students. They wore red pants and T-shirts. Day-glow orange jackets lay on the couch behind them. They both smiled nervously.

"Let's sit over there," I said, motioning toward the couch along the wall. They followed, but remained standing in front of me. "Tell me how many people were on the airplane."

"There were four, pilot, co-pilot and two passengers," the dark haired line boy, introduced as Rick, said.

"Yeah, two pilots are required on the Lear," Juan added.

I looked at Sam Hughes. "Do you have the names of the four?"

He picked up a sheet of paper. "Figured you would ask. Pilot was Jacob Stanislaw, the co-pilot Jerome Clark and the passenger Vladik Yakov and Josef Urni."

I entered the names into my tablet and then turned back to the line boys. "Do you have any idea why the plane crashed?"

"No. She looked fine, but we didn't take care of the Lear. The pilot was in a hurry though, kept asking how much longer, while we refueled, but most of them do that," Rick said.

"Yeah, some are real impatient," Juan added, with a quick look at Sam Hughes.

I held my cell phone out to them. "Was this man one of the pilots, or maybe a passenger?"

They both examined the photo and then shook their heads.

"Never seen him before," Rick said. "That the guy they found at the crash?"

I ignored his question, instead asked one of my own. "Was anybody else around?"

"Old Everett Cummins, he's St. James' mechanic," Rick said.

"Devlin St. James," I asked.

"Yeah, the Lear jet belongs to him," Sam Hughes said. "We keep his planes here. Do the grunt work, but only Everett Cummins takes care of the mechanics."

"Was Mister Cummins here because of an issue with the Lear?"

All three shook their heads.

"I'm afraid we can't answer that," Sam Hughes said.

"Were you here the entire time, up until the Lear took off," I asked.

"No," Rick said. "The pilot said they were waiting for someone who was running late, that we could go."

"I saw him take off about twenty minutes later," Juan said.

I nodded. "How many airplanes does Mister St. James own?"

"Two -- well, one now."

I nodded, made another note in my tablet. "I'm going to have an artist come and work with you on a description of all four of the people you saw board the airplane."

"Sure. Is that all," Rick asked.

"Yes, and thank you."

They grabbed their jackets and hurried out of the office.

"They're good kids," Sam said. "I'm sure they'll try to help."

"Let's hope," I said. "Thank you for your time, Mister Hughes."

"Anything I can do. Just let me know."

He walked me back to my car, then turned and went back into the hanger.

I glanced at my notes. Not much there. It was time to head back to the office and check out the names on the four men.

*****

I frowned at the monitor screen. Of the four men, the pilot, Jacob Stanislaw, was the only one with any information. The other three didn't exist, well not as Jerome Clark, Vladik Yakov, or Josef Urni anyway. Not a photo of any of the four. That made the upcoming time with the lineboys and sketch artist even more important.

Jacob Stanislaw was thirty-five. His last known address was in Vallejo, California. We had a field agent in the area checking on it.

I tapped my front teeth with a pen. I couldn't start looking for the other three until I had an I.D. and the sketch artist and couldn't meet with the line boys until tomorrow. Maybe it was time for another visit with our mystery man. I turned off the computer. Would he recognize the four names? The bit about him claiming the clothes not being his was interesting. If he told the truth, someone had gone to a lot of trouble to keep his identity a secret, who and why?

I smiled. The briefs had really irritated him, definitely a boxer-shorts guy. Well is our John Doe's amnesia for real. I'd know soon enough. If it was how could I jog his memory? Maybe a visit to the crash scene? To accomplish that he'd need some clothes and it wouldn't hurt our bonding for me to supply them. It seemed a good place to start. I pushed back from the desk, stood and picked up my

16

purse.

*****

I flashed my badge toward the young woman behind the counter as I walked to the elevator. Inside, I punched a button. On the second floor, the doors opened. Halfway down the hall a man stood. He glanced at me, then quickly away. It could be nothing, there were many rooms on the floor, but all of my senses went on alert.

I walked toward him. He stepped back, into a pool of darkness. At hat shadowed his face. I could see he wore a visitor's badge, but the number written on it, 458, told me he was on the wrong floor. "Afternoon."

He nodded without speaking.

"458 is on the fourth floor. Are you lost? Maybe I can help."

"Bathroom," he muttered, but it was enough for me to hear his foreign accent, German or Russian maybe. Could he be Vladik Yakov? "Down the hall, make a right. I'll walk with you."

The elevator opened behind him. Without answering, he turned his back to me and stepped inside. With his head still down, he pushed the button.

I frowned as the elevator door closed. Who was he? Why the interest in our guy? I fished in my jacket pocket, brought out my cell phone and called the office. Harry answered. I told him what had happened."

"Discription?"

"Maybe six foot, slender build, he made sure that's all I got. He could be Yakov, or even Jerome Clark. Our John Doe might be a loose end. I think we need to move him to somewhere safer."

"I trust your instincts, Gail. Make it happen. Does he need a babysitter?"

"I don't know. Let me think on it. I'm heading into his room now."

Chapter Three
Morgan Garrett

LYNDON SCARSDALE, CALIFORNIA'S newest senator had hired me before his election. Chasing down the senator's daughter is what had brought Darcie and me back together. I hadn't seen Scarsdale much after the election, and then he'd went off to Washington. For reasons I wasn't any too sure about he'd kept me on the payroll. I guess that's what comes with being rich.

Tuesday isn't my regular day to report in, but the Senator had called and asked me to make an appearance, so here I am.

Mrs. Scarsdale answered the door. "Mister Garrett, how nice to see you. Lyndon is in the library. You know the way."

I did, smiled as I walked away.

I knocked on the library door.

"Come in," Lyndon Scarsdale said.

He wasn't alone. A man sat in an over-stuffed, green plaid chair across the room. We'd never met, but I knew Devlin St. James on sight.

Scarsdale introduced us. "Morgan, this is Senator St. James."

"Ex senator, son. Now I'm just a farmer from over in Santa Ynez."

Yeah, sure, a farmer. Devlin St. James was one of the most powerful men in California. He'd been a tall, imposing figure in his prime and traces of that man remained. At eighty-seven years of age, he could still dominate any room he occupied. He had served four terms as the United States Senator from California; in addition, he had been ambassador to Japan, and Undersecretary of State. At one time his name had been bandied about as a presidential candidate. I didn't know why it had never happened…something about him turning down the offer.

"Glad to meet you Senator," I said.

"Lyndon tells me you are a pretty good man at solving

mysteries?" St. James un-wrapped a cigar as he spoke.

"I have had some luck. "

Scarsdale jumped into the conversation. "I want you to see if you can help him out. You heard about the crash at Nojoqui Falls?"

When I nodded St. James spoke. "That was my jet, and my mechanic is missing."

"I don't think I can do much about the crash. The NTSB will handle that, but I could look into your mechanics disappearance. Tell me about him." I pulled out my Blackberry. "What's his name?"

"Everett Cummins. He was eighty last month. I threw him a party. Everett has been with me for over twenty-five years."

"Do you have his address?"

"He lives in Santa Maria. You can call my secretary for the needed information. Everett said he was taking a week-end vacation, but he has been gone too long."

I nodded. "Who services your plane?"

"That's Lear jets," St. James said with a touch of arrogance.

"Then who services your *jets?*"

"Global Air. They have an office at the Santa Maria Airport."

I wondered why Santa Maria and not Santa Barbara, but I kept the question to myself. I glanced at Scarsdale. "How much time do you want me to put in on this?"

He looked pleased that I'd turned to him. "Whatever Senator St. James needs, if you don't find Cummins after a bit we'll see."

St. James lit his cigar, puffed on it and then blew out a white stream of smoke toward Senator Scarsdale. "Young man I want to stress the name, St. James, means something in this country. You will conduct yourself with such in mind."

"Of course, sir. You can rest assured that I am very discrete." Right up until it comes time not to be, I silently added.

*****

One thing about having a boss in Santa Barbara, I always have the return drive to Santa Maria to think about what he lays on me. Today's request seemed straight forward. It shouldn't be hard to find out about St. James' mechanic. Everett Cummins was eighty. I couldn't see him hiking the Alps or anything. I'd start by talking to St. James' secretary.

It was funny St. James had been in Scarsdale's library. Not ha-ha funny, but strange funny. Just a couple of weeks back I'd read a story

mentioning him in the Sunday supplement. A Russian Jewish emigrant, Asa Kaminski, had been interviewed in Cleveland. He'd told the reporter he had information about the long time missing General Harden Hathaway. The general's disappearance had remained a mystery since 1945, but the reporter said Kaminski had shown him a WWII helmet with Hathaways' name inside and hinted he knew what had happened to the general. They'd had another meeting scheduled, but Kaminski died.

The article also said Devlin St. James, then a twenty-five year old first lieutenant, had served as an aide to the missing general. St. James had even been decorated for his bravery when they'd liberated the death camp at Ohrdruf, the same camp where Asa Kaminski was interned. Nothing was said about why St. James had been noted in the article, but the reporter must have had his reasons.

My cell phone rang. It was Darcie. I looked for a place to pull over. I was tempted to just take the call, but my love was a stickler for following the law. Who would have thunk it? I saw an exit, took it and pulled to the side of the road. "Hey, beautiful," I said.

"I take you're not in a meeting."

"Why would you say that?"

"You are so crazy."

"But I'm also handsome and a sex machine. "

"One out of two isn't bad," Darcie answered.

"Ouch. Which one?"

She laughed. "Checking to see if I need me to pick anything up from the store for your dinner-making tonight?"

I mentally went through the list of what I'd already purchased. "Some garlic bread. I forgot that."

"It's Italian, then?"

"Not saying. It's a surprise. Remember?"

"We could just go out, you know with your drive to Santa Barbara and all…."

"Nope. I'm cooking. Tonight's gonna be special."

"Oh, Morgan, they're all special."

"Ah shucks, Ma'am, you're making me blush, but I'm still not telling you more. You just be at your place at 6 PM."

"Fine, just fine. I'll see you tonight." She ended the call.

I laughed as I closed my cell phone. Darcie so hated when things didn't go her way.

Since I was already off the road, I decided to give St. James' secretary a call. "Miss Nina Cramshaw," I said when a voice answered.

"Miss Cramshaw has left for the day, a family emergency. Maybe I can help?"

"Devlin St. James asked me to speak with Miss Cramshaw about..."

The voice cut me off. "Then by all means you must speak with her. She will be in tomorrow morning at nine o'clock."

I barely got out, "Thank you," before the call ended.

Well, no help there. I wasn't far from the Santa Maria Airport. Maybe there were some answers in that direction.

My GPS took me right to Global Air. The hangar stood behind a no-nonsense-looking fence, I drove up to the gate, pushed a button, expecting someone to answer, instead the gate slid open. So much for airport security, 911, and the whole program. I drove in and parked.

The huge hangar doors were open and a Lear was being towed onto the ramp. I watched for a moment and then stepped inside. I was amazed at the hospital-like cleanliness. The gray painted floors shined with a military appearance. "Hey, who's the boss around here?" I shouted at a young man in red coveralls as he jogged by.

"That's Mr. Hughes, in the office on your right."

I started to say thanks, but he was gone before I could speak.

The man sitting behind the desk wore a leather jacket and a tan ball cap with Oklahoma Sooners blazoned across the front. He looked up as I entered. "How did you get in here?"

"Uh, well I pushed the button and the gate opened."

"Damn that girl. I've told her not to do that. How can I help you?"

"Morgan Garrett. I'm looking for Everett Cummins."

"Cummins? He's on an extended vacation as far as I know. He works for Devlin St. James, not me."

"Any idea of where he'd go?"

"Hell no. Like I said, he doesn't work for me. Although I'm sure St. James wishes Cummins was here now, what with his Lear crashing and all."

"About that, mind if I ask you a few questions?"

"What's it got to do with Cummins?"

"Maybe nothing. It belonged to St James. Cummins was his

mechanic...."

Sam Hughes shrugged. "I don't know much. I wasn't here when it took off, or when it crashed."

"Who was?"

"Couple of the line boys."

"Could I speak to them?"

"Sure, but I think they are out refueling a customer. Let me check."

Turning to the microphone on his desk he called, "Rick?"

When he got no answer,he started out of his seat, at the same time the radio blared. "We're on the way in, and we've finished Mr. Clay's fueling."

"Come into my office when you get here."

There was no verbal answer simply a double click on the radio. After a short wait a young man entered the office

"Rick Kaminski," Hughes said with a motion of his hand. "This is Morgan Garrett. He's looking for old Everett. Has a couple of questions about St. James' Lear."

Kaminski? I looked closer at the kid. He had to be about nineteen. Skinny, dark hair, cut close to his head. His arms were bare and I could see a tat of a cross with flowers growing around it on his forearm. how many Kaminski's could there be? Another coincidence? I didn't like coincidences.

"Was Everett Cummins here the day of the crash?" I said.

"Yes, sir," the kid answered.

"Did he leave before the jet took-off?"

"I don't remember seeing him around, but Juan and I were in another hangar when they took off, so he could have been."

"How did he act? Did you notice anything?" I watched the kid frown.

"He just stood around."

I turned, noted a beautiful, red, bi-wing in the back corner of the hangar. "That's a dandy. Yours?"

"I wish. It belongs to Cummins," Rick Kaminski said.

"He's a pilot?"

"Yeah, but he doesn't fly anymore. He's eighty you know."

"Thanks for talking with me. Where's the other guy? Juan was it? Could I speak to him?"

"He went to the joh...oh, here he is."

22

Another young guy came into the office. He looked at me as he spoke, "You cops are sure all over this crashed plane, but the lady was prettier."

"I'm not a cop and I'm not here about the crash. I'm interested in Everett Cummins. Do you know where he went on vacation?"

"No, he didn't talk to us peons much."

"Behave Juan; the man is trying to find Mr. Cummins." Sam Hughes warned.

"Well I don't know anything about the old man." Juan said.

"Okay I guess that's it, thanks again for your help."

"Any time," Sam Hughes said.

I nodded and headed for the hangar doors.

In my car I sat for a moment and watched the hangar. Rick Kaminski came out, glanced my way and stopped. He took a couple of steps toward me and then turned and walked back into the hangar. Kaminski. He had to be related to the guy mentioned in that story. St. James is mentioned in a bit about a missing general where an Asa Kaminski has the missing general's helmet, and now there's another Kaminski working where St. James keeps his planes. Just what the hell was going on?

My phone rang. "Hello."

"Mister Garrett," a woman's voice asked.

"My phone, so yeah, it's me."

There was a pause. "Nina Cramshaw here."

St. James' secretary. "Yes, Miss Cramshaw."

"The senator called, said you needed Mister Cummins' home address."

By senator I knew she spoke of Devlin St. James. "Yes, Ma'am. Sorry to have been a bother on your day off."

"Part of my position. "

She gave me an address east of Miller. "Thank you."

She hung up with no further words.

I glanced at my watch, still plenty of time before my date.

*****

Everett Cummins' place turned out to be a small apartment complex, shaped like a U with a courtyard full of roses and green lawn. A large oak tree stood in the middle of it, shading a wood bench. Without much hope I tried the front door. Of course it was locked. Now what? I glanced around. Would he have stashed an

extra key? Maybe a neighbor had one. I'd started to walk to the next unit when someone yelled from across the courtyard.

"It's about time somebody showed up. I called and told them Mister Cummins was missing two days ago." The words came from a small, silver-haired, woman. As she spoke, she made her way toward me with the help of a spiffy looking green and chrome walker. She selected a key from a large ring she carried on a chain around her tiny waist and unlocked the door.

"Ma'am, I'm not a cop," I said.

She went very still and then with a quickness that surprised me, she reached in the pocket of her sweater and pulled out a can of pepper spray. "Then who the hell are you?"

"Whoa, hold it right there." I backed up two steps. "I'm a private investigator. Everett Cummins employer asked me to see if I could find out why he didn't show up for work."

"Who's Everett's boss?"

I knew she knew and this was a test. "Devlin St. James. Everett works for him as a mechanic."

She lowered the pepper spray. "You have some ID?"

I showed her my P.I. license.

She nodded. "Something's wrong. First Ev misses our dominos night and then his son arrives and hightails it out of here ten minutes later."

"Son?"

"Yes, I let him in. I recognized him from the photos Ev has, and he'd told me he was coming; excited about it I'll have you know. By the way I am Mrs. Delila Willoughby; my late husband was Colonel Nash Willoughby, and he left these apartments and a nice annuity to see me through my declining years."

"Delighted to meet you," I said.

"It all seems right fishy, wouldn't you say?"

I nodded.

"Do you want to go in…look around? Maybe something will tell you were Ev is?"

"I sure would. Mrs. Willoughby, how long has Everett Cummins lived here?"

"Ev moved in here the month after the Colonel died, that would be in 2007."

She unlocked the door and stepped back.

I walked inside.

What I could see was a living room with brown leather sofa, matching recliner and newer looking television set on a metal stand. Off white blinds shielded a window. The air smelled like pine cleanser.

"Cozy huh? It's got a full kitchen and good size bedroom and bath. We remodeled it last spring. Ev picked the colors."

"Do you mind if I take a look in the bedroom?" Through the still open door I heard a car honk.

"That's Miriam. We're going to the mall." She looked me over again, slowly, then handed me the key. "Lock up when you leave. Drop the key in the mail slot."

"Thanks. I won't be long."

At the door she stopped and looked back. "You must find Everett. I don't have a good feeling about all of this."

Mrs. Willoughby shut the door behind her.

I stood where I was and looked the room over again. On the wall above the sofa some photos hung. I walked to them. The one in middle showed an older guy standing next to the airplane I'd seen in Global Air's hangar. No surprise there, they'd said it was his, There was a younger guy standing next to Cummins with his hand on his shoulder. The other two photos were of Everett again with the same young man posing in front of the Eifel Tower, and then Everett with a pretty red-head on a boat with a lot of water behind them.

I walked into the bedroom. An un-opened suitcase lay in the middle of a made-up bed.

I opened the bag. It had a number of pockets and two zippered inner compartments. Inside the first section I found underwear, t-shirts. The second had jeans, polo shirts and tennis shoes. I tried one of the zipper compartments and fished out a passport. I flipped it open. The young guy's face from the photos stared back at me. His hair was longer, but it was definitely him. I looked at the name. Jonathon Wayne Cummins. Interesting, but I was looking for Everett Cummins not his son.

I looked around the room, my gaze skimmed over a desk, then jerked back to a sheet of paper lying there. I went to it. It was a note.

The senator called. Needs me to take a look at something on the Lear. I'll be back by six. Make yourself at home. It'll be great to see you, son.

25

Mrs. Willoughby said the son had left right away. So why hadn't he waited? I'd have to ask Mrs. Willoughby what time the son had arrived.

I searched the other compartment and found an international driver's license for Jonathon Wayne Cummins.

I read the note again. So Cummins went to check something on St. James' Lear jet and hasn't been seen since. The senator hadn't mentioned that detail. I glanced at my watch, almost five. I needed to get to Darcie's.

I locked up as promised, dropped the key in Mrs. Willoughby's mail slot and then headed toward my car.

Chapter Four
Darcie Carmichael

"DAMN YOU, MORGAN. Why don't you just tell me what you are up to?"

"You got something against surprises?" Wes said coming through the open door of the office we shared.

"Yeah, I do. They're highly over rated."

"What the hell does that mean?"

I turned, frowned out the window. "Don't mind me. I'm feeling a tad-bit cranky."

"You getting any sleep, partner?"

"Why would you ask that? You've been talking to Morgan." My voice rose with each word. The last one was almost a shout.

"Whoa. Whoa." Wes crossed to the office door and closed it. "You want the Captain to send you home. This is only your first, full day back on the job."

I felt my fingernails digging into my palms and forced myself to relax my hands. Avoiding Wes' eyes, I crossed back to my desk. "I'm sleeping."

"How much and how often?"

"Wes, I don't need another mother."

"Why don't you give me an answer then? You still having nightmares about Sherice?"

Leave me the bloody hell alone, the words were right on the tip of my tongue, and then I looked into his face. All I saw there was worry. I tried to make light of it. "Nightmares? Only when I'm asleep."

"Damn-it, Carmichael. Mayo's death wasn't your fault. The bullet I took wasn't your fault. The bullet Morgan took wasn't your fault. It was Sherice. *She* used the shafra to cut Mayo's throat. *She* fired the gun that took me down."

"I know, Wes. I know."

"No, you don't. You still think you could have stopped her earlier. Hell, no one knew Ice was a woman. We all thought it was a man." He took a deep breath. "You talk to Morgan about the nightmares?"

"When my screaming wakes him up." I forced a laugh. "We're quite a pair. If it's not me having the nightmares, it's him. In the old days if we had a night with no sleep, it was because we were…well you know."

"The two of you seeing anybody about them?"

"No.

"I know someone if you want to, she's good."

My hands shook as I opened my desk drawer. "Let's don't talk about it anymore. Okay?" I didn't wait for his answer. "What's the latest on the gang-bangers?"

Wes heaved a theatric sigh. "I haven't busted nary a one all week. You got any plans for the weekend?"

I shrugged. "Morgan and I talked about taking Becky to the dog park. That's about it. You guys want to bring Miracle and join us?"

Wes grinned. "Thanks, but Jackie's spending the weekend with her grandparents and you know what that means."

I held up my hands in warning. "Yeah I do, and no details, please."

"No sense of humor, Devonshire. No fun at all." Wes pushed back his chair and stood. "What you doing tonight?"

"Seeing an old friend first for a drink, then Morgan and I are having dinner together. You remember Gail Crane?"

"Yeah, FBI, right? Quite a looker."

"She just got back from a week in Hawaii, we're catching up."

"Hawaii sounds a great place for a honeymoon, don't you think?"

I looked at him hard. "Guess so. I haven't really spent any time thinking about honeymoons. You and Janey having a second one?"

"Janey and I never had a first one. She'd like that."

"Well, if you need a place to leave Miracle, I'm offering."

"Thanks. May take you up on that." He turned toward the door. "Gonna grab a doughnut from the break room, you want?"

"I'm fine." I watched Wes walk from the room. He'd brought up honeymoons. Had Morgan talked to him about our mystery dinner? What would I say if Morgan did ask me to marry him? Was I ready for a commitment like that? Yeah, he'd kicked the booze, but it was

still a battle for him. What if he lost? I couldn't go through that again.

I glanced at the clock, 4:30. An hour to go. My cell phone rang. "Detective Devonshire."

"Darcie, I can't make it for our drink. Had a case dropped in my lap. Rain check?"

A wave of disappointment swamped me. I'd been looking forward to talking with Gail. She had a way of cutting through the bullshit. We'd only known each other for a year, but it seemed like we'd been friends forever. "Sure. I understand. You call and let me know when it's a good time for you."

"I will for sure. It's been too long."

"How was Hawaii?"

"Hot, wet and reeking of pineapple."

I laughed. "Did you meet anyone?"

"None worth writing home about. How's that man of yours?"

"Morgan's fine. What can you tell me about your case?"

"Watch the evening news. It involves that private plane crash. Damn, my desk phone's ringing. I've got to take it."

"Yeah, you do. We'll talk soon." I ended the call.

Now what? I opened the file the Captain had dropped on my desk. It was a missing person case. Everett Cummins hadn't been seen by his landlady for a couple of days. An old, grainy, black and white photo had been attached to it. The guy was at least in his mid-seventies, on the short side with white hair. His face looked like a roadmap of lines. He smiled into the camera and it looked natural, like it belonged there. "So where are you? Are there grandkids missing you tonight?" I looked for any personal contact number. There wasn't one. His was employed at Global Air as an airplane mechanic. Global Air should be in the phonebook. As I reached for it, Wes came back into our office.

"It's quitting time."

"Just gonna make a call."

"You really want to keep Morgan waiting?"

"It's only five."

"Surprise him. Janey calls it being spontaneous." He grabbed his jacket. "I'll walk with you."

Chapter Five
John Doe

WHY DO I know some things, but when I try to delve deeper, my mind's a blank? I have this uneasy feeling, like I should be doing something, but what? It's there, but when I try to pull it forward it slips away. Damn. I guess my only option is to roll with it, at least for awhile.

These doctors don't seem to have any answers either. I've heard their talk while they think I'm asleep. Myself, outside the wreckage, four burned bodies inside, they're all wondering if I had anything to do with the four.

What happened before, or why the plane crashed I didn't know, but it wasn't due to me, somehow I knew that. I frowned at the window. Just how much of the attentiveness from the FBI agent has to do with those questions? Does she think I know more than I'm saying?

The nurse finished fussing with my bed and turned to me. "There now, I'll just get this IV pole out of the room. The doctor says you don't need it anymore."

"Thank you." I watched her move toward the door.

She smiled at me and said, *"Au revoir,"* with a little wave of her hand.

"Ont une bonne journée...." I stopped speaking, stunned to realize I spoke French. Good God, what did that mean?

The nurse blushed. "Oh, I'm sorry. That's all I know."

"When will the doctor be here?" I was excited. Could this mean my memory was returning?

"The resident is making his rounds, but the psychiatrist won't be here until later."

"I need to see him now. Can you call him?"

The nurse hesitated in the doorway. "I'll pass your request on."

I stood, walked toward her.

She stepped back, seemed uncertain of what to do. "Are you

okay? Maybe you should return to the bed and rest."

"I've had enough rest."

The nurse edged toward the door. "Well, if you need anything…."

"The doctor, I'd like to talk to him, please."

The nurse walked out.

I moved to the window. What did it mean that I spoke French? Was it my native language? Okay. France. "The Eifel Tower, champagne," I spoke the words aloud. Neither meant a thing to me. "So French equals…." Africa jumped into my head. "What the hell?"

That was even screwier. Have I ever been to Africa? No. Yes. Geez, I wasn't sure one way or the other.

A knock sounded on the door. Before I could say come in, it opened.

The resident, I couldn't remember his name, sauntered in with a young woman by his side. Speaking as if I was deaf he said, "This is a white male six foot one, 190 pounds. He was brought in yesterday and claims complete memory loss. No trauma or other signs of injury." He hesitated for a moment, looking down at the chart he carried. "All vital signs are normal, an interesting case. Mister Wilkins is across the hall. He's recovering from a cardiac incident. " He turned, and he and the girl marched away.

"Hey, I'm not claiming anything. You think I don't want to remember." I shouted at their backs, but neither of them bothered to acknowledge me. "Damn, I want out of here."

"I think I can make that happen." The female FBI agent came in the door. She carried a shopping bag in her right hand. "That is if the doctor says it's okay."

"Good luck with that. He isn't anywhere around."

"That's okay. I brought my own. He's right behind me."

Someone tapped on the door. "May I come in?" A silver-haired man came into my room.

"Doctor Fields, this is our John Doe." She looked at me. "Doctor Fields is a specialist in retrograde amnesia. He's out of the University of California at Los Angeles, but was returning from San Francisco and agreed to stop by."

Her own doctor, huh? Does she think I'm *claiming* loss of memory too? "Retrograde amnesia. That's what I have?" I said.

Doctor Fields walked to the end of my bed and picked up the

chart hanging there. He read for a minute or so. "The doctor's feel you are capable of learning, so it's retrograde, rather than anterograde. I've seen your test results, the MRI, CT and EEG are all normal. It's looking like a classic case of Pure Retrograde Amnesia caused by trauma." He lifted his head, looked at me. "You still have no memory?"

"Little stuff pops into my head, like speaking French and knowing the clothes I wore aren't mine. I think I've spent some time in Africa, but that's all."

"Africa? French?" The FBI agent said.

"Just happened."

"I see."

The doctor looked at my chart again. "Physically you're in great shape. They found no drugs in your system…"

"I don't mess around with drugs. I don't even drink that much."

Doctor Fields stared at me for a moment. "I meant, it doesn't seem you were drugged in anyway prior to your being found beside the jet."

My face heated. "Can I be cured?"

"With most cases time is the cure needed. We could try hypnosis."

I shook my head. "I'll pass on the hypnosis." I swung my legs to the side of the bed. "Then there's no reason for me to remain in the hospital?"

"No physical one."

The FBI agent looked at the doctor. "So he's free to leave?"

"No medical reason to keep him." Doctor Fields looked at me. "If your memory returns too quickly, or if it becomes overwhelming, you should arrange for therapy."

It seemed to me I would need therapy more if it didn't return, but I just nodded.

"Great, then I'm springing him." The agent held out the bag to me. "Clothes, including boxer shorts. Guessed at the size."

I was stunned. "Uh…well…thanks."

"Couldn't take you out of her naked." She turned toward the door. "I'll wait in the hall while you get dressed."

"Sure…uh, it was Miss Crane, wasn't it?"

"Gail Crane. You can call me Gail."

"Okay, Gail, where are we going?"

"Out to the crash site. We've still got three hours of daylight. Maybe it will help with your little memory problem."

Did I hear mockery in her tone? Her facial expression told me zip, but she was FBI. I nodded. No matter her reasons, I needed answers and it seemed about a good a place as any to start.

****

We were in the agent's tan Ford sedan and on the way to Nojoqui Falls. My new jeans, tee-shirt and athletic shoes felt like they belonged on me. I must not be a suit-wearing kind of guy. These clothes are great, but where are my others, and where do I live?

"I need to call you something," Gail said. "John Doe just isn't cutting it." She glanced at me. "How about Jerome?"

"God no."

She laughed. "Not the Jerome type? How about Duke?"

It sounded right, but not right. "Why Duke?"

"I rescued a dog once, a French poodle. I called him Duke."

"You named a French poodle Duke?"

"Yeah, I did. He just didn't seem all that French. Wasn't one of those small ones, he stood five feet tall at his head, with fur black as a moonless night. God, I loved that dog."

Loved. She'd said loved. "You don't have him anymore?"

It took a moment for her to answer. "He's at the Rainbow Bridge, the area they have reserved for heroes. Duke took a bullet for me."

"Sorry to hear that." It surprised me to realize I knew about the Rainbow Bridge. To be sure I asked. "The Bridge, that's where our pets go when they die."

"Yeah, that's right." She glanced at me again. "So what else is up there we can pry free."

I smiled. "Have no idea."

"What did the other doctors say as to why you have some memories, but can remember nothing about yourself?"

"They say the brain's like a storage bin," I said. "We move things from our receptor section and put them in cubby holes. Mine has locked the personal cubby holes, or maybe lost the key, and I don't have conscious access any longer."

"How do you know when your subconscious will know something," Gail asked.

"I don't. Someone says something, and I realize I know about that subject. This morning I discovered I speak French."

"I know you mentioned that to Doctor Fields. It happened just like that, out of the blue?"

"One of the nurses said, *'Au revoir,'* and the next thing I knew I spoke to her in French."

"Have you tried any other languages?"

"The ones I could think of, Spanish and Italian."

"And?"

"They're foreign to me."

"You try Russian?"

"Nyet." I felt her tense beside me and I smiled. Okay enough with jerking her chain. "Don't worry, that's all the Russian I know."

"So you have a sense of humor?"

"Maybe, but I can't remember any jokes. It's like walking into a room and wondering why I came in. The doctor tells me everyone has those feelings on occasion and it doesn't indicate anything serious. It just means that piece of data is lost for a moment."

"I sure hope it's not serious, because I've done that," Gail said.

"No worry. You're bright and highly focused. I've known a lot of women like you. "

She glanced at me. "Really, you remember someone like me?"

"No. I don't know why I said…well, yes, I do. I have known women like that, but I don't know where or when."

Gail slowed the car. I saw the sign for Nojoqui Falls as she turned left off of Highway 101.

"Somewhere in those cubby holes is all of your life," she said. "Keep working on it; I'm sure you'll find the key."

"From your mouth to God's ears. You're much easier to talk to then the doctors at the hospital."

"Why thank you." She slowed and turned again.

The road wound through hills with tall, brown grass. Trees, mostly oak, grew on both sides of the road. It had been foggy in Santa Maria, but here the late afternoon sun had me longing for my aviator shades.

"Do you know anything about airplanes? Lear jets in particular."

She glanced at me when I hesitated in answering. "I haven't flown the Lear 45, but I've flown the smaller Lear."

"You mean as a passenger?"

"As a pilot. I think I have flown several different airplanes. I feel I know how to do it, but I can't remember ever flying an airplane."

34

"Well, that's a breakthrough, don't you think?" Gail smiled.

She had a great smile. I caught the flash of a dimple. "I didn't know until we started to talk. I wish I could remember more."

We turned at a sign that read Nojoqui Falls County Park.

It was a pretty area with tall, spreading trees. Beyond the parking lot I could see picnic tables and a playground, but in no way did it spark a smidgeon of memory. There were five other cars in the lot. Gail parked the car next to a line of yellow tape. "We'll check in with Dave Kelicoe first. He's with the National Transportation Safety Board. Looks like they've made some headway since yesterday, they've isolated most of the airframe. Any of this mean anything to you?"

I gazed about the site. It was like I'd never been there before. I shook my head.

A man walked in our direction.

"Good morning Mr. Kelicoe. This is the gentleman they found next to the jet."

"They tell me you have no memory of the crash," Kelicoe said turning to me. His face remained expressionless too, except for the nerve twitching in his jaw. He's not a hundred percent on board with my amnesia either.

"Not a bit. Do you mind if I look around," I asked. "Maybe something will come to me."

"Go ahead," Kelicoe said. "I trust you'll tell us if you recall anything."

"Sure. Why wouldn't I?" I wandered about the crash site, mindful of where I walked, careful not to touch anything. The pieces of the blue and white jet had come to rest partially in the creek-bed formed by the runoff from the falls. The grass around the frame had burned streaming away from the aircraft. The Lear had come down between two large trees, and had landed nose low. That's strange; any pilot worth his pay would have kept the nose up for impact. I could see where the left wing had separated. The right engine had come off and spread its own fire trail.

I looked back toward the falls, envisioned the path of the Lear. It would have just cleared the top of the falls, before coming to rest here. I shook my head. No one could have survived the break-up of the fuselage; at least those poor guys were dead before the fire broke out.

Well, I hadn't learned much. I'd been a pilot at one time, that was something, but who the hell was I, and how had I ended up outside that plane, and without a scratch?

Gail came to stand beside me. "It's getting late. We need to head back to Santa Maria."

I hated the thought of another night in that hospital room. I didn't need to go back, they'd said so. "Can you check me into a hotel? It doesn't have to be fancy." I felt my face warm. "I can't pay you, but I'm keeping a tab in my head. I'll give you back every red cent."

She waited until Kelicoe walked away before saying. "I've already made a motel reservation for you. You're our only lead. The bureau's picking up everything. Don't worry about it."

Their lead to what? Damn, I wanted answers, and for now this seemed to be the only way to get them.

Chapter Six
Morgan Garrett

I HESITATED AT Darcie's front door. Maybe this wasn't the best thing to do. Things were going alright between us. Why rock the boat? Was I moving too fast? I shook my head. Okay big guy; you got yourself into this. Now let's cook dinner. I opened the door.

From the bedroom I heard Darcie's basset hound, Becky, kicking up a fuss.

"Just a minute," I said.

She quieted. Becky and I weren't the best of friends yet, but we were coming to an understanding. "Let me get the rest of the stuff and then I'll let you out."

I went back to my truck, grabbed the two tote bags. Darcie would be happy I had used the totes instead of plastic bags; she was big about going green.

In the kitchen I popped the chicken, eggs, milk and salad stuff into the refrigerator. I planned to fix Southern fried chicken. I knew Darcie liked it and had found a recipe on the Internet.

"Okay, Becky, your turn." I walked to the bedroom and opened the door. The basset hound stood there for a moment, just looking into my face, before she sauntered by. A lot different from the boisterous greeting she always gave Darcie.

"What do I have to do?" I said to her swaying backside. "It's been three months and you still look at me like I'm on probation. You've got to like me. I don't stand a chance with Darcie if you don't. " Becky stopped, glanced back at me, and lo and behold, the end of her tail wagged, just a little, but it was a wag. I felt a wave of relief. "You want a cookie?" Too many treats were forbidden, but that tail wag deserved a reward. I followed her to the kitchen right to the dog-cookie jar. "Let's keep this between me and you." She took her small bone, walked to her cushion next to the couch and settled down.

Some men see cooking as un-manly and make a big issue out of the inability to boil water, but Darcie and I had always shared the duty when we bunked together on assignments. I glanced at Becky. "I had a good thing with your momma back then. Damn, what would it have been like if I hadn't let booze screw things up? We'd probably both still be with the company. Sherice would have never entered the picture." I rubbed at my side where the scar still puckered skin. "But hey, then maybe Darcie wouldn't have you, and she always wanted a basset hound."

I fished out a skillet from the center island. I had decided to prepare sautéed green beans with mushroom and onions. Darcie had a thing for mushrooms. Personally, I hate them. They're too damn slimy, cooked or raw.

The refrigerator held a six pack of *Amber O'Doul's* I'd put in last night. It's not bad at all for a non-alcoholic brew. That was one of the hardest things I had to face, that I was an alcoholic. I still found it hard to say straight out when I attended my AA meetings. Hi, I'm Morgan and I'm an alcoholic. I pushed the thought away and pulled the recipe I'd printed out from my pocket.

****

Becky jumped off her dog cushion and charged the door in full voice. I glanced at the clock. It was only five thirty, but Darcie walked in anyway. I heard her greet Becky with the usual baby talk.

"What smells so good?" she said, coming into the kitchen.

"Southern fried chicken, or it will be in about another twenty minutes. You're early."

"Gail couldn't make it."

I knew she wouldn't say anymore. We had a pact. No talk about work. I'd tucked a towel around my waist and Darcie whistled as I turned to face her.

"You look sexy as hell. There's something about a man in an apron."

"It's not an apron."

She grinned. "Whatever. Give me a kiss."

I did, we made it a long one.

I stepped back. "Why don't you change and head out to the patio with Becky and relax."

"What? No small talk."

"Need to keep an eye on my masterpiece."

38

Darcie laughed.

I watched the two of them walk toward the bedroom. I knew they'd spend ten minutes or so curled up on the bed together. So far I hadn't been invited to take part in this ritual, and I wondered if I ever would be.

The oil popped in the skillet and I turned my attention back to the chicken.

****

Darcie pushed back from the table and groaned. "That was some bloody-good chicken."

I emptied the last of my O'Doul's. "You want another?"

"I'm fine."

I stood, started clearing the table.

"Damn Morgan, enough. Why all of this?" She motioned toward the table.

"Can't a guy cook for his girl?"

She continued to look at me. I guess the time had come. I settled back into my chair. "I wanted to talk to you about something, well, really I wanted to ask you something."

I saw her go tense.

"The last months have been good, right?"

She nodded.

"We've been together almost every night, mostly here at your place. Your parents talk to me again." I grinned at her.

"Mom just barely." She attempted to return the grin, but it looked forced The first month after Mayo Gerardi's murder had been a hard one for her mom.

"Becky's warmed up to me She gave me a tail wag today."

"I knew she'd come around," Darcie said.

I took a deep breath. "Darcie, I think we should move in together."

She went very still, then reached for her bottle of beer and finished it in one long drink. She looked across my shoulder, then down at her empty plate. Something was weird here. What was going on?

"Darcie…?"

"You want to move in here with me?" she said.

My mouth felt dry and I wished for another bottle of beer myself, and not a non-alcoholic one. "Too much, too soon?"

Darcie laughed. She pushed back from the table and stood. "Let's get this mess cleaned up." She grabbed our plates and headed to the kitchen.

Puzzled, I picked up the empty platter and followed. What had just happened? She hadn't given me an answer.

Darcie stood at the sink and stared down at the dirty dishes. She had a sad look on her face. My heart stuttered at seeing it. I placed the plate on the counter, went to her and wrapped my arms around her waist. "I'm sorry. If it isn't what you want I understand. This is your place..."

She turned in my arms, placed a finger against my lips. "No. It's a great idea. One step at a time, that's the best way to go. When do you want to move in?"

I felt like a weight floated off my shoulders. "How about tomorrow?"

"Tomorrow it is. Now let's get this mess cleaned up and head to bed."

I glanced at the clock. "It's only eight. A little early for sleep."

She grinned at me. "Who said anything about sleeping?"

****

The dream had me. I wanted to wake up, but couldn't. I was there, living it all again.

The Middle Eastern sun beat down on the Hummer and made it at least a hundred and ten inside, but I felt a cold sweat break out along my backbone. Something was wrong. I felt it all the way down to my toes.

"This is the corner," Darcie said. "He's supposed to be here with the information."

"We can't wait." I looked out the narrow opening of the windscreen. "What's that kid doing?"

The boy, who looked to be about nine, started running toward us. There was a satchel on his back. Please let it be full of books.

"Eddie," I yelled to our driver. "Get us the hell out of here."

Two men appeared on the roof of the house to our left. I felt the thud of the shells impacting the armor plating almost before the rat-tat-tat of automatic fire reached my ears.

In front of my face the windscreen splintered. Through the spider web of cracks, I watched the kid. He pulled a wire from the back of the satchel and then swung it.

Damn. Damn. Damn. I pushed my M-16 through the shattered window and fired a short blast, followed it with another.

The kid went down in the dirty street -- and exploded, his blood and body parts splattering all over the front of our Hummer.

I screamed. "Dear God, I shot a kid." I screamed again, couldn't stop. "Darcie, Darcie I just shot a kid. I just shot a kid."

"Morgan. Morgan. Wake up." The words were shouted into my ear. "It's not real. It's over."

I jerked my eyes open. Darcie leaned over me. I pulled her close, held her and trembled as I waited for my heart beat to return to normal. I buried my face in her hair. "When's it gonna stop? It's been over six years."

She rubbed my back in small circles. "I don't know, Morgan. I wish I did."

I heard the despair in her voice and knew what she thought about, what if her nightmare about Mayo went on for so long?

I reached over my head and turned on the light. 11:05 glowed from the bedside clock. "Let's catch the news?" I reached for the remote, turned on the television.

The TV reporter held the microphone in front of a slightly built man of uncertain age who looked nervous, but resigned. "This is Dave Kelicoe from the National Transportation Safety Bureau. Thank you so much for speaking with us." The reporter flashed white teeth toward the camera. "The private Lear jet that crashed at Nojoqui Falls, there was a man found alive at the site, have you identified him?"

"No. The man has no memory of who he is, or why he was at the crash site. We have determined he was not the pilot or co-pilot when the jet left Santa Maria. You will have to direct any other questions to the FBI."

"Amnesia?" The reporter said. "Do you believe…"

"I've nothing more to say." The man turned and walked away.

"I bet that's Gail's case," Darcie said.

I nodded. "The jet belonged to Devlin St. James."

"How do you know that?"

"The late senator was at Scarsdale's. St. James' mechanic's missing. I'm looking into it at Scarsdale's request."

We both turned back to the television in time to hear Kelicoe say. "We have a photo of the un-indentified man." He held it up. "If

anyone recognizes him, we'd appreciate a call."

"I'll be damned," I said, sitting up higher in the bed. "I know who he is."

"You do?"

"His name's Jonathon Wayne Cummins. I saw his passport at Everett Cummins' place."

"Did you say Everett Cummins?"

I looked at Darcie. "Yeah. He's St. James' missing mechanic."

"He's also my missing person case," Darcie said.

We both looked at the television screen. The news had moved on to the weather.

"And the man found at the crash site is his son," I said.

Darcie reached for her cell phone. "Got to let Gail know."

She held the phone to her ear and then snapped it closed. "It went straight to voice mail."

I heard a bark of demand. Darcie had moved Becky to the spare bedroom when the nightmares had started, her screams upset the basset hound. "We've awoken her highness."

Darcie kicked the quilt aside. "I'll go soothe her."

I watched, with much appreciation, the sway of Darcie's naked back side as she walked away.

The news had segued into a late night talk show and I flipped it off. So Darcie and I looked for the same man, Everett Cummins. The guy with amnesia was Cummins' son. I'd been hired by St. James to find Cummins, and the crashed jet belonged to St. James. I didn't like some of this, too many damn coincidences.

Darcie came back into the room. Damn, she was beautiful. I felt myself come to attention as she moved toward the bed.

She saw the sheet tenting above my groin and smiled. "You look alert."

"Let's say some parts of me are very awake."

She pulled the sheet aside, smiled down at me. "Well, since you are up." She slid into the bed and we reached for each other.

****

The ringing of Darcie's cell phone jarred me awake. Sun streamed through the cracks of the blinds.

She unwound from me and picked up the phone. "It's the captain." She flipped it open. "Devonshire."

I watched her face as she listened. A frown creased her brow. She

nodded. "I can be there in an hour and a half." She closed her phone, looked at me. "A car's been sighted over a cliff in Monterey county, Big Sur area. It's registered to Everett Cummins."

I kicked the quilt aside. "I'll go with you."

Chapter Seven
Gail Crane

I STRETCHED, FELT each muscle rev up for the day ahead, and for the first time in a long time I looked forward to what it would bring.

Duke's case intrigued me. No way was this guy a murderer. His face appeared in my mind and I felt my cheeks warm. Who did I kid? The man interested me as much as the mystery. My head cautioned to take it slow, there could be a wife and children, somewhere. I laughed softly. Judging by my accelerated pulse, my heart wanted to tell my head to shove it.

Out of habit I flipped open my cell phone. Damn, dead battery. I knew I'd charged it yesterday morning. I needed a new phone.

I stood, moved to my desk and plugged the charger in. There were two missed calls, both from Darcie Devonshire, one at five thirty this morning and another at six. I checked for messages.

Darcie's voice said. "Gail, call me. I've got some information for you." Message two from Darcie sounded more urgent and tinged with exasperation. "Gail, it's about your mystery man. You need to know this."

I punched in Darcie's cell phone number. She answered on the first ring. "What's going on," I asked, listened with surging excitement as she told me about Morgan's discovery. Duke was Jonathon Wayne Cummins. "What's the address of the apartment?" I wrote it down. "Thanks so much. Give Morgan a big kiss for me."

Darcie ended the call before I could ask where she was off to at seven in the morning.

John Wayne -- The Duke -- no wonder the name I'd picked for the mystery man had seemed so right. Cummins. The name sounded familiar. Then I remembered where I'd heard it. The line boys at Global Air had mentioned an Everett Cummins as being St. James' mechanic. Were he and Duke related?

44

I replayed my conversation with Darcie in my head. She hadn't mentioned Everett Cummins by name; just said Morgan had been following up on information about a case. I needed to get to the office and see what more I could discover about Jonathon Wayne Cummins.

Twenty minutes later I logged on to the FBI website and typed in my name and password. I entered Jonathon Wayne Cummins. Tapping my front teeth with a ball point pen I settled back to wait.

Unease rippled inside my stomach. What would I discover about Duke? He said he didn't feel he had a wife, but he could, and kids too. I frowned into the air.

A glance back at the computer monitor showed me information from both the National Crime Information Center and Automated Identification Division System. It relieved me to see the NCIC showed Duke had no criminal record; the other screen gave me what I needed.

Jonathon Wayne Cummins. Date of birth, July 23, 1965 in San Diego, California.

That made him 45 years old.

Mother…Hannah Lewis Cummins. Deceased September 2001. Breast cancer.

Father…Everett Cummins.

Humm, he'd remarried in February 2010 to Bethany Spangler age 35.

I sat back in my chair. Spangler. The name sounded familiar. I did another quick search. Devlin St. James had a stepdaughter, Bethany Spangler. It had been a smudge on the St. James' name for him to marry a widow with a nine-year-old daughter, but the Spanglers had the same lofty reputation as the St. James. The wedding had been another, if not Camelot affair, damn near close.

Could it be the same Bethany Spangler? I did a quick search. Found a photo of her. Another search gave me the Santa Maria Times write-up on Cummins' marriage, bingo -- the same Bethany Spangler. At seventy-one, Everett Cummins had married the 35 year old step-daughter of his boss. I looked for a divorce decree -- found none. They were still married.

What did that make Duke? St. James' son-in-law? I shook my head. Went back to Duke's information.

No siblings.

Graduated from high school, went on to college at Oregon State University and received a B.S. in Engineering.

I skimmed the rest.

Present employer, a French airline consultant firm, LTD International De Consultants en Matiere D'Aviation. The past three years he'd been in Africa working as an advisor for a Nairobi start up airline.

That explained him speaking French and his knowledge about Africa.

Jonathon Wayne Cummins received his first pilot's license at eighteen. Okay, he was also a pilot, no real surprise there.

He didn't have a permanent address, all his mail went through the French company. I could get into his email account, but the thought bothered me, and it didn't seem warranted, at least not yet.

I noted no mention of a wife or family and felt a bag of tension drop from my shoulders.

A letter of recommendation from a US conglomerate, written to the French company, glowed; they hated to lose Duke -- Duke? His nickname was Duke. I felt the hair on the back of my neck rise. Whoa, get a grip girl. No mumbo-jumbo stuff going on. It was a fluke. Me choosing his real nickname to call him by.

I pushed back my chair, stood. So I knew his name, his place of business, his father's name -- but I still had no idea how he ended up beside the crashed Lear jet without a scratch on him, and in someone else's clothes.

I glanced at the clock, ten-thirty, late enough for a visit. As I walked toward the door, I pushed down a surge of expectation. "Slow girl. Slow. It's a case, just a case." But I lied and I knew it.

*****

I took the 101 South onramp and pressed down on the gas pedal. By the time I'd entered the Broadway exit, I'd convinced myself to take a wait-and-see approach. Duke wasn't going anywhere soon, and for all I knew he could be gay. That would explain no wife or family. I pulled into the motel's parking lot, turned off the car. Damn, he'd better not be gay. I ran fingers through my hair, fluffed it a bit. Checked to make sure I hadn't spilled any coffee on my blouse, and then headed toward his motel room.

I knocked. No answer. Frowning, I knocked again. Where could he be? A thought flashed through my head, the foreign guy I'd

spoken to at the hospital. My hand lifted to the gun in my shoulder harness. "Duke. Duke, it's agent Crane. Are you in there?"

Chapter Eight
Duke Cummins

I WOKE TO the sound of an irate male voice urging his family to, "Get moving." A car door slammed. It took a moment for me to remember where I was. I looked around. The motel room was cliché décor, but the bed hadn't been bad and much better than the hospital room. It was nice of Gail Crane to book it for me, but I couldn't live in a motel room. Did I have a place in Santa Maria, a house, condo? Neither felt right. Damn. Why was I even here?

The bedside clock read seven-thirty, time for breakfast. These motel chains usually put on a good spread. I didn't bother to wonder about why I knew; instead I kicked the covers aside, stood and headed toward the bathroom.

*****

I poured a second cup of coffee and walked back to my table. Now what? Where do I begin? The jet had to have flown out of somewhere nearby. Maybe someone had seen me? But I didn't know the name of the airline. Would Gail tell me, or was that a big FBI no-no? She'd given me her cell phone number. I could call. I pushed back my chair. I'd noticed the hotel had a computer hooked to the Internet in a room off the lobby. I could do some surfing, maybe check out Africa since I knew I'd been there.

*****

"Sir. Sir."

I looked up from the computer monitor. One of the check-in clerks stood there.

"Sorry," she said. "We've let you use the computer much longer than usual since no one else needed it, but this gentleman has been waiting for some time."

I hadn't noticed the guy standing behind her until she gestured toward him. I took in his clothing, hair and shoes, all very American, but still something about him said European even before he said, "I

48

won't be long upon it."

He had a Russian accent. I recognized it at once.

"Sorry," I said, glancing at the lobby clock. It was ten-forty-five.

I stood and backed from the table. He smiled as he took my place, but it didn't reach his pale-blue eyes. They reminded me of a shark's. Something else I realized I'd come in close contact with at some time in my life. I nodded and walked away.

A woman stood in front of my motel room door. I heard her call out, "Duke. Duke it's Agent Crane. Are you in there?"

"No. I'm right behind you."

She jumped and then whirled around. "Damn," she said. "Make some noise."

My gaze went to her hand. It rested on a gun. I recognized its make, a Glock. "Are you planning to shoot someone?"

She lowered her hand. "Habit," she said, but her explanation sounded lame, and from the color flooding her face she knew it.

"Would you like to come in?"

"I would. I have something to tell you."

She stepped back and I unlocked the door, opened it and followed her in.

Gail walked to the chair by the table and settled into it. "I know who you are."

I looked into her face and waited.

"Your name is Jonathon Wayne Cummins."

I repeated the name in my head, tried different variations, John, Johnny, Jonathan. None meant anything to me.

She went on. "You work for a French airline consultant firm, LTD International De Consultants en Matiere D'Aviation. You'd been working for them in Africa as an advisor for a Nairobi start up airline.

Yes, that felt right.

"You're also a pilot."

I'd already figured that one out.

"Does any of this ring a bell with you?" Gail said.

"Not the name."

"There's more. Your father is Everett Cummins. He lives here and is a mechanic for Devlin St. James. It's possible that's why you were in Santa Maria."

Everett Cummins. Everett Cummins. I sought a face, a memory

to go with the name, some surge of emotion. Nothing. I turned, walked to the window and looked out.

"Duke, or should I call you Jonathan?"

A cubby hole in my brain released another bit of information. "The only one who called me Jonathon was my mother."

Gail remained silent, and I knew she sought a way to give me the information that had just slipped to the forefront of my mind. "My mother's gone. She died from breast cancer."

She nodded. "Your father's remarried."

"Is he?" I turned to face her. "What's his address? I'd like to pay him a visit. Maybe he has some answers." I looked down at my hands. Were they like my fathers, or did I inherit them from my mother?

" Let's go." She walked to the door and I followed.

Chapter Nine
Pieter Orloff

I WATCHED CUMMINS and the agent, Gail Crane, climb into a car as I neared. I had no reason to rush, there were two places they could be headed, Global Air, or the old man's apartment.

She glanced up as I walked by. It made no difference; the agent would not recognize me from our quick meeting at the hospital, for today I am Count Pietraski, with long, dark hair and close-clipped beard. I allowed our gazes to meld, smiled in slow appreciation of her features as I passed so near I could see the blush stain her cheeks. American women, they boast of their free-thinking, but still color at the admiring glance of any male.

I heard her car start as I rounded the corner, and sprinted the last few feet to my own.

On the street, I stayed two cars behind. It took only a moment to know their destination -- Everett Cummins' place. I dropped even further back. My cell phone rang and I answered.

"Orloff, you're late calling in." Devlin St. James' tone was as bullying and boorish as ever.

"Nothing has changed."

"I don't care. When I tell you to call at a time, you call."

When I did not answer, he went on.

"Where are you now? Where's Cummins?"

"He and the FBI woman are going to Everett's."

"What? You said he'd never remember. The drug..."

"He will not. Someone must have found something."

"The damned FBI."

"Perhaps." I shrugged. "Or the private investigator you so foolishly hired."

"I had to do that -- make it look good. Everett has been with me for too many years for me not to search for him. For Christ-sakes, he's married to my step-daughter."

"How is Bethany?"

"Fine and gallivanting around France the last I heard."

I smiled. "Maybe you should locate Bethany."

There was a long pause and then.

"Why? What have you done? I said to get Everett out of the way…"

"And I have, permanently."

"Damn-it, Orloff. You're going too far, first Kaminski and now old Everett."

"Our contract said I am to tidy up, and you were not to question my methods. Do you remember?"

"I remember," St. James snapped. "But murder? Everett wouldn't have said anything. Hell, I'm not even sure if he knew anything."

"You did not complain when we took him away."

St. James did not reply for a second or two. "That was necessary. He was upset about his son, which was your fault. Did you expect him to stand there and let you kill his boy?"

"He should not have been there," I said.

"You sure that drug will make him forget anything he saw that night?"

"I am positive."

"They why not use it on Everett?"

"I had no more. It left me with little choices."

"But murder? Why not pay-offs, family threats? You have contacts."

I laughed. "That's a politician's way, and as for blackmail senator, you wish to leave yourself open for two blackmailers, instead of one?"

I could picture red flood the old man's face, knew his blood pressure spiked. He was a fanatic about his family's good name. "One stupid mistake," I heard him mutter. "How long do they expect me to pay?"

"Your mistake," I replied, "was to pay the money. You should have killed Asa Kaminski when he first contacted you."

"Maybe, about that reporter. He's making noise…"

"I will take care of him."

He didn't protest my words. How his song had changed, yet good, for it bound him tighter to me.

I drove by Everett Cummins' place. Saw the agent's car.

Watched them exit. What did they seek? Could something inside spark the younger Cummins' memory? It hadn't happened before with the drug. "I have arrived," I said to St. James. "I will talk no more."

"What?"

"I must concentrate."

"You report in at one o'clock today. You hear me. Not a second later."

"Yes, Senator," I said, with forced meekness -- and then ended the call. He would sputter in outrage when next we spoke. It was something I had to tolerate. St. James must believe he held the reins; right up until I strangled him with them.

Chapter Ten
Darcie Devonshire

MORGAN AND I stood on the bluff looking down to where the surf pounded against a two-toned, gray, Buick sedan, wedged between algae-stained boulders. We had arrived on the scene thinking the body would already be recovered, and had been surprised to find the deputies and the highway patrol still milled around.

"Shit, they haven't done a damn thing. We could be here all day," I said.

"Cheer up. It won't be all day. The fog'll be rolling back in a couple of hours and that'll put a stop to everything." Morgan grinned.

I glared at him. "That makes me feel so bloody much better."

"Don't go all hyper on me, Devonshire. We wait."

"I don't do wait." I walked over to the young patrolman who'd responded to the anonymous call. "Officer, what's the plan?"

"Called the district office. San Luis Obispo's sending a helicopter rescue team to get the body out. They're already in the air. "

"You sure there is a body?" When he didn't answer, I went on. "When's the tow truck getting here?"

"I don't know if one has been sent for."

"You'll have to winch the car up. You know no one's getting down there."

He frowned. "Like I said, Detective, I don't know."

Morgan arrived beside me. "Darcie, let's sit in the Beamer. I'm freezing my ass off." He grabbed my arm and led me to the car. Inside he handed me coffee. "Drink."

"That shit's cold." I said.

"Drink it anyway."

"How do they even know it's Everett Cummins?" I took a sip of my tepid coffee.

Morgan shrugged. "The Buick's registered to Cummins, but it's possible there could be someone else inside. Hell, there might not be any one in the car at all."

I glared at him. "There damn well better be."

The low thump, thump of a helicopter's blades came to me. "Air rescue's here." I opened the Beamer's door.

The helicopter circled the Buick twice and then hovered above.

"Good thing the wind's not blowing," Morgan said.

A side door in the helicopter opened. A man in a harness stood there. He backed out, hung suspended from a cable. A moment later, he started down.

The man landed on the rocks, slipped as a wave hit not three feet below him.

"Damn. I wouldn't want that job," I said.

The man made his way to the driver's side door and opened it. A minute later, he looked up and shook his head.

"Well, someone's in there," Morgan said. "And they're dead."

"But, is it Everett Cummins?"

The man pulled a limp body halfway out of the Buick and then fastened another harness around its waist. He made an up motion with his hand, and the two of them ascended. At the helicopter's side they were both pulled in and the door closed.

I turned toward Morgan. "Now we'll just see who we have."

With a rush of air, the helicopter landed across the road from us. I shifted back and forth as I watched them lever the body free and place it on a stretcher. I could see it was a man, older, judging by the gray hair. "Come on. Come on" I murmured.

The San Luis Obispo county coroner bent over the body. He was a new face to me. I wished it had been Jack Laurie, then I wouldn't have to stand here twiddling my thumbs with professional politeness.

They pulled a wallet from the man's pant pocket.

Okay, that was it.

I pushed my way into the crowd of deputies. "Got an ID?"

"Everett Cummins, just like the car's registration," one replied.

I called back to Morgan, "It's him." I walked to the man who stood beside the body of Everett Cummins. "How did he die?"

"Well, he didn't die in the crash. He smashed into the windshield, but look at his face, no blood. He was dead before the car hit bottom. I think the autopsy will show he died from blunt force trauma to the

parietal and occipital plate, that's the back of the head."

I glanced at him to see if he was being a smart ass, but he looked as if he just thought out loud.

"I want a full tox work-up on him."

He finally looked up at me. "May I ask who you are? This has to be paid for, you know."

"I am Detective Devonshire, Santa Maria Homicide."

"He died from a blow to the back of his head."

"I want to be sure that's all it was. I'd also like a full report on the Buick when you have it ready."

"You're really hot on this thing." He looked at me intently. "Why?"

Morgan walked up beside me. "Everett Cummins worked for Senator Devlin St. James. I work for the Senator, and he is very interested in this case. I suggest you conduct this investigation with that in mind. If the detective here wants it, then we want it. Okay?"

Morgan was throwing a lot of weight around, and I wondered if he really had that authority.

The coroner's eyes narrowed, but then he nodded. "We'll give you any help and information we can."

"Thank you."

The ambulance pulled away with Everett Cummins' body and I turned back toward the cliff.

Morgan and I watched the old Buick being hauled upward. The car's fender hit a large boulder and created a small landslide. When it finally stood on the side of the road, I turned to him. "I want to see inside."

"Why," he asked.

"I…I don't know. I have to look."

"Okay, but look from over here. If that cable snaps it'll cut you in two."

"I'll watch it." A gust of wind made me shiver as I walked toward the car. Well, I blamed it on the wind anyway. The Buick had been a beautiful, classic automobile. I could see the love and attention Everett Cummins had lavished on it. From the back it didn't look bad at all, the light gray paint gleamed on the trunk and the chrome bumper glistened.

I made my way to the driver's side door.

The front of the Buick was another matter. The grill and fenders

were twisted; the bare metal looked almost obscene as it peered from the areas of pristine, glossy paint. A spider web of cracks spread across the windshield.

Careful not to touch anything, I leaned, looked in through the driver's side window. The gray, broadcloth, bench seat looked brand new. No blood on it, ditto for the steering wheel and instrument panel. Everett Cummins had for sure been killed outside the car, placed inside, and then the Buick sent over the side.

"Okay, you looked." Morgan said from behind me. He took my arm. "Now move back over here and stay out of the way. What did you expect to see?"

"You could eat lunch off of the front seat." I frowned. "Someone bashed Everett Cummins in the head and ran his car off a cliff. Why? And then his son is found beside a wrecked jet, not a scratch on him, but with no memory." I stared at the Buick. "Devlin St. James just happens to hire you to find Cummins, who is his lost mechanic, and also just happens to own the jet."

"Lots of unanswered questions," Morgan said. "I say we head back to Santa Maria and find the answers."

Chapter Eleven
Morgan Garrett

THE RETURN RIDE to Santa Maria was a quiet one. Darcie let me drive the Beamer, a serious sign my love had some major stuff going on inside her head. I didn't know what she thought about, but I mulled over the two senators and just what they were up to. That kid I'd met at Global Air, Rick Kaminski, how did he and his grandfather fit into the puzzle? I glanced at her. "Home or police station?"

"Home first. I'll check on her majesty and you can get your own ride."

I nodded. "What's your first move?"

"I'll see if the Captain can pull some strings and get the Buick brought here. Play up the senator angle you started…."

I pulled into the driveway and cut the engine. "If not there's always the FBI card in the hole." Darcie didn't reply and I looked at her. "Why the frown?"

"Gail's cool, but sharing with the feds has gone bad before."

"These things are all tied together; her, the now, not so mystery man, our homicide, Devlin St. James' involvement. You won't be able to keep the FBI out of it. Besides, they have deeper pockets and more resources at their beck and call."

"I know," Darcie said, and judging by her sour look the knowledge didn't make her happy.

I decided to play Switzerland. "Let's see how things go. No sense getting riled before you have to."

Her comment was to exit the Beamer. With a sigh and shake of my head I followed. "I'm going to be late tonight."

Halfway to front door, Darcie looked back at me. "Santa Barbara? A call on Senator Scarsdale?"

"A fishing expedition," I said as I walked toward my truck.

"Well don't bite off more than you can chew."

At the truck's bumper, I looked back at her. "Well, we're just full

of metaphors today, aren't we?"

"We're full of something," Darcie said. She walked in the door and closed it behind her.

I'd just started the truck when my cell phone rang. "Morgan Garrett."

"Mister Garrett, this is Rick Kaminski, we met at Global Air yesterday."

"Yes."

"Are you a private investigator?"

"Why?"

"I overheard part of your talk with the boss. You're working for Devlin St. James?"

"Senator Scarsdale's my boss."

"I'd like to talk with you about something."

I heard the unease in the kid's voice. "What?"

"Not over the phone and not here at Global."

"This have anything to do with Everett Cummins?"

Again the long pause before the kid said, "It might."

Where to meet with him? There was O'Grady's Pub, but I sensed we'd need more privacy. "How about here in thirty minutes?" I said, and gave him my soon to be new address.

"Thank you, Mister Garrett."

He hung up. Polite kid. I wondered what had him so skittish. I guess I would find out.

I climbed out of the truck and walked to the front door. Inside I heard Darcie and Becky. "Change of plans," I called. She and the basset hound came from the kitchen.

"What's up," Darcie asked.

I told her about Rick and the phone call. "You remember that write up about an Asa Kaminski, and the missing General Harden Hathaway? It was in the Santa Maria Times a couple of days ago."

"Kaminski died, but before he did, he showed the reporter an old helmet with Hathaway's name inside, and told 'im he had more information about the general."

"Devlin St. James was General Hathaway's aide. St. James was even decorated for his bravery when they'd liberated the death camp at Ohrdruf, the same camp where Asa Kaminski was interned."

"Devlin St. James again." Darcie frowned into the air. "He rose to glory fast after that. How do you think Rick Kaminski ties in?"

"I don't know, but I'm betting he and Asa are somehow related."

She reached to pat Becky's head. "Company's coming, now you behave yourself." Darcie leaned toward me, gave me a thorough kiss, and then turned toward the door. "I want a full report after dinner tonight."

I gave her a sharp salute. "Yes, sir."

She grinned back at me before she walked away.

*****

I was listening for it, so I heard when the car arrived in the driveway. "Our company's here," I said to Becky. "Rick seems like a good enough kid, but you are on guard duty, okay? He'll never figure you for a vicious attack dog."

Becky wagged her tail.

The doorbell peeled and she was up on her feet and charging toward the door in full voice before I could turn around.

"Good girl," I said as I opened the door.

Rick Kaminski looked beyond me, toward Becky. "Does the dog bite?"

"Yes, but I have her under control." It was hard not to smile. "Come on in. We'll talk in the kitchen."

I turned and walked away. Halfway down the hall, I looked back. Becky lay across the doorway and the kid still stood outside. "Come on, girl."

The basset hound stood, sauntered toward me and I could have sworn she smiled as she passed. I looked at Rick. "Coast is clear."

He came toward me. "I'm a little scared of dogs. Got bit as a kid."

A little ashamed, I said. "She's a sweetheart. Loves almost everybody." Becky went to her bed and settled onto it. "Want something to drink. I could put on some coffee."

"No. I'm fine Mister Garrett."

"Call me Morgan. Now what do you want to talk with me about?"

"My grandfather, I think he was murdered."

His words didn't surprise me. I'd halfway expected them. "Your grandfather being Asa Kaminski?"

"You read the article."

I nodded. "You know anything about a connection to St. James?"

He frowned. "I'm not positive there is a connection...except in

60

Pappa's head.

I raised an eyebrow.

"But that doesn't mean someone else didn't believe there was," Rick said. "Pappa felt threatened." He looked away from me. "I didn't know how much until I received the letter."

I nodded again and waited.

"The letter arrived a week ago. Pappa asked an old friend to send it to me if he was killed."

"You mean died?"

He shook his head. "The letter says, killed."

"You bring the letter?"

"A copy of it, but I'm not showing it, unless we have an agreement."

"Agreement?"

"That you'll find out who killed him."

I frowned. If St. James was involved, this could be a conflict of interest. What the hell. I worked for Scarsdale, not him, and besides this could help me find out more about what had happened to Everett Cummins. His death looked like a murder to me too and my gut said he and Asa Kaminski were somehow connected. I always listened to my gut. "I get a hundred bucks a day, plus expenses. "

Rick reached into his pant pocket and then handed me a hundred dollar bill. "This'll get things started."

I took the money. "Now show me the letter."

Rick pulled some folded sheets of paper from his jacket pocket and handed them to me.

Ricky,

If you are reading this, I am dead. Just know I always loved you. Sometimes we make mistakes and they follow us for the rest of our lives. I never intended to take the path I did, but Mama needed medical care, a specialist. They made promises, try this, try that, all costing much and you know, my Ricky; it did not matter in the end.

I looked a question at him.

"My grandma died from surgery complications, they screwed up the anesthesia, left her with dementia. They gave her all kinds of experimental treatments. Nothing helped, but Pappa wouldn't give up, not until she took her last breath."

I nodded and went back to the letter.

Then the third notice came from the bank about my home, they

were going to take it from me, Ricky. I couldn't let that happen. It was all I had left of Mama. I needed money. I needed it soon. Devlin St. James has much of it. You see I do not say senator. The man should have never been elected. In fact the bastard should never left Ohrdruf alive. Blessed God, there were many who didn't, General Harden Hathaway being one of them.

I frowned, read the words again. No one knew what had happened to Harden Hathaway, or maybe there was someone who did.

I was there that night, Ricky. I saw. It was early morning. I'd eaten something that messed with my guts and was making my way to the latrine. In the middle of a field I heard the general shouting.

I saw them clearly in the moonlight. General Hathaway was yelling he'd see St. James dishonorably discharged. He was a disgrace to his uniform. St. James was blubbering, saying everything was a mistake...a misunderstanding. He didn't know the girl was twelve. It wasn't rape. She'd asked for it. He couldn't be kicked out. It would kill his father.

At that time the St. James name meant nothing to me. He was but one American soldier among many.

The general turned his back and the coward St. James struck General Hathaway with a shovel. One of those folding ones the Americans all carried. Hathaway fell and St. James struck him again and again. I turned and staggered back to my bunk.

I don't know how long I lay there, staring into the dark, my heart pounding, it seemed like hours, yet must have been minutes. I heard the door squeak open, saw a figure of a tall man framed in the doorway with something draped across his shoulders.

He came toward me. I closed my eyes, even as I stilled myself for a fight for my life -- but instead I heard a dull thud. I waited, counted the seconds until I heard the door close. I opened my eyes. I saw it then, the general's still form. That is when I smelled the sharp, acrid smell of gasoline. A moment later the back wall erupted in flames. Fire. Fire, I screamed, pulling myself to my feet. Smoke filled the room. I heard the cries of terror. I stood, took a step toward the door and stumbled over something. I picked it up. It was a helmet. As I placed it on my head, the door slammed open.

Hurry, hurry, a man's voice shouted.

All who could rise staggered toward the door. There were many

who could not. A man ran past me. I saw then it was St. James. He scooped an old man from his bed and carried him out. I tried to help the man in the next bed, but he was unable to rise and I was too weak to lift him. It was hell, Ricky, the flames, the smoke, the screams. It was a miracle I got myself out.

In minutes all was over, the building a smoking pile of rubble.

Later I removed the helmet and looked inside, saw General Hathaway's name. I hid the helmet among my clothes.

Ricky, I intended to tell what I'd seen, but the next morning many bodies were pulled from the still smoking rubble, and none were identifiable. Everyone praised St. James' heroics, and they were right. He did risk his life to bring many from the burning barracks. I convinced myself I was wrong, and even if not, it was no concern of mine.

That afternoon we were shipped away.

Years passed, my Ricky. I thought only of surviving. I met your grandmother, married, and had children. Many years later, after urging from your grandmother, I did send a letter, told what I thought I'd seen, just in case they wanted to look more into it, but I never received a reply. So I put it behind me.

Then the sickness took your grandmother, and they wanted our home, her rose garden, the apple tree with all of our initials carved into it. I couldn't let that happen.

I sent Devlin St. James a letter, told him what I'd witnessed that night; sent along a photo of the helmet. I said I wanted $25,000.00 for my silence. I didn't really expect him to get the letter, didn't expect him to pay, but ten days later a cashier's check showed up in my post office box. I paid off the mortgage, Ricky boy. I should have left it at that, but I was angry, angry and bitter. St. James had everything, I had nothing. So I sent a second letter, and a third. Each time he paid.

It was then I noticed the dark car. I don't know why, dark sedans aren't a rarity, but in my heart I knew I was in trouble. They've been in my house. I feel it. They are playing cat and mouse with me. So I write this letter and leave it with Amos. If they kill me, he is to send it to you. Ricky my boy, don't believe what they tell you. Yes, I grew greedy, but it is St. James who is my murderer, just as he was the murderer of Harden Hathaway. I've included a key with the letter. Go to bus station in town. I've left you the helmet. Do what your

63

heart tells you is right.

Love you with all my soul,

Pappa.

I looked up. Rick had walked into the living room and was petting Becky's head.

"How did your grandfather die?"

Rick walked to me. "According to the doctor at the VA hospital he choked on a fish bone."

"You don't believe them?"

"The doctor had witnesses when they pulled it from Pappa's throat."

I lifted an eyebrow.

"My Pappa hated fish. No way would he ever have eaten any without a lot of help."

"What about the helmet? You got it?"

He nodded."I flew out there. The helmet's in a safe place and yes Harden Hathaways name is inside."

I frowned at the sheets of paper. "It's only his word."

"Then why did he pay Pappa, not once, but three times?"

"St. James has a big bug up his butt about his family name," I said. "And he can afford to."

Rick took a deep breath. "I want to know who killed my grandfather. I don't care who it is."

I thought of Everett Cummins. Had it stumbled onto St. James' secret? If St. James had killed once to protect his family name, we'll, not only once, he burned that building too. How many had died then? No, he wouldn't think twice about killing again? I nodded at Rick Kaminski. "I'll see what I can find out."

Chapter Twelve
Duke Cummins

GAIL PARKED THE car in the shade of a huge oak. She pointed at a unit in-between two others. "That's the apartment. The big house must be the owners." She reached for the door handle. "I'll be right back."

I watched her walk to the front door. In a few moments it opened. A few moments more and Gail and an elderly lady came toward me. I climbed from the car.

"Well it's about time you came back young man." The women said. "Where's Ev? He with you?" She looked in the back of Gail's car.

"You know me?" I said.

She frowned. "What kind of a question is that? No, I don't know you, but I know you're Everett's son Duke, and you arrived her three days ago, and then hightailed it out only a couple of minutes later. "

"How did I get in? Do I have a key?"

"Not unless Ev gave you one. I let you in. He told me you were coming." She looked from Gail to me. "I'm not liking this one bit. First that private detective's here, now a FBI lady, and still not nary a policemen. I called them about Ev a good two days ago."

"His disappearance is being looked into by Detective Darcie Devonshire," Gail said. "I know her well and am sure everything that can be done is being done."

"Uh…Mrs…?"

"Willoughby. Mrs. Nash Willoughby, but you can call me Delilah."

"Well, Delilah, would it be okay if we went inside and looked around?"

"I'm sure that would be fine, you being Ev's son and all. Let me get my key."

I watched her walk back to the front door. "Do you know how

long my father has lived here," I asked Gail.

"No, I don't."

The unit had been freshly painted and the well-tended flower beds were starting to fill with blooms. "It looks nice." I looked toward the house. "From what Mrs. Willoughby said, I've been here at least once before. I wonder if it's been more often."

"I could find out, but why don't you just ask her."

Mrs. Willoughby came out her front door. Gail and I stood in silence as she made her way to us.

She held out the key. "Here you go young man."

"Thank you. Mrs. Wil…"

"Delilah."

I smiled. "How long has my father lived here?"

"Four years."

"Have I visited before?"

She didn't say anything for a long moment, and then turned and looked at Gail. "What's going on here?"

"Mr. Cummins had an accident. The trauma has erased some of his memory," Gail said.

"Oh, you poor boy. You think a visit inside will help?"

"I hope so, Delilah," I said.

She patted my arm. "Well, no. You haven't been here. Ev said your job in Africa had kept you away, but you kept in constant contact with letters and email." Mrs. Willoughby leaned toward me. "Ev also thought you didn't come around because of that so-called wife on his." She sniffed loudly. "He was so excited about you being here now." Mrs. Willoughby turned and glared at Gail. "That's why I know something's wrong. He'd never stay away, not with Duke coming."

The front door of the house slammed open and a woman's shrill voice yelled. "Delilah, your daughter's on the phone."

"That's Emma. She's my Bridge partner. We've got a hot game going on tonight. We're working on our strategy. You just bring the key to me when the two of you are finished."

With that she turned and walked away.

My hands shook as I fit the key into the lock. Why I had no idea. What did I expect to discover inside? Was there something about my life I didn't care to remember? I walked in, felt Gail follow. She closed the door. A brown leather sofa and matching recliner

dominated the small, but neat room. A newer looking television was on a metal stand, and off-white blinds shielded a window. A wooden end table, next to the recliner, held a remote control and a television guide. What type of programs did my father favor? I waited, but the cubby hole in my head released nothing.

Behind me Gail remained quiet.

On the wall above the sofa some photos hung. I walked to them. The one in the middle showed an older guy standing next to a beautiful, red, bi-wing. There was a younger version of me standing next to him; he had his hand on my shoulder. "Is that my father?"

"Yes. He's younger there, but that's him."

I looked closer. We had the same nose, the same embarrassed grin. My father didn't seem to like his photo taken either. "I remember the plane. He spent every waking spare minute restoring it. I helped whenever I could. Mom complained a lot, but I knew she didn't care. What made dad happy, made her happy." I looked at Gail. "Do you suppose he still has it? Maybe he took it out and had to make an emergency landing somewhere."

"It's possible."

The other two photos were of my dad and me posing in front of the Eifel Tower, and then him with a pretty red-head on a boat with a lot of water behind them. She looked younger than me. "Is that his new wife?"

"Bethany." Gail confirmed.

I looked around the room again. There wasn't one thing to show a woman had ever lived here. "Wonder where she is now?"

Gail shrugged.

I walked into the bedroom. An un-opened suitcase lay in the middle of a made-up bed.

Was it mine?

I opened the bag. It had a number of pockets and two zippered inner compartments. Inside the first section I found underwear, t-shirts. The second, held jeans, polo shirts and tennis shoes. I tried one of the zipper compartments and fished out a passport. I flipped it open. My face stared back at me. The passport had been stamped a lot. It seemed I did quite a bit of traveling. I searched the other compartment and found my international driver's license along with a large stack of traveler's checks. It felt good to see them. Now at least I could pay my way for…whatever. My gaze skimmed over a

desk, then jerked back to a sheet of paper lying there. I walked to it.

It was a note.

Duke,

The senator called. Needs me to take a look at something on the Lear. I'll be back by six. Make yourself at home. It'll be great to see you, son.

"Don't touch it, please," Gail said from the doorway.

"I probably already have."

"We'll ignore yours and Mister Cummins' prints."

I turned to look at her. "You think something has happened to him, don't you?"

"He's connected to all of this. Your father is St. James' mechanic." She came to stand beside me, read the note. "Now we know St. James called him to the airport before the Lear took off."

"And he planned to be back by six o'clock. He wasn't."

"You must have gone looking for him."

I smiled. "Or maybe I went out for a bean and cheese burrito. I like them."

"My favorite too, but no, you went looking for him." She frowned. "No one saw you at Global Air though."

"Or they didn't tell you if they did," I said.

Gail nodded. "That's always possible." Her cell phone rang. She walked back into the living room. "Agent Crane," I heard her say.

There was a long moment of silence and then her voice lowered and I couldn't hear anymore.

I walked around the room in silence. Something had to feel familiar. For Christ's sake, the man was my father. I felt nothing, except a mild curiosity.

My father seemed to like the beige color family, the bed coverings, the drapes, even the round rug beside the bed were in all hues of beige. Did I like beige? It seemed okay, but I felt I tended to lean more toward the blue family.

"Duke."

Gail's voice came from behind me. I felt myself tense. There was something about the way she called my name. I turned, stared into her face in silence.

"That was Darcie. I'm afraid I have some bad news."

"They found him, didn't they?"

She nodded. "Darcie got a call about a car over the cliff south of

Big Sur. She went and was there went they pulled it up. I'm sorry…your father was inside."

I closed my eyes, let the works sink in. My father was dead. I waited…waited for something. I felt sad that a man had lost his life, beyond that, nothing. "What do I do now?" I laughed shortly. "It's not as if I can identify the body."

"They'll get someone else to do it."

Quick, hot anger had me balling my hands into fists. Who had done this to me? Stolen my memories, left me an empty shell. God damn them, I couldn't even mourn my own father. I'd find who and when I did…. "I'd like to take another look at that Lear they found me beside."

"I can arrange that. It hasn't been moved from the field."

"When?"

"How soon do…"

"Now," I said.

"Let me call Dave Kelicoe and fix it with him." Gail walked away from me and pulled out her phone.

I looked around my father's living room again. It was a nice place. I wondered if Mrs. Willoughby would let me move in here. It would be better than a motel room and it felt right to do so. Gail came toward me.

"Dave's there now and says we can come on out."

"Good. I want to stop and speak with Mrs. Willoughby. She needs to know about Dad and I have something I want to ask her."

Gail nodded and we both headed toward the door.

Mrs. Willoughby answered almost before the bell finished chiming. The smile on her face faded as she looked into mine. "You found Everett,' she said.

"We did. He..."

"Ev's dead, isn't he?"

I nodded. "A car accident."

Her lips trembled and a tear slid down her cheek. I reached to touch her arm. "I'm so sorry." It was so surreal, me comforting her, like she was the family and me a friend.

She took a deep breath. "I'm sorry for you to Duke. Not the visit you had planned on."

I forced a smile and shook my head.

"What now," she asked.

"I'll let you know about a memorial." I hesitated and then went on. "I'd like to stay in the apartment. It…"

"Of course you can. Ev has it paid for the rest of the month. After that you can stay for as long as you want to rent it. Everett would like…" Her voice broke and she looked away.

"Thank you, Delilah. I'll be back tonight." I pocketed the key.

She nodded, backed into the house and softly closed the door.

I turned to Gail. "I'd like to see that plane now."

Chapter Thirteen
Gail Crane

I COULD FEEL Duke's eagerness to get out of the car and see the wreckage again. The cynical part of me wanted to know why. Was he afraid there was some evidence that would damn him? He hadn't seemed too shocked when I'd told him about his father's death. Had he already known? Did he have a hand in it? Damn. I believed his amnesia was for real, but I didn't know for sure.

I parked in front of the yellow tape and Duke was out of the car before it rolled to a complete stop. He started away, almost at a run.

I followed more slowly.

Duke had stopped at the side of the airplane. I walked to him. Twisted pieces of blue and white aluminum reached out the full forty-nine feet of its wingspan. The fire had destroyed parts of the fuselage, but had done very little damage to the wings. He seemed troubled by the sight before him, and I assumed he was trying to remember something, but his words told a different story.

"Look at that," he said, his voice almost a whisper. "That beautiful, sleek jet, relegated to this ignoble ending. It's near sinful."

He stood for several seconds in respectful homage before he moved closer to inspect the shattered Lear.

I watched him move from the tail section, toward the wing. He stopped to look at one item, then another, with what I recognized to be a trained and practiced eye. Before Duke reached the separated pilot's cabin, he had stooped and probed each inch of the Lear with a measuring gaze. At one point he even lay on the ground and looked under the wing.

At the front section, Duke waited until I caught up and then turned to me. "I'll bet they don't find anything mechanical wrong with this bird."

"Why do you say that?"

"I guess it's more a feeling than anything tangible. Where she's not burned, she's too clean, well maintained. There's no sloppy work evident anywhere. The twist of the safety wire shows care; the parts and components are clean, not just surface clean, but clean in the hard to reach areas. A meticulous mechanic has cared for and maintained this bird, and believe me I have seen both kinds."

"That would have been your dad," I said.

His face took on that odd, lost look I knew meant he remembered something and couldn't quite put it in its proper place. After a slight hesitation, he walked across to look at the area where he had been found by the firefighters

Walking up to stand behind him, I said, "This is sort of where you were born, isn't it?"

"It's one hell of a bassinette."

"Give it time, you'll remember."

"No," Duke whispered, "I don't think I will. What the hell," he added in a more positive tone. "I'm alive and life goes on."

"Does anything come to you about the crash?"

"No, but that's not why I wanted to see the jet. I know I've been involved in a crash before. I wanted to see if I could trigger some past memory. It didn't happen, so we may as well keep moving."

We continued around the Lear until we reached the air-stair door. I heard voices and looked toward the sound. Dave Kelicoe and a group of mechanics walked toward us.

"Dave," I said, "how's the investigation going?"

"Better, now that you FBI people have got out of my hair."

"Be nice now." I smiled, determined to be a diplomat.

"This door wasn't on the jet when it crashed," Duke said as he leaned forward and ran his hand over the smooth aluminum.

"What?" Dave said. "How do you determine that?"

"Look at the opening; it's warped in the middle section. Now look at the door. It's straight, and notice the top, it's bent and dirty like it hit the ground. Where was it found?"

"Not anywhere near the wreck," Kelicoe said. "Two kids brought it to us yesterday. We'd looked all over for this thing."

"So the door was blown off in flight," Duke asked.

"Well, we don't know for sure yet."

"I don't have time to wait for a year or so for you to be sure. This is personal for me, real personal."

I watched Dave Kelicoe's face flush and decided the right time had come to say our goodbyes. "Thanks, Dave. If we come across anything more we'll let you know."

"And I'll attempt to get my report to you." There was a long pause before he added, "Before next year."

There wasn't anything to say to that, so I tugged on Duke's arm and herded him toward the car.

Chapter Fourteen
Darcie Devonshire

"DEVONSHIRE," THE CAPTAIN bellowed as I walked past his office.

"Yes, sir?"

"I had a call from the SLO county sheriff. They're sending the Buick. Should be in the garage tomorrow, but tox report will take a couple of weeks." The Captain looked at me in suspicion. "What the hell happened?"

"Just the spirit of cooperation, I played nice."

He grunted. "Well, fine. I take you found the missing Cummins?"

I nodded. "Found him, but it's more than a car accident. Has all the makings of a homicide."

"Damn. That's all I need with all of these blasted budget cuts. Why didn't you leave it to them?"

"Because it's my bloody case. You assigned it to me."

The Captain shook his head. "I told you to check it out. See if it was our missing person. Stamp case closed. Not to bring a homicide back and drop it on us."

"The FBI's got an interest in it also. I'll inform Agent Gail Crane. We can work it together." The words galled me, but seemed to please him.

"You do that."

I turned and walked away.

Wes sat at his desk across from mine. He had a frown on his face. "What gives?" I said.

He looked up. "Just had an interesting conversation."

"With who?"

"Our old pal, Tomas Flores."

"Flores. He back from Mexico?"

"Yep. He wants us to meet with him at the Metro Club."

"That so. Are you?"

"He asked for both of us."

I wouldn't have the Buick until tomorrow and there was nothing else on my desk. I did need to speak with Gail, but it could wait a tad bit longer. "What did Flores say?"

Sounds loco, but he swears someone has come into Santa Maria and is taking over the drug trade, uniting all of the gangs."

"Not going to happen. Those guys can't agree on whether it's day or night."

Wes frowned. "If it's true we're in big trouble. Bad enough we have gangs, but to get them all working together...."

"Who could pull something like that off?" I said.

He pushed back his chair. "I guess we'd better find out."

*****

I hadn't been back to the Metro Club since the Ice case, hadn't even driven by. It didn't look any ritzier. Wes and I parked on the street and then walked toward the front door. A cardboard sign, splotched with what I was sure I really didn't want to know, leaned against a dingy window. It proclaimed the club, open. We walked in. The place might as well have been closed. I didn't even see anyone behind the bar.

A side door opened and Tomas Flores walked toward us. He motioned with his hand. "Back here."

I looked at Wes. He shrugged and we followed Flores. He led us through a storage area and then into another smaller room. It had a desk and a computer, so it had to be the business office. There was a banker's chair behind the desk and two other wooden ones against the wall. A huge girly calendar hung behind the desk. The semi-nude redhead made Dolly Parton look flat-chested. Wes whistled and then grinned at me and wiggled his eyebrows.

Men.

I turned to Tomas Flores. "Enjoy your vacation?"

"It was fine."

"Been to see your Tisa," Wes asked.

"She not know I'm back."

"Let's keep it that way," Wes said with a stern look.

Flores shrugged. "That all history."

Wes walked behind the desk and settled in the chair. "Why'd you call? I don't think it was for my engaging conversation."

"You got big problem. Makes Juan Sebastian look like fly-shit."

75

Wes leaned toward him. "Say what?"

"Someone taking over Sebastian's area?" I said.

"Much more. He got Santa Maria, Nipomo, Arroyo Grande and Pismo Beach already. He trying for all, Paso Robles to Oxnard."

Wes snorted. "We're talking gangs here. They hate each other."

"Juan gone. No one taking control. Lots of little fish. One big shark comes in…." Flores shrugged again. "He not just make promises, he's delivered. More money than has been seen around here for mucho time. They've recruited…many have joined."

"Who is he," Wes said.

"You won't believe me. You have to see for yourself."

I frowned. Someone with enough brains and brawn to make the gangs work together? Santa Maria's gangs had been quiet the past three months. We'd thought we were making headway. No drive-bys, no knifings or murders in almost a month. Anger rushed through me. Bloody hell, what had been going on right under our noses? Judging by Wes' flushed cheeks, he thought the same. "So, why have you come to us?"

Flores wouldn't meet my eyes. "I need help. They sweet talk Almeta, my baby sister."

"What do you mean?" Wes said.

"This gringo hombre, he's not a local, he flashing lots of money. Buy her dresses. He drives new car. I know they'll hook her on drugs and put her to work."

"Gringo?" Wes said. "The guys white?"

"As the snow."

Wes scowled. "Turning 'em into working girls, huh? Not much hooking in Santa Maria."

Flores smiled. "Yeah, right. You want I get you a date in less than twenty minutes."

Wes looked like he wanted to argue, but I cut in. "Why don't you go get your sister and bring her home?"

"She over eighteen. Won't listen to me, besides Almeta not in Santa Maria, maybe Santa Barbara, I'm not sure."

"Well, shit," Wes said. "What do you expect us to do? Santa Barbara is out of our area."

Tomas Flores looked first at Wes and then at me. "That didn't stop you before."

I watched Wes' face flush with red.

"You've got connections." Flores said to me.

"What's in it for us, if we do help?" Wes said.

"I know some big stuff going down right under your noses."

"Are you involved?" I said. Flores didn't answer, which as far as I was concerned was his answer. "What types of things?"

"Protection, some counterfeiting, and other stuff."

"Shit," Wes said. "You're talking white-collar crime."

"Guy on Main, he say no to their offer of protection. He got jumped the other night. He not dead, but damn near close."

"Who," I said.

Flores shook his head. "Not saying more. Not until we have deal. You find my baby sister."

"So you'd like be our inside guy?" Wes said. He looked at me. "You think the Captain would go for it?"

"If he believes it." I looked at Flores. "We need at least one name we can check out."

"They can be much hurt if they talk to you. Why you think they stay quiet."

Wes stood. "No name, then we can't help. Come on Darcie. We're wasting our time."

"Wait," Flores said. "I can give you more. He's big and dirty up to his nose. Don't know if he's the shark, but maybe."

"Who?" I said.

"Politician."

"Well, hell. As if that's a surprise," Wes said, and then laughed.

"Local?" I said.

"Santa Barbara."

Wes frowned. "Santa Barbara again."

Flores looked at me. "You already involved."

Santa Barbara. It could only mean one thing. Morgan. "Is it Scarsdale?"

"Devlin St James likes young Mexican girls," Flores said. "The crashed plane, the dead old man, Cummins, it all tied together."

How did Flores know about Everett Cummins? "Bloody hell," I said.

Flores smiled. "We got us a deal?"

"I have to run it by the Captain, but yes, I'd say we do."

Chapter Fifteen
Duke Cummins

AT THE DOOR of the car I turned, looked back at the mangled blue and white jet and just like that a memory assaults me.

In my mind's eye a scene of trees and bushes whip past the windows of a cockpit. I'm flying. The air is full of the sound of trees and brush rushing past the windscreen, the sputter of a faltering aircraft engine, a radial piston engine, mixed with the banging and slapping of the heavier tree limbs as the airplane descends into the thick forest.

The airplane comes down in the trees, the impact bone crushing. I'm slung forward in the shoulder harness; a tree limb crashes through the co-pilots window, spears Jean Claude in the neck and drives his body into the partition behind. I see the green, upholstery padding torn from the metal by the force of the tree as vivid as if it was before my eyes this very moment.

With the vision of the tattered green upholstery, the memory faded.

"What's wrong," Gail asked. "You said Jean Claude and something in French." She looked at me with an odd expression.

"I remembered crashing an old DC-3 in the jungle," I said. "It was vivid, and clear, but now it's gone."

"Try to concentrate on the memory. Maybe something will come back."

"No, whatever it was is gone now."

"Who was Jean Claude?"

"I don't...I'm not sure, maybe my co-pilot? That's dumb, he was my co-pilot and he's dead, but, I...but I don't remember him. Shit, this is driving me crazy; not remembering. Gail, I've got to find out where I stand. I need to find my father's lawyer, or who his executer is, and what about his wife."

"She goes by the name Spangler, not Cummins. St James will

know where she is."

"Then I need to talk to him, but first can we go see that man at Global Air? What was his name, Hughes?"

"Sam Hughes. Why do you want to talk to him?"

"He has my father's airplane for one thing. Another is he may not have been there when the Lear crashed, but he would know how my father worked."

"Let's go."

*****

Global Air looked, smelled, and felt like home to me. The faint odor of jet fuel, combined with oil and grease, wrapped me in a cocoon of familiarity. I hesitated inside the door long enough to cause Gail to ask. "What's wrong?"

"No, nothing. I just…nothing." I turned toward the man in the ball cap who had walked up.

"I'm Sam Hughes. Ms. Crane said you wanted to speak to me. You're the guy from the Lear I hear."

"Well I was found there, but I seem to know next to nothing about that. I have discovered I know quite a bit about aviation, even though I can't remember specifics about myself. I thought maybe you could tell me a little about St. James' operation?"

"I didn't have much to do with his daily workings. I housed his birds and sold him fuel. That was about it."

I glanced at Gail. "It turns out I'm Everett Cummins' son. I hoped you could tell me what kind of man he was?"

"Was? What do you mean was?" Sam Hughes looked from my face to Gail's and then back.

"Mister Cummins died in an automobile accident," Gail said.

"Oh, God, I am so sorry."

I didn't say anything, so he went on.

"Everett was pretty fussy about his airplanes. My mechanic's work was never good enough for him. Take the Stearman back there." He gestured toward the red bi-plane I had seen in the photograph. "He wouldn't even let the line boys move it out. He did it himself. Course he didn't fly much anymore. Do you know how old he was?"

"Eighty. I believe."

Hughes' cheeks colored. "Well, of course you do."

"About the Stearman," I said. "Is the rent paid? Does he owe

you anything?"

"I'd have to check, but ole Ev was as good as gold. I suspect he's paid for at least this quarter."

"Could I look at the bird?"

"Sure, I reckon it's yours now. Say, what kind of license you got anyway?"

"I have an air transport rating on my Commercial instrument and multi engine ticket. I have a flight instructor license also. My log book's in my bag." I hadn't seen it at the apartment, but I knew it was in there.

We walked to the bright red bi-plane.

"Go ahead. I know you want to get inside," Hughes said.

I climbed into the cockpit. I could see meticulous care displayed everywhere I looked. My father had babied and expended great love and tenderness far beyond normal maintenance requirements.

I looked up and saw that Sam Hughes watched me from the edge of the wing.

"You interested in a job?" he said.

"A job? You mean flying?"

"I'm shorthanded right now. One of my guys went back to the east coast. I planned to post the opening tomorrow morning. I'd need to see your log book of course. You got any time on a King Air? I use the King Air and the Lear 45 on my charters."

"I've flown both. Got a...hey Gail, is it okay if I take a job?"

"Duke, you're a free man. You don't have to ask me, but what about your old job?"

"I'm not going anywhere until I find out what happened to me." I turned to Sam Hughes. Yes, Sir, I'd love a job."

"Be here tomorrow morning then. Bring your licenses and your log book." Sam Hughes turned and walked away.

"Gail, do I have a social security card? I'll need one."

"We can check easily."

"How about that, a job."

"Come on. Let's go," she said. "You need to get settled into your new place."

Walking back to her car I know I had a dumb grin on my face that I couldn't make go away. I still planned to find out how I'd ended up beside that cockpit with no memory, but a job made me feel more like the man I'd been before it was all ripped away.

Chapter Sixteen
Morgan Garrett

BY THE TIME I parked in front of Senator Scarsdale's house, I had about mulled over Rick's grandfather's words to death.

The camp at Ohrdruf is near Weimer Germany. I've been there. When I'd visited it looked pretty normal, but I knew when the Fourth Armored Division had rolled into that valley in April 1945, it was far from it. They'd found people starving; sick and mistreated beyond belief. The Army's main interest had been to get the inmates fed and medicated. By the time the third Army CID team started to look into General Harden Hathaway's disappearance, the starving Jews, Asa Kaminski among them, had been transferred to other locations.

Had Devlin St. James killed Harden Hathaway? Did his damn family name mean so much to him? I shook my head. What did I tell Scarsdale? Not a damn thing. I needed more proof than a letter from a self-proclaimed blackmailer.

I climbed from my truck and headed toward Senator Scarsdale's door.

The housekeeper answered the doorbell.

"The Senator is on the back terrace. I will show you."

Scarsdale sat on a wrought iron chaise with a drink in hand, and across from him lounged Devlin St. James. I had no idea they were such buddies and I did a quick re-think of what I would say.

"Morgan." Scarsdale waved toward another chair. "Sit down, Join us. Would you like a drink?"

"Iced tea would work." I nodded toward St. James. "Senator."

"Mister Garrett. I had no idea you would be dropping by this afternoon."

Scarsdale took a sip of his drink. "Didn't I mention that when you called this morning? Thought I did when you invited me for a round of golf."

St. James pulled a cigar from his shirt pocket. "You might have. My memory isn't as sharp as it was two years ago." He clipped the end of the cigar. "Do you partake, Mister Garrett? I have another."

I shook my head. "Never developed the taste." I noticed he didn't offer a cigar to Scarsdale.

The housekeeper arrived with my iced tea. She carried a tray with sugar, honey and a small plate with a selection of yellow, blue and pink packets. There were also slices of lemon in a small bowl. I declined all and took my glass of tea.

St. James lit his cigar, puffed, blew a stream of smoke into the air as he settled back into his chair.

I faced Scarsdale. "I can come back later, Senator. I've nothing much to report. Everything's running smoothly with your security team."

"Good. Good. The new girl is working out?"

"Yes, sir. I partnered her with Jimson. They're a good match."

St. James cleared his throat and Scarsdale glanced his way.

"Any news about Everett Cummins?" my boss said. "Senator St. James is of course anxious."

I looked at St. James. He did seem concerned, but why was that? I watched his face as I spoke. "Everett Cummins has been located. It isn't good."

"Everett's dead, isn't he?"

St. James' voice, like his face showed no emotion. "He is, Sir. They found him and his car half-way down a cliff, north of San Simeon."

He blew more smoke into the air. "They're sure it's him?"

"Positive."

"Dear God," Scarsdale said. "How did it happen?"

"Details are sketchy."

"Where's Everett now?" St. James said.

"I'd guess he'd be in San Luis Obispo's morgue. They'll probably want to do an autopsy to determine cause of death," I said.

St. James stood. "The man was eighty years old and driving an ancient automobile. He lost control. What other reason could there be?"

"You know cops," I said.

"I'll have Everett moved to Santa Maria, arrange for his services." St. James stuck his cigar into his drink. "His wife will have

to be found."

"Wife?" I said.

"My step-daughter, Bethany, she's in Europe."

A wife, young one too. I filed that fact away. Did St. James know about Cummins' son?

St. James stuck his hand out in my direction. "Thank you Mister Garrett. I wish the news were better, but it's good to know. Where do I send your check?"

I shook my head. "No check. I work for the senator."

"If that's the way you prefer things."

Time to nudge the hornet's nest. "I could look into it a little more."

"Why?" St. James said. The word seemed casual, but I saw his lips tighten before he turned toward Scarsdale. "I can't take you away from the senator for any longer."

"Just something I heard one of the officers say."

"You heard?" St. James said.

"Yeah. Didn't I mention I was there when they pulled the car up?"

St. James stared into my face. "You didn't."

"What did you hear?" Scarsdale said.

"Something about there being no blood in the car. " I shrugged. "Seems a little strange. It looked like he'd gone into the windshield…but no blood."

Scarsdale leaned toward me. "They suspect foul play?"

"They were mistaken," St. James said. "Who would want to hurt old Everett?"

"Morgan could find out for you." Scarsdale said.

"That isn't called for. I'm sure it was an accident." He looked at me again. "I won't take up anymore of Mister Garrett's time."

"No problem if that's what Senator Scarsdale wants."

St. James let a frown slip out, before he schooled his face into a deadpan expression. "That won't be necessary. Everett wouldn't want so much bother." He started toward the door. "I'll see to everything. Thank you for your time, Mister Garrett."

See to everything? I just bet you will. I watched him walk away.

"Well, I'm glad that's over," Scarsdale said. "Not the death of course, but at least St. James knows what happened to his friend."

Friend? I doubted it, but yeah, St. James did know what had

happened to Everett Cummins, and I planned to know too. It tied in with Asa Kaminski and probably with Cummins' son. I just needed to figure out how.

There wasn't much more to say to my boss, I'd done what I'd come to do. "I'll report in again on …"

"I have something more to talk to you about."

"What's on your mind, Senator?"

"My investment counselor made a strange statement to me on Thursday when I paid my regular visit. He handles my campaign funds which are separate from my regular investments. With the campaign now at rest, for a while anyway, I don't see him too often. This last visit, he indicated he was having a hard time in Santa Maria, some unexpected expenses. He sounded as if he thought I could do something about it." The senator frowned. "He's been sound in the past, but I want you to look into it. I need to know if I should pull my campaign money."

"I'm not much on high finance Senator; maybe you need someone else to…"

"No, no one else. I need to keep this quiet."

I frowned. "Is all of the money there?"

"I believe so, yet, how do I know for sure. Just do some research into what he's doing right now. See if there's a hint of anything that could be an embarrassment to me or my investors."

"How did you meet him?"

"Oh, Senator St. James highly recommended him."

St. James again. "What's this guy's name?"

"Morris Frost. He has an office on Cook Street in Santa Maria. It's most likely nothing, but I'd feel better if you looked into it. I'm on my way back to Washington so call me there if you find anything."

"Why an office in Santa Maria? Why not here in Santa Barbara?"

"I've been with Morris for three years now. I've always received a good return on his suggested investments. I saw no reason to change when he relocated."

"Okay. I'll look into it."

We said our goodbyes and I headed back to my truck. I'd exited the Scarsdale's driveway when my cell phone rang. It was Darcie. I pulled to the curb and answered.

"Hello, Sweet thing."

"Morgan."

Darcie used her, in-full-cop-mode, voice, and alarm bells went off inside my head.

"What's up?"

I listened as she filled me in about her and Wes' talk with Tomas Flores. I waited until I knew she had finished before saying. "You think it's legit?"

"I do."

It made sense, a lot more than Kaminski being taken out over a helmet. St. James couldn't have people looking too close at him if he was playing house with some bad-boy druggies, even worse if he was the head bad-boy. Had Everett Cummins gotten too close? "You talked to Gail yet?"

There was a long pause. "I called you first since you're already having dealings with St. James."

"Not any more. I've been dismissed. The esteemed senator doesn't wish for me to look any deeper into Everett Cummins' unfortunate accident."

Darcie snorted into my ear. "Of course he doesn't."

"This has to do with Cummins' son too. That's Gail's…"

"I bloody well know. I'm calling her right after you hang up. Morgan, she may not want you to get involved."

"Too bad, my new client wishes else wise. I'd prefer to work with the FBI, but…."

"Well, this Santa Maria detective will be overjoyed to get in bed with the great Morgan Garrett, PI."

"You're such a flatterer. I'll see you at home."

"Not home. We don't talk work at home. Meet me at Café Noir. Let's say four o'clock."

I looked at my watch it was one thirty. "You got it, Sweet thing."

Darcie laughed and ended the call.

*****

I drove easy, kept at the speed limit as I passed the rolling hills that had once teemed with cattle, but now had become wine country. How had they decided these hills were better for vineyards? I enjoyed the drive. It gave me time to think.

I'd sure like to meet St. James' step-daughter, Bethany; I bet she's a pistol. Marry an old guy like Cummins and go off to Europe and wait for him to die, or maybe she didn't wait. Now there was a

thought.

Dropping into Santa Maria I decided to check out Morris Frost's office.

Cook Street seemed quiet and lazy and I was comfortable waiting in my truck. I had another hour before my meet with Darcie.

So far I had seen no one go in or come out of Frost's office. With an internet search on my blackberry I'd already learned Frost was recently re-married and his new wife waited for him in a plush house down in Orcutt, south of town. His divorce had led to his move into Santa Maria. A nasty affair, affair being the operative word, seems he had trouble keeping it zipped.

Now what is this? I sat up straighter in the truck. A Hispanic street punk, with his big shirt hanging outside his shit-kicker pants, walked into Frost's office. Now that's interesting. He didn't look like he'd be much in need of an investment counselor. I noted the time. Ten minutes later the Hispanic came out in a hurry and walked to the curb. As soon as he arrived, a dark, maybe black or blue, chopped-top hot rod picked him up and sped away. Now what was that all about?

Five minutes later, a slight man exited the office. He had to pass me. I looked down, pretended an interest in my cell phone, but glanced up as he came abreast of the truck. Yeah, he matched the photo from the internet, Mister Morris Frost. He looked scared shitless and I could see he sported a split lip and a swelling eye. A gift from the Hispanic? This had all of the makings of a denied protection offer, or was it something else. I thought of Darcie's words about someone new uniting the local gangs. Not good. Just how deep was St. James into this? More questions, and I'd start by asking my love a few of my own.

Chapter Seventeen
Gail Crane

"I NEED SOMETHING to drive," Duke said to me. We'd just passed a rental lot. I nodded, made a turn at the next corner and doubled back. As my car idled in the parking area, he turned to me.

"Thanks so much for everything Gail. If you hadn't taken me to Global Air, I wouldn't have met Mister Hughes."

I wanted to say, it was my job, but I knew it was much more. "You're welcome, Duke."

He climbed from my car. "Can I call you?" and then, "would you like to have dinner with me? I'm buying." He patted his back pocket.

His invitation floored me and then I smiled. "I'd love to."

Duke's expression grew serious. "Gail, there is a lot about my life I don't know, but more and more as I go along I'm learning who I am deep down and I, well... I don't know how I ended up by that jet, but I don't feel I was involved in its crash."

"I hope not Duke. I really hope not."

He looked like he'd expected a different response from me, but right now it was all I could offer.

"I'll pick up the car and then I think I'll take my father's, no, my, Stearman up for a ride." Duke hesitated. "Gail, I don't know the policy, but will you keep me in the loop about the crashed jet?"

"You're a big part of my case, Duke. Of course I will."

He nodded and turned away.

"Duke," I said. "I'm very sorry about your father."

He didn't say anything for a long moment and then. "I'm sorry too."

I watched him walk away my stomach a jumble of emotions: the thrill of Duke asking me to dinner, a fierce ache at the sadness in his face. What must it be like, not to be able to mourn your own father? To not have a solid past, only brief flashes of memory? Tears filled my eyes and I blinked hard. Well, it was my job to fill in some of the

blank spots, get the answers, no matter where they took me and I'd start at my office.

*****

I'd just logged into the bureau's site when I heard a tap on my office door. I looked up. Darcie stood there. "Come on in."

"I can come back later."

"No, the timing's fine." I stood, met her halfway and we exchanged a hug. "It's great to see you."

"Yes, but it would be better away from our offices."

"Amen to that." I looked closer at her. Her entire demeanor screamed this was no pleasure visit. "What's up, Detective?"

Darcie settled in the chair across from me.

I raised an eyebrow.

"It's about the Nojoqui Falls incident. You're the closest thing I know to a liaison between the FBI and us."

I nodded, waited.

"You know about Everett Cummins, what you don't know is how they found his body."

"Car accident," I said.

Darcie frowned. "I don't think it was an accident."

"Go on."

"His head hit the windshield, hard from the way the glass looked, but there wasn't any blood in the car."

"Shit," I said. "Homicide then?"

Darcie nodded. "I asked for a complete toxic screen, and for them to send the car to Santa Maria."

"And?"

"They are, but…."

"Would you like it to come here?"

Darcie hesitated before answering. No, she really didn't want the car anywhere near the FBI. My dear friend hated to give us even an inch of control. I got it, I was the same way.

"The Nojoqui crash and this is related," Darcie said. "I feel it."

"Makes sense, Everett Cummins knew something, it got him murdered. Duke must have seen something too, but why didn't they kill him?"

Darcie shrugged. "That's for you to find out."

Her words raised some questions in my head and I didn't like them.

"There's more," Darcie said.

I waited.

"You remember during the Ice case last year? I told you about Tomas Flores."

"The local drug dealer that went to Mexico."

"He's back. He called for a meet-up at the Metro Club with Wes and I." Darcie stood, walked to the window. "Flores says someone big has moved into Santa Maria. He's uniting the gangs."

She faced me. Darcie looked pissed, no not pissed, she looked insulted.

"They've branched out into white-collar crime, added a protection racket and prostitution to their resume."

"Who is it?"

"Flores only gave one name, and he isn't one-hundred-percent sure about it."

I waited.

"Devlin St. James. Flores also says it's all tied together. The plane crash…he called Everett Cummins by name. He knew he'd been killed."

"Shit and double-shit," I said. "But no way can I move on this without proof."

"Wes and I'll get it. This type of crap doesn't happen in my bloody town."

"There'll be more," I said, "probably identity theft and Medicare fraud. Thank you for the information. The bureau will look into it."

"Where do you want San Luis' finest to park the car? It'll be here tomorrow?"

It was my turn to hesitate. St. James' possible involvement changed everything.

Darcie jumped on my slight pause. "Everett Cummins' murder is my case."

"I work for the FBI, remember. F stands for federal," I said. "That means all of the states."

Darcie's lips tightened. "I didn't have to tell you."

"I would have found out."

"Maybe, but when?"

My face heated. Diplomacy, use Diplomacy. Hell, I'd suffered through more than one class outlining the techniques. I took a deep breath. "Let's don't turn this into a pissing contest."

Darcie looked startled, and then laughed. "We're big girls. We can share."

Yes, we'd share, as much as the bureau would let me. "We use a local garage. I'll sit it up and call you. You and Wes can be there if you want, but the FBI will use our specialist."

"We want," Darcie said.

I waited, it was her turn to make nice.

"Wes and I are talking to Flores tomorrow. Soon as we know more I'll call."

I could have Flores picked up. The bureau would expect me to, but Flores didn't know me from Adam. Darcie and Wes would get it all from him sooner and easier. There was one other little issue. "How does Morgan tie into all of this?"

Darcie only missed a heartbeat before she answered, but it was enough. "What makes you think he does?"

I sighed. "Tell him to be careful. There's a limit on how many times a line can be crossed."

"Senator Scarsdale's his boss, not St. James."

I held her gaze with mine. What wasn't she telling me? Her phone rang and broke the tableau.

"It's Da."

She answered it. "Hey, Da, can you hold for a bit?" Darcie looked at me. "We'll talk soon."

I nodded. "And thanks for the information, Detective. It puts a whole new spin on things."

Darcie turned and walked out the door.

Just how much of a spin? I reached for my telephone.

*****

The bureau's info sites are a wealth of information, but sometimes like now, it was way too much. The screen spilled data about Devlin St. James faster than I could take it in. The ex-Senator was way too damn pure to be real. No one's family escapes without one or two little skeletons.

I'd almost had enough nicety-nice to make me gag, when a murder in Montreal, Canada scrolled by my field of vision.

UNIDENTIFIED BODY FOUND IN LOCAL HOTEL APPARANTLY THE VICTIM OF A ROBBERY. HAD THE PHONE NUMBER OF A SANTA MARIA CALIFORNIA MAN. NO FURTHER DATA. LA OFFICE HAS BEEN NOTIFIED.

LA office? "What are we? Chopped liver?" I grabbed my phone. Yes, I was a bit territorial.

"Shind…"

"Harry," I interrupted before he could finish speaking. "What is going on with LA? Are they withholding information from us?"

"Hold on Gail. What are you talking about?"

I took several deep breaths before reading him the report and then giving him the quickie version of Darcie's visit, omitting St. James' bit for now.

"I don't see what one has to do with the other."

"The dead guy had a Santa Maria phone number, that's our jurisdiction."

"That's a stretch, but okay. Let me make a few calls and I'll get back to you."

Chapter Eighteen
Duke Cummins

THE RED POLY-FIBER covering of the Stearman Model 75 gleamed in the afternoon sun as I watched Rick and Juan roll the aircraft toward the hangar door.

"Hey, Mister Cummins, she's sure a beauty," Rick called. "Old Ev wouldn't let us touch it. He did all this himself."

"Just don't get any hangar rash on it."

The airplane was called a Stearman by aviation buffs everywhere, but had been built by the Stearman Aircraft Division of Boeing Aircraft Company. I knew this one had gone from military trainer, to crop duster, to being my father's pride and joy, now it looked like it was all mine.

Everett Cummins. My father. God that was hard to comprehend, but he'd loved this bird. It showed the same meticulous care I'd seen on the Lear.

I moved toward the engine and started my preflight walk-around; the whole process felt both strange and familiar.

I settled into the seat. It felt comfortable and yet I knew I had never been in this ship before. Shit, will this strangeness ever go away?

"Contact, switches hot," I yelled to Rick and Juan as I started the Pratt & Whitney R-985 engine, smiled as it fired off immediately and settled into its natural guttural, round engine, roar. I signaled to Juan to pull the chocks and then watched as he darted under the leading edge of the wing to remove the yellow wooden blocks that served as brakes when the aircraft sat idle.

I checked to be sure Juan and Rick were clear, taxied forward a few feet and applied the brakes to make sure both operated normally. Satisfied, I called the tower to request clearance for taxi to the takeoff runway.

As I zigzagged my way down the taxiway, I heard a voice in my

head.

The pilot's forward visibility in airplanes with a conventional landing gear is restricted by the nose and engine rising in front of him. This presents a special set of problems. The landing gear configuration, known as a tail dragger, makes it necessary to use the steerable tail wheel to zigzag a course down the taxiway.

I recognized the voice, the moderation, the slight drawl. Did it belong to Everett Cummins, my father? I waited, listened for more, but it was gone.

I pushed it away. I was going up, and nothing was going to spoil the moment. "Santa Maria tower, this is Stearman three zero tango ready for take-off."

"Roger, three zero tango, hold short. We have a Cessna one fifty on final."

The small Cessna trainer glided past my windscreen.

The tower operator called. "Three zero tango, into position and hold.

I taxied onto the runway.

"Three zero tango, you are cleared for take-off."

Easing the throttle forward I felt the leap of the Stearman, like an eager young colt ready to run.

I climbed to 2500 feet and swung toward the ocean, away from the Air Force missile base at Vandenberg.

Beyond the rolling sand dunes I could see waves shimmering in the distance.Morro Rock jutted above the haze. Banking right toward the Nipomo Mesa I reduced the power and descended toward the nearly dry Santa Maria riverbed.

I felt relaxed and contented. This is where I belonged.

Looking at the tiny cars on the 101, I thought of Gail. She was like that, all hustle and bustle. Me, I'm more laid back. That I knew. I looked forward to our date this evening. I had known Gail only for two days, but it seemed much longer. I enjoyed being with her and I'm pretty sure she felt the same way, but I could have it all wrong. She's an FBI agent. I might be nothing more to her than a case, and shit, I don't even know who I am, not really. I know my name; where I worked, who my father was, but I don't feel any of it. Could we ever make it work? "But God, I do like being with her."

Sudden anger burned inside my stomach. Who had taken my life away from me, and why?

Maybe a fly-over the crash site at Nojoqui Falls would show me something.

I turned eastward.

As I neared the site, the scar the Lear left on the landscape was clear and visible. The aircraft had torn through trees and underbrush. The place where it had come to rest still bore a black burn on the almost denuded terrain.

Making a second circle over the area I was struck by an oddity in the crash path. Normally in this type of accident, the aircraft travels for some distance along the ground. This path was short, as if the ship had crashed, nose-down. Any pilot worth his stuff would have kept the nose up as long as possible.

Orbiting the site I stared at the scar on the land. With each new view I was struck with the obscene crash of a perfectly good airplane, for no apparent reason. No. There had to be a reason; I just didn't see it yet. The one thing I was sure of, there was no one flying it when it hit the ground.

Bringing the wings level I turned to a heading to put me in the traffic pattern at Santa Maria. "Just enjoy the flight. There's nothing to do about it right now." I scanned the sky ahead looking for other traffic, turned the radio volume up a notch. It was time to go back.

Chapter Nineteen
Darcie Devonshire

"WHAT'S UP, DA," I asked as I walked from Gail's office.

"I know you're at work, Cupcake. I wouldn't bother you, but..."

"It's fine Da. I'm on a break."

"Well my timing couldn't be more perfect then. Animal control just called. Someone has dropped off a basset hound, a senior male. In pretty bad shape, they're going to put him down if..."

"Put him down. Why?" I interrupted.

"They're full, overcrowded. The older ones don't get adopted."

Tears filled my eyes and I blinked. Morgan hadn't even moved in with me yet. He and Becky were still coming to terms with each other. I didn't have any idea how either of them would take to another member being added to the family.

"Could you foster the old guy for awhile? The closest rescue is inland, of course they're full too, but they'll put out a call for some family to adopt him."

I had to swallow before I could answer. "I'll go get him right now."

"Thanks, Cupcake. I'll drop by to meet him as soon as I can."

*****

I turned into the parking lot of *Santa Barbara County Animal Control*. My stomach started to churn before I even turned off the motor. I'd only been here one time, with a neighbor who'd lost a cat. Her Mabel hadn't been here, but the sight of all of the pets that needed homes had haunted me for days. I'd left in tears. No matter how unpractical the urge, I wanted to give everyone of them a home. I couldn't, but at least I could for this one.

I climbed from the SUV, took a deep breath and walked toward the front door. I was happy to see a lineup at the counter. From the overheard conversations they were all there to adopt, not to give up a pet.

Thirty minutes later my turn came. "Hi, I'm Darcie Devonshire. My dad called me about the senior basset hound you took in."

The women flipped though the stack of papers she had beside her. "Oh yes, the owner surrender." She looked up at me. "You know he's not a youngster?"

That's what senior means, I wanted to say, but I smiled instead. "My dad told me."

"He's also a basset hound. They can be..."

I cut in. "I have one of my own."

She pushed an application toward me. "You need to fill this out."

I nodded, took it, and stepped back.

It didn't take long. Soon I stood again in line, a much shorter one now. The same lady took my application, gave it a quick once over.

"Looks good, you'd be a fine home for any dog."

"Can I take him now," I asked.

"Don't you want to spend some time with him in the back?"

I shook my head. "I know I want him. He can go with me today, can't he?"

"There's nothing to prevent it. He's up to date on his vaccinations and already neutered."

"Can you tell me why he's here?"

"Oh, he didn't bite anybody or anything like that. He seems to be a real sweet old guy." She looked down at a sheet of paper. "His original owner died. Her son took him three months ago, but they lost their home and had to move in with his wife's family. All of them hate dogs. So he's here with us now."

Tears clogged my throat. I had to swallow before I could go on. "Well he's got a forever home with me." And just like that, I was a foster failure before I'd even been a true fosterer.

She looked up at me then, and really smiled. "I'm so glad to hear that. All I need from you is his adoption fee."

I wrote the check.

"You wait here. I'll get him."

I walked to the cat cage and watched three kittens play tag with each other. I'd thought about getting a cat, but so far Becky hadn't seen one she didn't want to have for dinner. Maybe a kitten would work.

What was the name of our new family member? I realized the lady had never said. He must have one. I looked toward the window

and saw her coming toward me leading a tri-color, lumbering giant. My God. He was way bigger than Becky. From nose to tail he had to be close to five feet long.

They came through the door and his brown eyes looked right at me. "Hello, Big Guy." I held out my hand. He sniffed it and wagged his tail. "Does he have a name?"

"Yes. It's Benbow. His first owner named him for that inn up by Garberville. You know it?"

I nodded. Nice inn, but the name would have to go.

"You have a leash?"

My cheeks warmed. I hadn't given a leash a thought. "Do you have one here I can buy?"

"You take this one. Drop it by the next time you're out this way."

"Thanks," I said.

She handed the leash with Benbow attached, to me. "He seems to know how to walk on one."

Benbow and I followed her back to the counter.

"He's entitled to a free check up from your local vet. "

I nodded. "I'll take care of that right away."

She smiled at me. "I know you don't plan to bring him back, but I have to tell you this anyway. You have some time to make sure he's going to work out, but if he doesn't then you have to bring him back to us. Understood?"

"I get it. He won't be back, though."

She bent to reach for something and then held out a small sack of dry dog food toward me. "He gets one of these also."

"No, you keep it for another dog."

She nodded. "It'll be put to good use." She handed me some paperwork. "Then that's that. You have a good life Benbow."

I could see we'd already been dismissed and her thought waves had moved on. I turned toward the door. "Let's go home, Big Fella."

At the SUV, I opened the back and then looked down at him. Now what? I hadn't thought about this either. With Becky she'd been trained to place her front feet on the entrance into the back, then I hoisted her hind-end. I sure couldn't pick this guy up and deposit him inside. "Well, what are we gonna do?"

He gave me a tail wag and then rose and placed his feet just where they should go. Smiling, I did my part and he was in. I kept a large doggie cushion in the back for Becky. He moved to it, gave it a

good sniffing, and then settled. He fit, but I didn't know how Becky would like sharing.

I took my place behind the wheel and glanced back at him. "What are we going to call you? Benbow's a nice inn, but it doesn't seem to fit."

He looked at me, then closed his eyes and sighed in contentment. Tears again filled my eyes. His paperwork said he was seven, but judging from his grey muzzle, Benbow, soon to be called something else, had to be about nine. No way would he have been high on someone's list to adopt. I'd bet that within a week he would have been on his way to the Rainbow Bridge. It hit me. Benbow. Rainbow. Too girly? No, just right and so fitting. "Rainbow," I said. He looked up, straight into my eyes. "Now I have to tell Morgan, and you have to meet your new sister, Becky."

I looked at the clock in the dash. Four-ten. I was late. I opened my cell phone and called Morgan. He answered on the second ring.

"Change of plans," I said by way of greeting. "Can you meet me at home?"

Chapter Twenty
Morgan Garrett

ANOTHER BASSET HOUND? I'd listened in astonishment. It turned to pride and understanding as Darcie talked. I got it. I did, but damn, Rainbow was moving in before I could. I finished my coffee and stood. Time to head home. I smiled at the thought. Home. Yeah, it was. Moving my stuff in was only a cherry on the sundae.

*****

In the driveway, I parked next to Darcie's SUV. A brown head popped up. So this was Rainbow. I moved toward him. "Hello, Big Boy. Why are you still in there?"

"Hey, Morgan."

Darcie stood inside the front doorway.

"We'll introduce them in the backyard. You bring Rainbow."

I glanced at the basset hound. "Maybe I should be the one with Becky. He doesn't know me."

"The big, bad, private dick, afraid of a little basset hound?"

"Little? Not hardly."

"Open the back. The leash is in the left corner. I'll stay right here in case Rainbow attacks you."

I did not find the amusement in her voice, amusing. I opened the back of the SUV. Rainbow did not move from his cushion. Now what? "He seems to like it in here," I said.

"Just call him."

Right. "Come on; let's go meet your new sister. I hope she warms up to you faster than she did me."

Rainbow stood and ambled to me. Well, I knew how I got Becky out. Here goes nothing. I reached for him, circled his middle with my arms, and lifted. Good God. He had to weigh at least seventy, but it was all solid muscle. I deposited him on the ground. "You stay right there." I grabbed for the leash, hooked it on in a rush. "You sure you want me to bring him into the backyard. Her highness is just getting

to like me."

Darcie didn't answer for a moment and then said. "Yes, I think that's the best way. I'll be in back."

"Yeah, let me be the bad guy," I murmured, leading Rainbow toward the rear gate. "We're coming in."

Darcie waited with Becky on the patio. The basset hound sniffed the air and her tail wagged at our arrival, both good signs. "Hey, Princess," I called. Beside me, Rainbow stopped, plopped his rear end down. Uh-oh. I looked at Darcie. "Does the new guy not play well with others?"

"I forgot to ask," she said. "He likes cats."

I groaned. "Super. We don't have any cats."

"I'm letting Becky go."

Becky sauntered toward us and I was proud of her sedate, ladylike behavior. A quiver ran through Rainbow and he pressed hard against my leg. "It's okay. She's not all that bad for a female."

"Hey, watch the chauvinistic crap," Darcie said, as she walked toward us.

Becky stopped in front of Rainbow. I reached and patted her head.

"Go ahead and let him off of the leash," Darcie said.

She scratched behind Rainbow's ear as I unhooked the leash.

"This is home. Go check it out," she said.

Rainbow walked a few steps from me, and looked back.

"I'll show you around," Darcie said.

She moved deeper into the yard, waited. Our newest family member did not follow. He still looked at me.

"I think he wants you to walk with him," Darcie said.

"Me." I tried to remain manly, but I felt a tug at my heart. "Why not? We males have to present a united front."

Side-by-side we did a tour of the yard. About half way through, Becky joined us. We finished our loop and the three of us walked toward Darcie who stood on the patio with a proud look on her face.

"I think it's going to work out," she said.

"We'll see what her highness thinks when it's time for the interloper to go home and he doesn't."

"Let's check Rainbow's reaction to the doggie door."

Darcie went inside and closed the sliding, glass doors.

Becky went on high alert as Darcie walked toward the treat jar.

Without a second glance at us, she rushed through the flap on the pet door.

"Okay Bow," I said. "Your turn."

He looked from me, toward the flap, then ambled to it and went inside. I felt a wash of pride as I followed.

"Want a cookie," Darcie asked.

"I'll pass." I grinned at her.

Darcie turned to Rainbow, held out the doggie treat. I almost laughed at the look of insult that showed on Becky's face. Rainbow gave Becky a look, took a step nearer toward Darcie. I heard a soft growl from Becky.

I looked at Rainbow. Come on, I silently urged, don't be a wuss. Rainbow faced Becky and a low rumble came from him. Becky looked shocked, but she lowered her backend and remained quite as Rainbow went to Darcie and accepted the doggie treat.

Darcie knelt and the two basset hounds came to her.

I watched her stroke and fondle their ears and a wave of emotion made my knees weak. God, I loved this woman. It made me sick to think about how close I'd come to losing her permanently to the booze.

A thought hit me like a sledgehammer, us living together wasn't enough. I wanted to marry Darcie Devonshire, make it all legal and binding. Oh, shit. The M word. We'd never talked about it. Not even when we were together with the CIA, then we believed making plans for the future would jinx whatever assignment we were on. Things were different now. Would she say yes? A part of me I didn't know I had ingrained, surfaced. I had to have her dad's blessing, not only his, but Wes' too. I wouldn't say a word to her, until I spoke with them. What kind of ring would Darcie like? Did she dream of a big wedding? I swallowed at the thought. I hoped not. I'd ask Gail. Women must talk about that kind of stuff.

"Morgan. Morgan."

I realized Darcie had said something to me. I snapped out of my thoughts. "Yeah?"

"We still need to talk."

"Yes, yes we do," I said and looked at her. There must have been something in my voice, because a strange expression flicked across her face.

"You okay? I know I should have checked with you first before

bringing Rainbow home, but there really wasn't any other choice."

"No. No. He's great. I was thinking about something else," I hurried to say.

"Not very pleasant from the look of panic on your face," Darcie said.

"Things go okay with Gail," I asked.

Darcie shrugged. "About as well as I expected them too. No talking work though, not here." She stood. "Let's keep that date we had for Café Noir."

I glanced at Rainbow and Becky. It looked like they had an uneasy truce in progress. "You think it's fine to leave them?"

"They're okay. We'll take the SUV. I'll drive."

*****

At Café Noir we ordered cappuccinos and grabbed a table in a quiet corner near the fish tank. I watched the goldfish and let Darcie choose the time to start our conversation. It wasn't a long wait.

"St. James is dirty," she said. "Sounds like he has been for a long time."

"Looks to be so."

She frowned. "We need proof."

"We'll get it. What does Gail say?"

"We're both making nice, for right now. "

A girl brought us our cappuccinos. I took a drink of mine. "How long's that going to last?"

Darcie sighed. "As long as it can. I hope it doesn't screw with our friendship too much. I like Gail."

"You think this Flores guy's going to be a help?"

"He will to get his little sister out of there. She's in a place called Harmony House. It's a so-called shelter for battered women"

"How will you get her out?" I said. "It sounds like that's where she wants to be."

"We'll bloody well get her to him. After that she's his problem."

I nodded, drank more cappuccino. "You said the pace is in Santa Barbara."

"That's right."

"Out of your reach." I dank more coffee. "You want me to get her?"

Darcie smiled down at her cup. "I can't ask you to do that, but if she showed up in Santa Maria, it would be a huge help." She slid a

photograph across the table toward me.

It showed a close-up, face shot, of a pretty Hispanic girl. "Consider it done. What's your plan for now?"

"Wes and I are going with Flores to talk with a guy that's being shook down for protection money."

"Your captain okay with it?"

"He will be." Darcie sipped from her cup. "What are you up to tomorrow?"

I told her about Morris Frost and his messed up face after the little visit.

"Sounds like he also said no to something," Darcie said. "Same thing?"

"Don't know…yet."

"How does Cummins' son tie into all of this?" Darcie said. "And Rick Kaminski's grandfather?"

"Both good questions. The link seems to be St. James. When is the FBI going over Everett Cummins' Buick?"

"Tomorrow."

Darcie rubbed at her forehead.

"Headache?" I said.

"A little one."

"Let's go home and I'll kiss it and make it better."

She grinned. "My feet are killing me too."

"Sweet thing, I've got the medicine for anything that's ailing you."

Darcie pushed her cup away and stood. "Well then what are we waiting for?"

Chapter Twenty-One
Gail Crane

GETTING READY FOR my date with Duke I felt like I was sixteen again and it was my very first. Let's hope it ended better than that one, a wrestling match in the back of Danny Church's old Ford Galaxy.

It was hard to decide what to wear when I didn't know where we were going. Should I opt for jeans and a sweater, or did it call for a slinky black dress and grandma's pearls. "Relax girl, it's just a date." I kept telling myself, but I wasn't listening. I changed from the black dress, back to jeans, then back again. I'd just reached to unzip the back of the dress again when the door bell pealed. Well then slinky dress and pearls it was.

Duke stood at the door in jeans and dark-blue polo shirt. He smiled. "Wow, you look fantastic."

"Thank you." I stepped closer and touched his arm. "Just, where are we going to eat?"

"I had a craving for some red meat and Rooney's Irish Pub was recommended to me. Have you ever been there?"

"Once, right after it opened. It's a great place. I love Guinness, but I'm over-dressed."

"No you are not. I'll change our destination to The Santa Maria Inn before I let you get out of that dress."

I smiled. "Well, if it doesn't bother you. One rule, we don't mention work. Deal?"

"That's fine with me."

We didn't talk much on the ride to Orcutt, but it wasn't a strained silence, it was a comfortable one.

At Rooney's we parked and Duke hurried around to open the car door for me. He let me take the lead as we walked toward the front of the brick building. There, I stopped and grinned in delight. "I don't remember that from before." I pointed to a small door off to the side

of the main entrance. A sign above it declared in a private entrance for leprechauns. "I love it."

Inside we were seated in a slightly raised area with a great view of the pub. Duke ordered us both Guinness' as the waitress handed us menus. Looking around I soaked in the Irish pub influence. The dark wood of the bar on the far side of the room was stunning. I wondered if they had brought it over from Ireland.

The waitress brought our Guinness'. I ordered *Beer-brined Roast Chicken* and Duke opted for the *Lost Sheppard's pie.*

*****

The dinner conversation flowed between us so natural I found I resented even the few interruptions by the waitress.

"Where are you from Gail? Are you a native Californian?"

"No, I am an Iowa girl who ended up in California because of the FBI."

"How did you pick the Feds?"

"I went to college in Oklahoma, a small one in Lawton. I applied when I was a senior there, when a recruiter came to lecture. I was surprised when they accepted me."

"Do you know that Joan Crawford came from Lawton?"

"That so."

"And the world war two flying ace, Robert Johnson."

"How interesting," I said, sounding anything but. "Have you ever been in love?" My out of the blue question surprised even me, but I realized I really wanted to know his answer.

He stared at me a long moment before answering. "I don't think so.There must have been women, considering my age, but I don't feel I've even been in love. How about you?"

"I thought I was once, but it didn't work out. His name was Tony. He was a stockbroker, a real wheeler and dealer according to him. It didn't take me long to see it was all in his mind. Underneath all the talk was, was a small boy, self-centered, and shallow." I frowned into the air. "I came home one night and found he had moved out and all I felt was relief that it was over."

"That happens I guess." Duke said and for the first time there was a moment of uneasy silence. He ended it with, "Would you like desert? I've heard the *Cinnamon Apple Bread* pudding is fantastic."

We'd ordered a bottle of wine to go with our dinner and now I held out my glass and said, "No desert, but how about a little more

wine?"

He nodded and poured wine into my glass.

It was when Duke was explaining some vague concept about an airline he wanted to start someday, when I realized even though I had no idea what he spoke about, I was hanging on his every word. Watch out girl, you're treading on slippery ground. You know nothing about this guy except the bare facts. You don't need another Tony repeat. "This wine is good," I blurted. "How did you know about it?"

"A lady at the grocery store. It's a local wine a former actor down in Los Olivos came up with. It's called Muscat Canelli. She said we should go visit the winery."

I felt a pang of jealousy. "I'm sure your new lady friend would love to go with you." God I sounded bitchy.

"Don't think so. She was picking wine for some guy in San Luis Obispo. He was with her. From their conversation I think she picks everything for him, including his underwear."

I took a long drink. "She doesn't seem to be your type. Have you met anyone who is?" Good one, Gail. Could you be any more blatant?

"Do you mean outside of present company?"

"I didn't know I was included in that category." The way I sounded I wouldn't blame him if I wasn't.

"Do you want to be?"

Hell yes, I thought, but I said. "Maybe."

"Then you just went to the head of the list." Duke stood. "Let's get out of here."

I scooted out of my seat.

Duke took my hand as we walked across the parking to his Ford Mustang and it seemed the most natural thing in the world. I thought again of my first date with Danny Church and us parking in the woods. Duke and I were a little beyond parking and necking, but I couldn't help but wonder what would happen next. Should I ask him in when we got to my place? Maybe ask him what he'd like for breakfast. "I like the car you chose."

"I like fast cars that handle. Maybe it comes with being a pilot."

I smiled. "Or not. I like fast cars too. My very first one was a 1967 red and white Mustang convertible. I named her Marilyn." I glanced at him. "I still have her."

His eyes lit. "You do? I'd love to see it."

"She's in the garage at home."

"You have a vintage mustang and you drive around in a tan sedan?"

"Work car. It's expected." I winked at him. "Want to come back to my place and check out my car?" I laughed. "That sounds about as cheesy as asking you to come by and look at some etchings."

Duke reached to grab my other hand. "Gail, I'm pretty sure I'd go just about anywhere with you."

He pulled me closer to him, lowered his lips toward mine. The kiss was gentle, exploring. Our still clasped hands rested against his chest and I felt his heart race.

The kiss deepened.

With a gasp I stepped back. "Duke…I…we don't even know each other…"

"I know, but it sure felt right." He reached behind me and opened the car door. "Now how about showing me that Mustang of yours?"

Chapter Twenty-Two
Darcie Devonshire

I KISSED MORGAN, rolled away from him and stood.

He opened one eye. "Hey, where you going? It's not even dawn."

I walked across the bedroom and opened the blinds. Bright sunlight flooded the room "Think so."

He yanked the coverings over his head. A muffled curse came from beneath them and then. "Alright. Alright."

I closed the blinds. "You don't have to get up. I'll check on Becky and Rainbow, get them fed."

Morgan's head appeared from beneath the coverings. "What time you getting home tonight?"

"The usual, about five thirty. You?"

"Not sure. I plan on doing some digging into Morris Frost's life and then..." he hesitated, "boxing up my stuff and moving in."

A wave of pleasure surged through me, tinged with a nip of unease. I'd been living by myself for a long time, well with Becky for the past year. What would it be like to share the house with someone full time? "Well don't hog the closet and you can have the bottom two drawers."

Morgan snorted. "I won't need a fraction of the closet and why the bottom drawers? I'm taller. What if my back..."

"I was here first. Squatter's rights."

"Darcie, this will work. I know it will."

"No doubt. It isn't the first time we've bunked together. It'll be great to have someone share the housekeeping duties."

He groaned. "Fine, but I don't do windows." Morgan leered at me. "Why don't you get back in bed and I'll show some of the fringe benefits of us living together."

I smiled. "I'm very aware of all of the benefits. Rain check. Okay?"

"Fine, but the forecast better call for a regular downpour damn

soon."

Laughing, I continued my way toward the bathroom.
*****

Wes was already in the office when I walked in. I couldn't remember that every happening before. "Morning partner, we clear to ride about the Flores business?"

"Cheerio, English. Yeah, Captain says check it out, but don't make it a full-time job."

"Flores?"

"He's meetin' us in front of Sears at the mall." He stood and grabbed his jacket. "My turn to drive."

In the car Wes turned to me. "You going to be there when the feds go over Cummins' Buick?"

"I bloody well will be."

He put the car in reverse. "Why the interest?"

"It's not right. He was dead when the car went over the cliff."

"I wouldn't know, since I wasn't with you." Wes' words were delivered with a pronounced chill.

"Morgan was looking for Cummins too. We were together when the captain called. I had to move on it."

"Guess it's just as well. I heard Morgan threw Senator Scarsdale's weight around. You couldn't have got that from me. That's right, right? You know how jumbled things get when they're repeated over and over."

I glanced at Wes. He stared straight ahead, the epitome of a spurned lover. I felt a pang of remorse. He should have heard all of the details from me. He was my partner. Well shit. I hated apologies, giving and receiving. "Sorry Wes, you're right. I at least should have called you when we returned." I looked at him again. He smiled now.

"That must have hurt."

I didn't bother to answer, instead I changed the subject. "We have a new family member."

"Oh yeah. Morgan move in?"

"Rainbow, another basset hound." I gave him the story of Rainbow's rescue.

"Well, I'll be damned. Good for you. Her highness handling things well?"

"They're still working through things, but so far so good."

We parked in front of the Sears store.

"There he is." Wes honked the horn and waved toward Flores. He looked at us, but didn't move. Then Tomas Flores turned and walked away.

"What the hell?" Wes started to get out of the car.

"Wait," I said. Two Hispanic guys detached from the portion of the wall draped in shadow and followed. Both were tall, mid-twenties, one sported a thin mustache, the other reminded me of the Pillsbury Dough boy with a tan.

"Shit," Wes said. "Now what?"

Flores went inside Sears.

I reached for the car's door handle. "Let's do some shopping."

We hung back but kept the men and Flores in our line of vision. In the lingerie section the two guys seemed to lose interest in Flores. They stopped in front of a table where bikini panties were displayed. The Pillsbury boy picked up a red, lacy, thong. He said something in Spanish too quick for me to understand and the other guy laughed.

"Wooh-wee," Wes said softly. "They like those. They are hot. You think Janey'd like?"

I had an identical pair, for special occasions. Yeah, they looked sexy, but I found them to be bloody uncomfortable. But Morgan liked them, a lot. "Do you recognize either of them?" I said.

"Nope."

"We need a photo for ID." I glanced at myself in a mirror. Navy-blue slacks and a white blouse, I could pass as an employee. "I'll distract them; you get the photo with your cell phone."

I sauntered forward, stopped in front of the display case. They still held the pair of panties. "They come in black and purple too," I said.

They looked startled and then the thinner one leered at me. "How about you model for us?"

"Against store policy." I forced a smile.

The other guy looked at my chest. "You're not wearing a name tag."

"I just arrived. I haven't clocked in yet." In the mirror behind them I watched Wes maneuver closer. He lifted his phone and on the way to his ear with it, he paused for a second. I saw the fat guy frown. I picked up a white pair of satin, bikini panties and waved them in front of his face. "What do you think of these?"

"Too virginal, you got anything crotch-less?" The skinny one

said.

"Or how about edible?"

I'd had enough of the boob-sey twins. "Oh, look at the time. Gotta check in. You guys have a nice day." I turned and walked away. I could feel their gazes glued to my ass.

Wes waited for me at the escalator. "Got it," he said. "I've already sent it in."

I grimaced. "Thank God. I feel like I need to shower with disinfectant."

He grinned. "Flores went up."

We found him standing in front of a display of hammers. "You talk to him. I'll keep a lookout for our two boys."

Wes came back in short time. "Wants us to meet him in the alley behind Nichol's Pawn Shop."

I groaned. This cloak and dagger stuff was getting old. "What about dumb and dumber?"

"He says he can lose them."

"Let's go." I turned toward the escalator.

The alley behind the pawn shop wasn't too bad as far as alley's go, the usual white dumpster and assorted empty boxes. It didn't look or smell like it was a nighttime home to anyone.

We waited in the car. A door opened and Tomas Flores came out. I noticed he didn't close it behind him. Wes didn't climb from the car. He made Flores come to us. I knew it was payback from the runaround we'd been involved with today.

Wes rolled down his window. "We ready to talk now? No telling what could be happening to your sister the past sixty minutes or so."

Flores flushed. "Dominick's scared. He's not sure he wants to speak with you."

"Your friend making good money?" I'd been in the shop a few times checking on stolen property and it hadn't looked very affluent to me.

Flores looked at me in puzzlement.

"He can afford to be paying for protection? It won't end. He does know that?" I said.

"What happens when they want more?" Wes said.

"Dominick say he can handle it."

Wes snorted. "I hope he's got health insurance. He's going to need it."

111

A thin, black, man stepped from the alley door of the pawn shop. He motioned toward us. "Looks like Dominick is having second thoughts," I said.

Wes' cell phone beeped and he looked down at it. "We've got an ID on the two bozos from the mall. Ricardo Dominquez and Felipe Juarez. Well, surprise. They've both been in trouble before. Small stuff, known gang ties. Last address was in L.A." He looked at Flores. Held out the phone. "They Juan Carlos' boys?"

"Never seen them before."

"Why were they tailing you," I asked.

"Don't know. Maybe I ask the wrong question."

"Well quit asking," Wes said. "You're no use to us if they're suspicious or you're dead."

We exited the car and Flores led the way to the back door of the pawn shop. "Detectives Smith and Devonshire." He motioned toward us. "This is Dominick Nichols."

"Mister Nichols," I said.

Wes nodded.

The black man glared at Flores. "Why did you bring them here? I told you no. What if you were seen?"

"We weren't," Wes said, "but we don't have to be here. It's your skin."

Dominick Nichols switched his glare to Wes. "Yes, maybe, but losing some skin is better than being dead."

The man was clearly petrified. He continually searched the alley even as we spoke.

"Come on in," he said, and then shut the door behind us. There were three locks on the door. Wes and I shared a look as Dominick engaged all three, then turned to the left and punched in a code to an alarm system.

"Precautions are fine and dandy," Wes said. "Doesn't do much good during business hours though, does it?"

The black man turned away.

We followed him into the front of the shop. Light flowed in from the windows. Racks of merchandise lined the pale grey walls. A long glass counter filled one side of the small room. It held watches, cell phones, old coins and a hoard of jewelry. I moved closer to a display of suitcases and guitars. There wasn't a speck of dust on them. Beneath the edge of a briefcase I caught a glint and leaned closer. It

was a shard of glass. I looked at Dominick. "Are they only destroying merchandise for right now?"

The black man's lips thinned, but still he did not answer.

"Won't stop there," Wes said. "First some stuff and then you if you still won't pay…."

Dominick again glared at Flores. "I don't know what you're talking about."

"Tell them, Dom," Flores said. "They can help."

"They can get Angela and the kids hurt." Dominick Nichols snapped.

"Mister Nichols," I said. "We can help…"

"You haven't before."

My face flushed. "We weren't aware of the issue."

Dominick smiled.

"Let's get out of here. It's all a waste of time," Wes said.

"No," Tomas Flores said. "Dom, tell them."

The black man turned, walked behind the counter. "I don't know what…" A bell jingled and Dominick jerked his head toward the door, at the same time I saw him rest his right hand on the handle of a hand gun setting on the lower shelf.

A mailman walked in. He must have felt the tension in the room, because he hesitated in the doorway before moving toward Dominick. "Morning, Dom," he said, before laying a stack of mail on the glass counter.

"Enjoying your walk, Keith?" Was the black man's reply.

I could tell the exchange was a daily one.

"Good enough. Good enough." The mailman looked into each of our faces. "Well you have a nice day." He turned and walked back to the door.

I wondered if he would be calling the station with a concern. Sure enough, I saw him pull out a cell phone as soon as the door closed behind him. He could be making a lunch order for all I knew, but I doubted it. He had looked too closely at our faces, memorizing. Why? What had he seen or heard on his daily route? I made a mental note to do some talking with mailman Keith.

I heard a moan and turned back to Dominick Nichols. He stared at a five by seven manila envelope in his hand.

Wes and I looked at each other.

"You've gotten one before?" Wes said.

113

"No, not me, but I know some who have."

Flores touched the other man's arm. "Dom?"

"Okay." Dominick swore beneath his breath. I think I heard him say interfering asshole as he tore open the envelope with shaking fingers. He pulled out three photographs. "Dear God." Dominick moaned.

"May we," I asked.

He pushed the photos toward Wes and me. I picked up a pencil and used the eraser end to separate them. The first two showed a boy and a girl. The girl looked about seven, the boy younger, maybe four. The girl stood in front of Alvin school, the boy sat at the top of a slide in a park I didn't recognize. The third photo pictured a pretty black woman standing beside a maroon Toyota Camry. I could see a Von's store sign in the background. "Your family?" I said.

"My wife Angela, daughter Krista, and my son, Alan."

I flipped the photo of the wife over. There wasn't anything written on the back. The picture was enough; no words of threat were needed.

Dominick stumbled back, collapsed into a chair. "They know you're here. God, what have you done to us, Tomas. Get out. All of you. Just get the hell out."

"No Dom, they can't know," Flores said. "Look at the post mark." He pointed at the envelope. It was stamped yesterday's date. "It's been at least three days since the photos were taken."

"He's right," I said.

The black man looked at me. "Then what will they do when they find out you were here?"

I didn't answer.

"You help us. We stop them. Threat gone," Wes said.

Dominick looked toward Flores. "You trust them?"

"I do."

"It started about six months ago. Some street punks came in, said they had a message for me for El Rios."

"Hold it," Wes said. "Who's El Rios?" He pulled out the notebook he always carried in his shirt pocket.

"I don't know. I'd never heard of him until then."

I glanced at Flores. "Do you know the name?"

He nodded.

I looked again at Dominick Nichols. "Go on."

114

"They said my shop would be safe as long as I paid the premium."

Wes snorted. "Premium? Like in insurance?"

"Yes".

"And if you didn't?" I said.

"There would be accidents, break-ins, fire, vandalism."

"You paid?" Wes said.

"I did."

I glanced at the photos. "What happened?"

"They keep raising the cost. El Rios' last demand is more than I clear in a year." Dominick wiped sweat from his forehead. "Last week I said I could pay no higher premium, and today I get these."

Wes glanced around. "You got a surveillance camera?"

"I do but El Rios never comes, just the two punks."

"We'll start with them."

"I'll get you the cd."

I watched Dominick walk into the back room.

"Who's El Rios?" Wes said to Flores.

"It's more than this." Flores gestured toward the shop. "There's the drugs, the girls, and computer stuff. You get my little sister, then I give you his name?"

"You little…"

"Do you have an address?" I interrupted Wes.

"I find out she's in Santa Barbara. This her picture too." He handed both to me.

"Where would you like her delivered?" I said.

Flores didn't answer.

"We can find out where you live easily, numb-nuts," Wes snapped.

"Bring her to the Metro Club. Call me. The phone number is on the paper. I will be there."

Dominick Nichols came back into the front of the shop. He held out a cd case toward me. "They are on here."

I took it.

"Now what?" he said.

"It's business as usual." Wes said.

"My wife. My children."

"You give El Rios his blood money," Wes said. "They'll be safe."

Dominick's shoulders slumped. I reached out, touched his arm. "Hang in a bit longer. We will stop him."

He nodded.

"Can we take the envelope too? There might be prints." I said.

"Yes. Please use the back door. I will lock up after you." Dominick led the way.

Flores, Wes and I followed. I knew a dismissal when I heard one.

Chapter Twenty-Three
Morgan Garrett

LEAVING THE HOUSE I shook off thoughts of Darcie and decided I would check out Scarsdale's financial guy again. Frost's office had parking in the front like a motel, only the driveway went on back and around the building. I'd just parked down at the end of the lot, to keep my private eye persona intact, when I got the big surprise.

The dark blue, low slung, hot rod from yesterday slid to a stop at the curb instead of using the available parking. The surprise came when out stepped an old friend limping on the leg I'd knee capped some months ago. He and his companion moved to Morris Frost's office.

Ten minutes later I watched the two come out again. That was fast. What was it all about?

Now what? Without much thought I decided to follow the two and see where it led.

Keeping two cars or more between us, I thought back to the day Gimpy and I met. I was trying to find the Senator's run away daughter. Mr. Gimpy had info I required, but was reluctant to provide. I had to work on his kneecap a little before he gave me what I needed. Seems it had left him with a permanent limp.

They drove along Broadway, then turned into a housing complex past Newlove. There were more automobiles than garages so cars were everywhere. It was hard to pick out the ones that would run from the junk yard heaps. Nice neighborhood. Grey paint seemed to be the favorite with most of it peeling and fading away.

The second guy with Gimpy I'd never seen before. I needed his photo for I.D. purposes.

I dug out my Blackberry.

Stopping beside a long row of the grey garages I watched the dark blue rod and waited for my quarry to give me a good position

for a picture. The big guy who stepped out from between the garages surprised the hell out of me.

He pounded on my hood. "Hey Gringo, what the fuck you do here?" Mister Charm had a two day growth of beard. He leaned down to look in my window and I grinned. They never learn. I always believe the best form of defense is a full frontal attack, so I opened the door and slammed the edge of the frame into his face. With a hoarse scream, he dropped to the ground. I scrambled out of the truck, circled to stand above him and watched the blood squirt threw his fingers. It looked like maybe I'd broken his nose. It was all quite fun, but the incident had attracted attention. The two I followed ran toward me.

"Hey you, wha…hey I know yous," Gimpy said, pulling up. Fear showed on his face, but his big partner keep coming.

"What you want man?"

The walking mountain was in full aggression mode, and right in my face. I don't like people in my face, especially his kind of people. I cupped my hands and clapped them on both sides of his head. That little move will rupture one or both ear drums, more important it hurts like hell. The guy backed up, holding his head as blood ran from his left ear.

"You." I pointed at Gimpy. "Why were you at that financial office?"

"I'm not telling you nothing."

"You forget who you're talking to, shithead? We've been down this route before."

"Hey you stay the hell away from me."

"Wrong answer." I spun, kicked out at Gimpy's bad knee. He went down screaming.

"Now you want to try again?"

Whimpering he looked at me, "Why my knee every time? El Rios said go there get the money. I go."

"Who's El Rios?" Turning I saw my door victim trying to get up. "Stay right where you are. You can get up when I tell you to. El Rios, who is he."

"He, he the jefe, but we all work for the Russian guy."

The crowd was building; I needed to get the hell out of here before they realize they had me out numbered. Backing into my truck I used my option to run away and fight another day.

A new jefe and some Russian guy? It didn't sound much like vintage Santa Maria. I'd been busy, but the day was still young. A visit to O'Grady's couldn't hurt. Its owner, my old friend Paddy, knew things, and had a better handle on street gangs than anyone in town. I rubbed at my throbbing hip. Damn. That spinning kick didn't useed to hurt so much. Darcie wouldn't like me going into the pub, not a good place for an alcoholic, but you go where the information is. I wouldn't lie about it if she asked me straight up, but I saw no reason why she would.

The lunch crowd was still in full swing and Paddy was busy at far end of the bar when I walked in. Spotting me he waved. He drew another couple of beers, placed them in front of customers, then poured me a cup of coffee.

"Morgan, boy' yo. Long time between visits," he said placing the coffee in front of me.

"Paddy, good to see you. You too busy to talk?"

"Not to you Laddie Buck. What's on your mind?"

"I've got a gang name I wonder if you've heard it? El Rios."

"El Rios? Yeah, he moved in to take Juan Carlos's place after you put him out of business."

"Actually Darcie and Wes did that."

"Yeah, sure. That's about all I know about him."

"How about 'The Russian'; or maybe just a Russian?"

"No, I haven't heard anything about any Russians."

A group of five came through the door. "I'll let you get back to work. Darcie and I'll call to have you over for dinner."

"That's sounds swell, Laddie. Want a cup of coffee to go?"

"No, buddy, but thanks."

I stepped out of O'Grady's and into the midday sun.

A Russian huh. How did that fit in? St James maybe, or did I have it in so bad for St James that I was reaching? Well, play it as it comes, follow the clues like a good little detective. El Rios. Now what kind of name is that? A gang moniker I'm sure. So, what I need is his real name. I needed to pay a visit to Morris Frost.

*****

Frost's office was quiet, no secretary or receptionist. The standard decorator's prints on the wall and a fake banana tree in the corner. The outer desk looked used, although nothing marred its top today. I moved on to the one office. I recognized Morris Frost from

yesterday. Up close I could see his bad comb over. It spread over his pate like fingers of seaweed floating without order.

"Good morning." I walked in and stood by his desk.

He jerked his head up. "Uh, good morning. Can I help you?"

"My name is Morgan Garrett. I work for Senator Scarsdale. Security. Who were the street punks I saw here earlier?"

"They, uh, you what? Who are you again?"

"Garrett, I work for Senator Scarsdale and I'm a little worried about the kind of clients you have."

"Clients…un, they are not clients."

"Yeah. What did they want?"

"I am sure that is my business. Did the Senator send you here?"

"I work for the Senator. Who were they?"

"Well, a local bunch. They were selling, uh, insurance."

"Yeah? Did you buy any?"

"They are very persuasive. I may have no choice."

I glanced down on his desk and saw a print-out of a young pretty woman. "Is that your wife?"

"Yes."

"They gave you that?"

His head went down. "Yes."

"Did they make a threat?"

"Not a verbal one."

"But they have been here before?" I stared at him, daring him to deny they had been in before.

"Just once."

"You called the police?"

He shook his head. "They don't want a lot. It's a small price for security."

He wouldn't meet my eyes.

"You're lying to me aren't you? You've been paying them for some time, now they have upped the ante."

His shoulders slumped. "Yes, and they demand more then I can pay. They say they will hurt my wife. What can I do?"

"First you need to get your wife out of town. Next you need to call the police. Tell them everything. This kind of shake down only works because people do what they want. Grow some balls. With your help the police can break this thing. How many people do they have their hooks into?"

"Some, I don't know every one of them. The beauty shop across the way for sure. I've seen them in there before."

"Who is El Rios?"

"He's the boss. I've never seen him."

"How about the Russian?"

"Never heard of him."

"Okay. Are you going to call the police?"

"I ah…yes, yes. Today. I'll call today."

Going through the door I thought, wait 'til Darcie hears this. She'll blow her English lid.

Chapter Twenty-Four
Gail Crane

I STOOD INSIDE the doorway of the local garage the FBI had leased to collect evidence from cars when needed. This was the first time we'd used it. The air smelled like oil and gasoline. It reminded me of the times I'd played assistant to my dad when he'd tinkered with our cars. I'd learned early the difference between a straight slot and a Phillips-head screw driver.

Everett Cummins' Buick had arrived about an hour ago. She was a beautiful car, two toned gray, and in excellent shape if you ignored the ruined windshield and caved in front grill and fenders. I expected Darcie and Wes to put in an appearance anytime now. I'd already gloved up, so I walked to the driver's side door of the Buick.

A young technician was on her hands and knees in the backseat. She held sticky tape and pressed it against a section of the gray broadcloth seat cushion as I watched.

I opened the front car door and peered inside. Most of the surface had a dusting of fine, fingerprinting powder, but nothing else. Not a sign of dried blood anywhere. I stepped back and moved to the front of the car. The windshield was a spider web of cracks. Cummins' head had to have hit it hard to cause so much damage. Scalp traumas bleed; there should have been a large amount of blood. FBI training stressed no conclusions before all of the facts were known, but no way was Everett Cummins still breathing when his Buick went over that cliff.

"Anything, Rachel?" I said to the tech.

"The inside of this car is cleaner than mine, and I had it detailed yesterday." She frowned. "I lifted one set of fingerprints and found some fabric threads beneath the driver's seat."

"No blood?"

"Not even any that had been cleaned up."

I nodded. "Thanks." I moved to the back of the Buick, looked

inside the open trunk. Pristine as the rest of the car. I suppose Duke will inherit. I wonder how hard it would be to restore the Buick to its prior condition. I knew from last night that Duke had a love for vintage automobiles. That thought took me right into reliving our series of goodnight kisses and my cheeks warmed. God that man could kiss. We'd both agreed without any discussion things would go no further last night, but I damn well wanted them too, and judging by Duke's reaction pressing against my lower stomach he had too.

"Agent Crane. Agent Crane."

My name being called, loudly, penetrated and I looked toward the door. "Yes."

"Two Santa Maria detectives are here."

"Yes, let them in." Darcie and Wes came toward me. "Detectives," I said.

"Agent Crane," Wes replied.

Darcie smiled and nodded. I saw her eyes shift to the Buick.

"Anything show that we hadn't already figured," Darcie asked.

"Doesn't look like it"

"No blood?" Wes said.

"Not even any detected with luminal."

Darcie walked to the front of the Buick. "Not bloody-well likely."

"Have your received a copy of the autopsy report yet," I asked.

Darcie frowned. "No, they're backed up as usual. I do remember Everett Cummins' forehead was pretty bashed in."

I looked again at the ruined windshield. "Makes sense, but I'm betting it wasn't the cause of death." I turned toward the door. "Let's talk outside." I led the way to my car. I noticed Wes and Darcie had parked their's next to mine. "Anything more from Tomas Flores?"

It made me happy that neither hesitated in filling me in on their visit with Dominick Nichols. "So they are branching out."

"You ever heard of El Rios," Wes asked.

"No, but I'll look into it. It would be good to have his real name."

"We'll get it for you, just…"

I interrupted Wes. "What does Morgan plan to do about Flores' little sister?"

"What makes you think I've asked Morgan to get involved?"

How could she say that with a straight face? I wanted to laugh, but controlled the urge. Wes managed to only grin at her words.

"So, when the girl is free, Flores will give you the real name of El Rios?" I said.

"He will," Wes said.

Darcie's cell phone went off. She glanced at the number. "It's the coroner." She lifted the phone to her ear. "Detective Devonshire."

I watched her face as she listened. It wasn't good news judging by her frown.

"Thank you for getting back to me so soon," she said and ended the call. "Everett Cummins' cause of death was a broken neck."

"Well that makes it official," Wes said. "We're looking at a homicide not an accident."

"Why bother to run the car over the cliff?" I said. "The killer had to know we'd see right away that Cummins was dead before being placed in the car."

"Time maybe," Wes said. "That is a pretty desolate stretch of road. It's a fluke the car was spotted so soon."

Darcie shook her head. "He could have buried the body, ditched the Buick, if he wanted more time. I think he's a bloody arrogant asshole."

"Damn, English, tell us what you really think," Wes said, then smiled.

My cell phone vibrated against my hip. I checked the caller. It was Duke. My cheeks warmed as I answered. "Agent Gail Crane."

"Gail, they've set a day and time for my father's memorial service."

"They?" I said.

"Devlin St. James."

"St. James set it up without speaking with you?"

"Under the circumstances he felt it would be better for him to handle the arrangements. How could I know what Everett would want, with my little memory issue and all?"

I heard the controlled anger in Duke's voice. Had St. James already claimed Everett Cummins' body? I didn't think the coroner mentioned that to Darcie.

"My father's wife gave them the go ahead to move him to Santa Maria," Duke said.

So Bethany Spangler was home from Europe. "When is the service?"

"This evening."

124

"What the hell. Isn't that a little soon?"

"St. James pulled some strings. It seems he has a tight schedule and my dear step mommy needs to get back to France, after the reading of the will of course."

"What time tonight? I'll be there."

"Seven. And thanks, Gail."

I could tell he wanted to say more. "Duke, what is it?"

"They wanted my father to be cremated."

"Who?"

"Bethany, but it's St. James who's calling the shots. I told her my father wouldn't want that. Dear step-mommy asked me, oh so sweetly, but how the hell would I know?"

Anger filled me. "If you don't want him cremated, then he won't be." Who did I know that could trump St. James' wishes?

Duke laughed. "He's not going to be. His will stated his desires for burial. He already has a plot. His lawyer said so."

"His lawyer. Duke, how…?

"I didn't. Delilah Willoughby did. She was with me at my father's apartment when Bethany called." He chuckled. "I guess she could tell by my words I wasn't happy. When I asked about a will and my father's last wishes she told me the name of his lawyer, Nelson Oates. He's the same one she uses, a friend of her late husband. I hung up on Bethany, called him, and he called her."

"I'll see you tonight, Duke." I ended the call, turned to Darcie and Wes. "They're having Everett Cummins' services tonight."

"I heard," Darcie said. "Wonder why the coroner didn't mention that Everett Cummins' body had been taken?"

"Seems like St. James is in an awful hurry to get him in the ground," Wes said.

"And to be cremated," Darcie said. "He probably was hoping to take care of it before the autopsy could happen. Score one for the good guys."

"The report gave us nothing we didn't already know," I said.

"But he didn't know that," Wes said. "Did the coroner say anything about the tox screen?"

"Are you serious? That'll take weeks. This isn't television," Darcie said.

"So why's St. James so spooked?" Wes said. "His push for a quick cremation screams he knows something about Cummins' death

that we don't."

"He's panicking, and that's in our favor," Darcie said. "Wes, you and I are going to be at those services tonight."

"Wouldn't miss it, partner."

*****

Back in my office I tapped a pen against my teeth and waited for the day to crawl by. It seemed like seven o'clock would never get here. I wanted, no, I needed to see Duke. He'd sounded so down. My desk phone rang. "Agent Crane."

"Gail." It was Harry Shindley. "Check your email. I called the L.A. office and got more information on that body found in the motel room. He was registered as Stan Jacobs from Omaha, Nebraska. Check it out. Oh, and they sent a photograph too."

"Thanks Harry."

He ended the call. I pulled up my email, opened the message and clicked on the attached file. Jacobs had been shot twice in the heart with a small caliber gun. Ballistics hadn't confirmed make or model. From the gunshot residue the gun had been very close to Jacobs when fired. I looked at the photos of the dead man, one a close up of his face, nothing memorable about him, except for the long scar running down the left side of his nose.

There wasn't much more, it seemed they couldn't match their photos with any living or dead Stan Jacobs. No surprise there. So who was the dead guy? I closed the file, made a mental note to follow up on it after I'd finished Duke's case.

I pushed back from my desk, looked again at the clock. Four-fifteen. Close enough. Maybe I'd get to the mortuary a bit early, see if I could help Duke with anything. I frowned again at my blank monitor, then opened my PDA and pulled up the notes I'd made from my interview with the line boys at Global Air. I read the list of people that had boarded the Lear. No Stan Jacobs listed. No mention of a scar on any of them either. I pulled up my appointment calendar. One of the bureau's sketch artists was to meet with the two boys tomorrow morning. Had I let Rick and Juan know? I found Rick Kaminski's contact information and punched his phone number in.

"Hello."

"Mister Kaminski, it's Agent Gail Crane. We spoke at Global Air."

"Yes Miss Crane, I remember."

126

"I'd asked you to meet with an FBI sketch artist. I have it on my schedule for tomorrow morning, but I can't recall if I'd spoken with you and Juan about the appointment." It embarrassed me that I didn't know for sure and excuses pressed against my lips, but I refused to let them escape.

"Yes, Miss Crane, the sketch artists called and let us know."

"Good. I'll see you tomorrow morning at ten then." I ended the call. Dwight had called for me. I remembered now that Dwight always double-checked his appointments, but I still owed him a drink.

I grabbed my jacket and purse and headed for the door.

Chapter Twenty-Five
Duke Cummings

THE FIRST THING I noticed inside the mortuary room was the low rumble of voices; the second was the soft, flowing notes of, Amazing Grace. The air smelled of the flowers that lined the walls and lemon Pledge. The memory of another funeral service came to me, a guy in Africa; they'd been playing the same song when I'd walked in.

A somber, dark clad usher leaned toward me.

"I'm Jonathon Cummins," I said.

He nodded and led me to the front pew. An older man sat there, ramrod straight. He must be Devlin St James. Not only had he taken over arranging the service, he was sitting in the family pew. I recognized the red-headed women next to him from the photo in my father's apartment. Bethany Spangler, aka -- Mrs. Everett Cummins. At least she was family, if only by marriage. I nodded at them and settled at the opposite end of the pew without speaking.

My father is dead and I have no idea who he was. It's like some awful joke. I tried to bring up some memory of the man and found nothing. I felt queasy and had the urge to get up, walk out and just keep walking. I could go back to Africa, put this all behind me. Where was Gail? She said she would be here.

I felt the presence of someone on my left and looked up into the pale face of Delilah Willoughby.

"Mrs. Willoughby, please sit here." I could feel the frail thin hand quiver as I took it to help her into the pew "So nice of you to come."

"Of course I came. I've known Everett for many years. I see she made it also." I looked at Bethany Spangler hoping she had not heard Mrs. Willoughby. A foolish hope since Mrs. Willoughby spoke quite loud and clear with no attempt at artifice or pretense. The younger woman kept her eyes on her lap, but I could see her cheeks redden.

I looked around the room. It was half full and more people were

arriving. How had they known my father? I spotted Gail toward the back.She sat with a man and a woman. They must be Morgan and Darcie. Her gaze met mine and she smiled. Gail looked lovely. I started to rise, but the service began and I settled back into my seat.

"Everett Cummins was a man well thought of in this community…."

The minister, a total stranger to me, spoke in a somber monotone. I wondered if he'd known my father. I folded my hands in my lap, waited and willed it to all be over.

A procession of people stood, said glowing things about Everett Cummins, Mrs. Willoughby among them. The minister twice looked at me in expectation, but I didn't rise. What could I say? I noted that Bethany didn't speak either.

The last to rise was Devlin St. James. He made his way slowly to the podium. Silence fell over the room.

St. James stood there for a long moment staring down at his hands. He lifted his head and looked slowly around the room. "Everett would be happy to see so many recognized faces. Although he hated memorials, dead is dead, he always said."

St. James' words struck a chord within me. Yes, my father had said those words, more than once.

"Everett Cummins was like a brother to me. I remember the joy I felt when he married my step-daughter Bethany," St. James said.

Joy? At her marrying a man fifty years older than her?

Beside me I heard a snort from Mrs. Willoughby. I looked across her, to Bethany, whose gaze met mine and I saw rage on her face. What was that all about?

St. James went on. "Everett was a proud Elk. He loved their Friday night dinners. I've heard he also liked to burn up the dance floor afterward.

A few soft chuckles greeted those words.

"I'll honor his memory by keeping my words few, but please join us after the service at the Elk's Hall to take part in a toast to my dear friend, Everett Cummins."

Devlin St. James moved back to his seat, and a short time later the ordeal ended.

I stood and helped Mrs. Willoughby to her feet. Following St. James and Bethany toward the double doors, I looked at Gail as I passed. Her smile was a beautiful thing to see.

*****

My father's single plot was in the newer section of the cemetery, all neat flat rows with metal headstones. I knew he'd already purchased his and had it engraved, all except the day of his death. I glanced skyward. If the minister kept his words brief we'd beat the setting sun by minutes. He did, and we all started toward our cars.

The end of a funeral is always an awkward moment. Everyone wants to leave, but they are unsure how to get away. Now I only had the farewell-to-do at the Elks to get through.

In front of me St. James stopped. "Would you care to ride with us in my lemo?"

Hell no, I wanted to say, but settled for. "Thank you, but I have my car."

He nodded and turned away.

Bethany's purse slipped from her hand. As we both bent to retrieve it she whispered to me. "We have to talk." Then she was trailing behind St. James like an obedient dog.

Standing in the rich green grass beside a small American flag I examined my new loafers, noted the dust and dew drops making mud on the polished leather.

"Duke, can I talk to you for a moment?"

I looked up. The man I'd seen Gail with at the service came toward me.

He stopped and held out his hand. "Damn hard place to meet, but I'm Morgan Garrett."

Morgan Garrett was a bit taller, and heavier in the shoulders than me, and his face showed a lot of mileage.

"I know this is off the wall, but can you fly Darcie and me to Vegas?"

"What?" He couldn't have surprised me more if he'd told me it would be raining cows tomorrow.

"Yeah, I know I get ahead of myself sometimes." He looked sheepish. "Gail told me you work for Global Air. Maybe we could work something out. I'd pay of course."

This was surreal. I couldn't wrap my mind around it. First a memorial for a father I couldn't remember and now a request from a man I didn't know. "It isn't my call." I managed to say. "Mr. Hughes is the boss. Flying can be expensive. I haven't even started yet.

130

What's going on in Vegas?"

"Marriage. Oh shit, don't tell Darcie. I haven't asked her yet."

Well since I didn't know Darcie that would be an unlikely event.

"Let me know. This is my cell number." He handed me a card and then spun on his heels and walked away.

"Jonathon, Jonathon Cummins." I heard a voice call from behind me.

I stuck the card in my pocket, then turned. Mrs. Willoughby approached, escorted by a tall, gangly man in the same age bracket as herself.

"Jonathon, this is Nelson Oates."

I held out my hand. "Glad to meet you sir."

He gave my hand a firm shake and released it. "I'm so sorry for your loss. I thought a lot of your father."

"Thank you."

"I hesitate to bring this up here, but since I've already had three calls from Mrs. Cummins, I'd like to request a firm appointment to go over your father's will."

Delilah Willoughby did not bother to hide her expression of disgust. "Never knew why Ev married that little…"

"Will nine tomorrow morning work for you?" Nelson Oates said.

"Yes," I said, "that will be fine."

"Good, Good. Come Delilah I'll give you a ride to the Elk's Lodge."

I watched the two of them walk away. I didn't figure the reading of my father's will would amount to much. I did hope his widow wouldn't try and take the Stearman from me, or maybe pressure me to sell it.

"Duke?"

I looked up. Gail walked toward me.

"I need a ride."

"You didn't drive?"

Her face flushed. "The Mustang quit on me half way here. I had it towed home and hitched a ride with Morgan and Darcie."

"What's wrong with the Mustang?"

"I have no idea. It just quit."

"You want me to take a look at it?"

"I'd love for you to."

I reached for her hand and gave it a squeeze. "We'll head back to

131

your place right after I put in a few minutes at the Elk's."

I stood at the bar, waited for my glass of white wine and Gail's Merlot. There was a good crowd. I'd moved through them, let Gail introduce me, nodded at their condolences, surprised to hear that most sounded sincere. I noticed St. James had settled himself at one of the white-cloth, draped tables and let people come to him. Bethany sat beside him. He was the king accepting the adoration of his subjects. What did that make my step-mommy, the court jester?

The bartender sat the two glasses in front of me. "Thanks," I stuffed a five dollar bill into his tip jar.

"Duke, we need to talk."

I looked up. Bethany stood there. It was the first time I'd really looked at her in person. She was quite the stunner. Red hair twisted into some kind of knot on the top of her head, gorgeous skin and striking green eyes. I couldn't help but admire the way she made that simple, black dress look like a million bucks. By the small smile that curved her lips, she knew the effect she had on men. Is that how she'd become Mrs. Everett Cummins? "So you said earlier," I said coolly.

"There are some things you need to know."

"I'm listening."

Bethany glanced over her shoulder. "Not here. Meet me later." She slipped a piece of paper into my hand. "Please, for my safety, keep this between you and me." She turned and quickly walked away.

Frowning, I placed the slip of paper in my pocket. It seemed a little cloak and dagger to me, but with everything that had happened I'd play along for now.

I walked back to Gail with our wine.

"What did she want?" she said.

I hesitated for only a breath, but caught the tightening of Gail's mouth as I replied. Bethany wanted to double check the time for the reading of the will tomorrow morning." I held the glass toward her.

"I see," she said, making no attempt to take the wine. "You know what, I'm feeling tired. I'm going to call a cab and head home."

"Thought I was going to take you and look at the Mustang?"

"It's late. Why don't we do it another time?"

Before I could answer she walked away. I let her go. I didn't mind some jealousy, but I wasn't sure that's what it was. Maybe it

was plain old suspicion? Whatever. I wasn't in the mood for it tonight. It had been a hell of a day.

Chapter Twenty-Six
Pieter Orloff

I WATCHED THE hills slide by as we descended into San Luis Obispo. I chose to go into SLO rather than Santa Maria to protect my low profile trip to Canada. No one needed to know I was out of town. Jacob Stanislov was a nuisance I had not planned on. When he called from Montreal saying the buyers had been detained and he needed more money, I knew there was only one thing to do.

I'd knocked. He'd opened the door, his final mistake. One should always check before opening one's door, better yet, he should not have opened the door at all. Remembering the surprise on his face made me smile.

"Orloff, what are you doing here?

"The jet?"

"It's at the airport. Everything's been taken care of. Just getting ready to eat, I thought you were room service. You want to join me?"

I detest meaningless conversation. I shut the door behind me, pulled the revolver from my jacket pocket and answered him with two quick shots.

Stanislov fell to the floor, the surprised expression still on his face. I'd worn gloves, so there was nothing to wipe down. Thirty minutes later I waited in my own room, not at the same hotel of course. I would have not been caught dead in such a place. Caught dead. I chuckled at my choice of words. The televised report was not long in coming. Jacob Stanislov's death was classified as another hotel mugging. Not surprising, considering its location.

"Sir, sir." The guy in the seat next to me said.

I looked up in questioning irritation.

"For the fourth time, could I get out? I'm going to miss my connection."

I could arrange for him to miss much more than that. I smiled and said, "Da, da."

I preferred to wait for the crowd to depart, but I stood and moved into the aisle.

Inside my car I turned on my cell phone. I had one voice mail.

"Meet me at the Garage." El Rios demanded.

*****

I drove slowly by the run-down, tin-sided building. I'd watched for any followers and had spied none, but caution was never out of place. I parked, exited my car and moved inside the building as fast as possible.

Almost blocking the entrance was the black hot rod of El Rios'. Two men I'd never seen before stood by the office door to my right. They spun in my direction, lifted guns. Stupid. Stupid. It was too late now. If I'd wanted them dead, they would be. They did not know me. I should have never been allowed through the door. Sloppy. Sloppy. Maybe El Rios was not the correct man for the position?

"Where is he?'

The youngest pointed at the door with his crutch. "Inside."

The office was daylight bright. I stood in the doorway for a moment and let my eyes adjust. When I could focus, I could see El Rios behind a scruffy old desk covered with auto parts and papers.

"We got the problems," he started without preamble. "You say keep violence down low, but some don't cooperate to good."

"What happened?"

"Hey *pregonero,* come in here."

The kid on crutches came in the door and stood stiffly. "Don't call me crier, my knee's really hurt."

"I'll call you whatever the fuck I want. This the Russian. Tell 'im what happened." El Rios moved from behind the desk. Picked up a big knife from among the papers and casually cleaned beneath his fingernails.

The kid paled. My KGB instructor had used the same tactic years ago. It was good to see it still worked.

"We are waiting," El Rios said.

"Yes sir. This gringo followed us from the stock broker to my place where I stay. He got Jose down and he kicked my knee. The same knee he broke last summer. His name's Garrett. He's no cop. He works for big shot Senator Scarsdale. Asshole Garrett's a mean son-of-a-bitch."

Garrett? Damn, you St. James.

El Rios pointed the knife at the kid. "Tell him ever thing. You talk. Tell him."

"He wanted to know why we went to that office. When I didn't answer him, he stepped on my knee, again, and I had to tell him El Rios sent us."

"What else did you tell him?" I was sure he had told everything he knew, which I hoped wasn't much.

"I told him nothing about you."

Disgusted, I turned to El Rios. "What are you going to do?"

"The gringo is a problem. I will make it disappear."

You can try, I thought, but said instead. "Do it. Quick and clean." I turned and walked away.

In the car I closed my eyes. What first? The Senator? Soon Gail Crane will talk to him. St. James must say the right things and I would see to it.

Chapter Twenty-Seven
Morgan Garrett

WHEN DARCIE ASKED me to help with Flores, my first reaction was not to get involved, but then, I already was, and seeing about Flores' sister would be a small thing. So here I am in Santa Barbara at eight-fucking-o'clock in the morning.

I didn't like the neighborhood. It was obvious gang-bangers ruled here. Even at this early hour punks stood in groups, leaned, against sad apartments and watched my car in suspicion as I drove by. In one of the houses a drape lifted and dropped back in place. Shit. Even eyes I couldn't see watched. One thing for sure I wouldn't be able to sit here and oberve the comings and goings. I needed time to think this out. I'd started to accelerate away when I saw my gimpy friend, still with his heavy duty companion. I pulled up beside them.

"Hey Paco, let's talk."

"What ya want?" The big guy said. I noticed neither came toward me, in fact Gimpy looked like he'd try to run at any second.

"I need to talk to my friend there." I pointed at Gimpy.

"He's through talkin' to you."

"Now you've gone and hurt my feelings." I glanced in my rearview mirror. We'd gained an audience. Not good. "Surprised to see you guys in Santa Barbara, and so early. This where El Rios is? You making a deposit?"

"Don't know any El Rios." The big guy showed me his yellow-stained teeth.

"It's not smart to lie to me. Seems like you should know that from our earlier get together." In the mirror I could see a group of gang-bangers walking toward us. "They make you feel brave? Just remember they won't always be around to help."

The big guy frowned.

The gang-bangers were closer. This sucked. I preferred the more physical way of getting what I needed from scum, but sometimes shit

happens. "Look, I just want some information. I'll make it worth your while."

He looked toward the approaching punks and waved them away. "We doin' business." He turned back to me. "Ask. Twenty bucks for an answer."

I nodded, pulled out my billfold and removed a twenty dollar bill. "Just one question. Which place is Harmony House?"

"Why you want to know?"

"I'm calling on a girl there."

"Not getting any hot-and-spicy at home huh?" He grabbed at his crotch.

So much for it being a shelter for battered women. Unless of course the clientele paid extra for the privilege. I wanted to kick his gonads up to join his tonsils, but I kept my answer to a short nod.

He held out his hand for the money. I gave it to him.

"There, the blue house."

The houses looked quiet, but then I noticed a face in the window.

"Call gimpy over here, then we're going to walk to the house and go in, and you both will be nice and polite. Any questions?"

The big guy motioned to Gimpy, who limped toward us. "We is going to get us a little harmony." He nodded toward me. "He's paying."

"Like hell I am," I said.

The big guy frowned. "You let us watch, then?"

"Oh yeah," I said. "I'll let you watch."

"You park in the back," Gimpy said. "We'll wait for you in the front."

They started toward the door. I parked my truck, grabbed my gun and climbed out. I didn't really expect them to be waiting for me and I didn't much care.

I stuck the gun in my jacket pocket and walked toward the front door.

The house was much like its neighbors, no driveway, no garage, a mesh fence with a missing gate and more weeds than grass. The blue paint had seen better days, but all in all it was no worse than its neighbors.

Gimpy hesitated at the door with big guy right behind.

"Is there a secret knock or something?" I said.

Gimpy opened the door and we walked in.

There wasn't much to see. We were in a foyer with faded rose wallpaper, cracked linoleum and a couple of wilted plants. No one came to great us but I heard noise to the rear.

"Keep moving; down the hall." I said.

We came to a door on the right. Locked; the same with the next door. The hallway ended at a kitchen. Still not a soul in sight.

I moved to the only other door. Still keeping one eye on my two friends, I jerked the door open and found a skinny little creep trying to hide behind a washing machine. His gaze jumped from the big guy, to Gimpy and then to me.

"I was going to pay. I was, but it ain't right. She's my woman. I shouldn't have to pay. You don't tell El Rios and I'll skim you off some good stuff."

I glared at the big guy. "Don't know El Rios, huh?"

He grinned and shrugged. "Where's Manny," he asked the skinny creep.

"It break time. He gettin' his bonus."

Anger gnawed inside my stomach. I could guess what Manny's bonus was. I backed from the room, slammed the door and wedged a chair beneath the door knob.

"Hey. What the hell. You let us out of here." The big guy yelled. I ignored him, walked back to one of the locked doors and kicked it open. The hole, no way could you call it a bedroom, was dirty and smelled like garbage wrapped in marijuana leaves. Ancient paint peeled in every corner. Two girls and I mean girls, one looked to be no more than twelve, lay on the floor in their own excrement. Their arms and legs were bare and I could see needle tracks the length of them. The lighter-haired one had a bad infection that swelled one arm. I'd lucked out. The darker haired girl looked like Anita. I compared her to the photo. A little worse for wear, not so young and fresh looking any more, but it was her.

"Wake up Anita." When I got no reaction I slapped her face. That brought her eyes open and a slurred groan came out with the foamy drool dripping from her mouth.

"Wha…wha you…? Where's Mickey? I need …." She tried to sit up. "Who're you?"

"I'm your savior. Get up."

"Fifty bucks," she said. "A hundred if you wanta play rough." She stood, swayed and I grabbed her by the arm.

We stumbled toward the door. I looked both ways. The sound of the three I locked in the laundry room came to me, but nothing else. I herded Anita's frail frame to the front door.

"What the hell," she said, and tried to pull back.

"Tomas sent me for you."

"Tomas?" She began to cry.

Looking out I could see no activity. I picked her up and ran for my truck.

I went about three blocks, then stopped to make an anonymous call to the police. When they asked for my name I said, "A concerned citizen." And hung up.

*****

"Wes, I've got a present for you. Can you and Darcie meet me at Pioneer Park in about twenty minutes?" I phoned from the side of the highway.

"We're at the station. I'll find Darcie and we'll meet you there. Have you got the girl already?"

"Yeah, and she's puked in my truck so I'll be glad to give her to you."

"Well you've been a busy boy. It's not even ten yet."

Looking over at Anita I could see she was in for a really bad time. Drug withdrawal is a real bitch.

*****

Wes drove up in his unmarked police. Darcie was not with him. "Where's your partner?"

"Couldn't find her and figured you'd like to be rid of your passenger rather quickly." Wes climbed out of the car and walked to me where I leaned against my fender. "Is the kid able to walk?"

"Yeah, but she's in bad shape. Looks like they were keeping her doped up. She's got a tough recovery ahead of her."

"She's Flores' headache now. We got her back. Thanks Morgan; you came through for us again. Was it a big problem?"

"Not bad. There won't be any repercussions, but there is something else I want to ask."

"You got it Morgan if I can do it."

"No, it's not that kind of thing. I…uh…well I want to ask Darcie to marry me and I want your blessing."

Wes' smile looked like it would split his face. "Well it's about damn time. You don't need my blessing boy. She loves you. So

140

what's the problem?"

"I've screwed our relationship before; I want it right this time. This is important to me and I feel doing it right is necessary, even essential. I love her and I know she loves me, so this has to be right."

"You're preaching to the choir Morgan, but if you need the words then okay, you have my blessing, one thing, if you hurt her…well, I'm not going to threaten you, but I will be very unhappy if you hurt her."

We stood there in the quiet afternoon, the sound of cars on Broadway a distant drone. The wind shaking the leaves in the trees seemed peaceful and held us for the moment. I had a friend here and that was a rare thing for me.

"Thanks Wes, that's what I needed. I have to go see her dad now."

"Help me get this kid in my unit." Wes turned and pulled Flores' sister out of my truck. He picked her up like she was a rag doll, clearly not needing my help, so I ran over and opened the door on his car.

I watched Wes drive away. Okay, I had his blessing, now I needed Darcie's dad's.

Climbing back in my truck, I decided my first stop was the car wash. Good God, warm puke smelled bad.

*****

Brady Devonshire and I had once been very close, but my drunken binge and Darcie's leaving me in Iraq had ended that. Now I hoped he would forgive me that behavior and accept that Darcie and I were back together for good.

Brady was a quiet and loving husband, father, a man to emulate. I had always respected him and made this call with a great deal of trepidation. I did not know how he would react, I could only pray. He answered on the first ring. "Mister Devonshire, it's Morgan Garrett."

"Morgan. Nice to hear from you." The words were neutral but I could detect a lot of reserve.

"Yes sir, I would like to talk to you about something important."

"Sure. What's on your mind?"

"I think this is better done face to face. Could we meet; or I could come by your house?"

"Here is fine. How about now?"

141

"Yes sir, I could be there in ten minutes."

"Very good, come along then."

*****

Parking in the driveway I thought of Brady's words to me seven years ago. Darcie and I had been visiting and he'd pulled me aside as we were leaving.

"Son, don't take life too lightly. It goes by fast and love is all we have."

I wished the hell I'd paid more attention to him then.

My stomach churned. I felt like I'd just wakened from a two-day bender. A feeling I'd hoped to never have again. "Come on, Garrett. It isn't as if he doesn't know about you and Darcie."

I got out of my truck, had to laugh at my shaking knees as I walked to the door. It opened before I could ring the bell. Brady Devonshire wasn't a big man, I towered above him, but I knew from experience how fast his presence filled a space, something Darcie had inherited.

"Morgan, please come in."

He led the way to the kitchen. A sure sign he figured something serious was going on.

"Coffee? It's a fresh pot."

I nodded.

"Take a seat."

I pulled out a chair, settled into it.

Brady Devonshire placed my coffee in front of me and then sat in the chair across the table. He didn't say anything, just looked into my face. I wasn't sure how to begin. We'd mended some fences, but there were still holes. I'd hurt his daughter and I hoped I hadn't ruined our relationship beyond repair.

"Is Mrs. Devonshire home?"

"Samantha is having tea with some friends." He drank from his cup. "Morgan, you have something on your mind. It's best to just to get it out."

"Brady I, I love your daughter. I have loved her for a long time. I have some flaws, well hell I have a lot of flaws, but loving her is not one of them."

He remained silent.

"Darcie and I have worked through the past. It'll always be there. We can't pretend it didn't happen."

142

He nodded.

"We've talked about living together; in fact I was planning to move in last night but…."

"Yes, it was bloody-well wonderful for Darcie to go to Benbow's rescue."

It took me a second to know what he talked about. "We changed his name to Rainbow," I said. "He's a great fella."

"My daughter's like that. She wants everyone one to think she uses her head first, but it's her heart that leads. Sometimes that can be a tad of a nuisance."

Quite an understatement. "It's one of the reasons I love her."

Brady stood. "Need a warm-up?"

"No, I'm fine."

He walked to the counter. "I know this is a modern world. Young folks like to try marriage on before they commit to the entire kettle of fish. Is that what you're asking? How I feel about you and my daughter living together?"

"Good God, no," I said.

He faced me. "Then what is it, Son?"

"I want to ask Darcie to marry me and I want your blessing."

He didn't say anything, just looked into my face, then walked to the patio doors and stared into the backyard. "Morgan you hurt her. What about the drinking?"

"I haven't had a drink in seven months. Killing that boy in Iraq is still with me and that will never go away but I am dealing with it. I need Darcie like I need air, but sir, she needs me also."

He nodded. "She's been happier the past months, more at peace."

"We complete each other." Oh God, that sounded so hokey, like something from a greeting card, but damn it was the truth."

Brady turned to me. "I know son, she loves you. You have my blessing."

I surged to my feet. "Thank you, Brady. I know I can make Darcie happy."

"Don't thank me too soon. I have to tell Samantha."

*****

I settled behind the wheel of my car. Two down and one to go. I knew Darcie would want Gail at the wedding. I went over everything in my head, what I'd done and what I still needed to do. I needed a ring, a thought hit me. How could I know Darcie would have

something appropriate to wear. Maybe she'd want a wedding dress. I remembered I'd written down the name of a bridal shop. I opened the consul between the seats and fished around inside. I didn't find the paper, but I did see Rick Kaminski's grandfather's letter.

I felt a rush of guilt. I'd taken the kid on as a client and really hadn't spent much time following through. Well I would change that right now. St. James was obviously the place to start, but how did I find the truth to a crime that old.

Johnny Scott came to mind. I hadn't seen him since I got out of the rehab center. He saved my life when he took me to that place. Dr. John Mason Scott and I go way back. I knew him even before Darcie. We were drinking buddies before he heard the angles wings and quit. I wasn't that smart. Johnny still had contacts in the pentagon.

I called him."Johnny, its Morgan. How are you Saw Bones?"

"Morgan. What are you up to?"

I had my Blackberry on speaker, the street outside was quiet, Johnny sounded like he was there in the truck with me. "Just wanted to touch base with you; I'm still working for Senator Scarsdale."

"Drinking?"

"Not a drop, pal and I hardly think about it more than once or twice an hour."

"It'll get easier."

"Yeah? How about helping me with something?"

"You know I owe you big time Morgan; all you have to do is ask. I wouldn't be here if you hadn't hauled me out of the burning hummer. You know that. Just ask boy."

"I think we're more than even. Anyway, what I need is someone in the pentagon who can give me information about a missing general from World War Two. His name was Harden Hathaway."

"That'll be a tough one. Why do you need this old stuff?"

"It ties into some people I am looking at right now. I don't have any proof so I can't make any accusations, not yet anyway. Do you know anybody that may know something about an old investigation like this?"

"Let me call my old boss; he's in Graves Registration now. He's a Brigadier General and a doctor; he may be able to put me on to someone. I'll get back to you."

With that behind me all I could do was wait.

Chapter Twenty-Eight
Gail Crane

FOUR-FIFTEEN, THE clock hands had moved five whole minutes since the last time I'd looked at them. Well damn. I give up. I kicked the covers off and got out of bed. I avoided looking in the mirror as I made my way to the bathroom. I knew my eyes would be dark-circled and puffy, lack of sleep always made me look like a raccoon. "You're being stupid, Gail. You hardly know the guy. He isn't worth losing sleep over." I bushed my teeth and headed for the kitchen and coffee.

"Besides," I continued my conversation, "you don't know what he said to her. It could be nothing. You're over reacting. Just because she looked at him like he was a leg of mutton and she a starved lioness, doesn't mean…." My vision blurred and I blinked, hard. "Shit. Just shit."

The coffee couldn't drip fast enough. Finally I poured a cup and settled at the table. "Okay, you are officially jealous. Now what?" I took a long drink. "The chemistry between Duke and me, it flows both ways. I know it does."

Then why were you tossing and turning all night? A voice nagged. I ignored it, drank more coffee. "Come on caffeine kick in."

Cup empty, I moved to the counter, refilled it, took another gulp standing in front of the coffee maker. The first caffeine jolt came.

I walked out to the patio. Stars spotted the sky. The neighbor's lights were one. What the hell were they doing up so early? Or maybe they always were. I lifted my face to the cool breeze. Someone fried bacon. I inhaled the odor with greed. I hadn't had bacon in months and suddenly craved some along with eggs, over-easy and whole-wheat toast. "What the hell. Control what you can." I'd shower and have breakfast at Pappy's, then I'd drop by the office before heading out to Global Air to meet with the line boys and the sketch artist."

*****

In Pappy's parking lot, I pushed down on the emergency brake and then turned off the car. On the drive over I'd changed my mind about bacon and eggs. I could almost taste Pappy's country-fried steak. My stomach growled and I grinned as I locked the car door behind me.

Inside the restaurant my appetite sky-rocketed at the smell of frying bacon and coffee, then did a nose dive as I saw Duke and Bethany Spangler standing in front of the cash register. I groaned and backed toward the door, but, *she*, saw me.

"Detective Crane," Bethany said. "Good morning to you. Another insomniac?"

Duke turned around. He smiled.

"That's Agent Crane," I said.

"Gail," Duke said. "What a surprise."

I bet. Why were they together so damn early? "Craving some of Pappy's country-fried steak," I said.

"Us too," Bethany said.

God, how could she sound some bright and chirpy, but maybe she a good reason to be in such a fine mood.

"That was the one thing I really missed in Europe, Pappy's country-fried steak, or maybe the biscuits and gravy." She touched Duke's arm. "Your dad brought me here the first time."

"You're out early," Duke said.

"Couldn't sleep," I answered, looking across his shoulder for the hostess.

"Us either," Bethany said.

Us? The coffee inside of me churned.

Bethany's smile was feline. "I was counting the cracks in the ceiling when I decided to take a chance and call Duke." She laughed. "I was delighted to find him awake. "

"I thought you'd be staying in Santa Ynez with your father," I said.

"Step-father," she corrected me and then, "no, I prefer the Santa Maria Inn."

"Bethany doesn't have a car yet," Duke said. "I know how that is."

I finally spotted the hostess. Thank God, she hurried toward us.

"I'm so sorry. It's crazy in here this morning. Table for three?"

146

she said."

"Oh no. We've already taken up way too much booth space," Bethany said.

I forced myself to smile at the both of them. "You have a nice day."

Bethany sniffed. "Not hardly. We're meeting with the lawyer for the reading of Everett's will."

"I'll call you later, Gail," Duke said. "How's the mustang running?"

"About the same as it was yesterday I imagine." I knew I sounded bitchy, but I didn't give a shit.

Duke looked startled at my tone, but Bethany smiled as she hooked her arm through his. "Well, we'll get out of the way and let you enjoy your breakfast."

I turned my back on the two of them and let the hostess lead me to my booth seat.

"Coffee," the hostess asked as she handed me a menu.

I nodded in silence and she walked away.

*****

I pushed the cooling mass of gravy-covered, steak around on my plate. I'd taken about three bites and knew another one would send me racing for the bathroom. I sighed. All my upbeat reasoning wasn't cutting it. Bethany wanted Duke. Why couldn't he see it?

The waitress stopped beside my table. "More coffee?"

"No, just the check."

"Would you like a to-go container?"

I shook my head. Pappy's country-fried steak had lost its charm for the moment. The waitress walked away. I reached for my purse.

"Gail? Gail Crane."

The words came with a French accent.

I looked up. A man stood beside the table, tall, blonde with ice-blue eyes, a mixture of Paul Newman and Robert Redford when they were in their prime. "Who wants to know?"

"You don't remember me?"

"I guess I don't."

He slid into the booth across from me. "Andre. Andre Gasualt. Veronica's step-brother."

Ronnie Gasualt, my college roommate. Yes, she'd had a step-brother. He'd visited a couple of times, taken us clubbing. Was this

him? That had been fifteen years ago.

"Andy," I said. "It's been a long time. You seem blonder now."

"Oui. Oui. I was so surprised to see you. I went home for Christmas. Veronica still speaks of La Mirage."

I groaned. I didn't want to remember La Mirage. Too many margaritas and I'd made a complete ass of myself. I still wasn't sure if I'd slept with him or not. He had said no, but the glint in his eyes.

"You must let me take you to dinner. I'm in town only for another night."

I hesitated. "Let me call you. I've got a tight schedule today."

"Of course. Of course. Here is my business card."

He reached in the pocket of his jacket and held out a card to me. The waitress returned with my check. He took it from her hand.

"I will get this."

"What? No you won't."

"Oh, but I will. In case you don't call. I can't leave Santa Maria without buying you a meal. Veronica would never forgive me."

I remembered then he never called Ronnie anything but Veronica, and that he hated being called Andy. Why hadn't he corrected me? He always had before. I took the business card. It took some doing, but I gave in gracefully. "Well, thank you." I slid from the booth. "I'll call you." I felt his gaze on my back as I walked away.

Chapter Twenty-Nine
Pieter Orloff

WITH A SMILE I watched Agent Crane walk toward the front door of Pappys. I knew she would be checking up on me. Well let her. Everything I had told her about Andre Gasualt would come back as truth down to the photo of me in this guise, just as I knew everything supplied to me about Gail Crane would be factual. My people were the best and I put my trust in them.

I admired the sway of her hips in the dark gray skirt. Gail Crane had the look that attracted me. Raven haired, with intelligent brown eyes, tall, with abundant curves, but it was her self-assured attitude that drew me. She was the type of women I yearned to bend to my will, and I would before my job here ended.

Her cheeks had colored when I brought up La Mirage. What had happened between her and the real Andre Gasualt?

I knew Agent Crane had not contacted Devlin St. James as of yet, but she would. The trails all led to him and the woman was not stupid.

It surprised me when I'd seen her garage door open and she had backed from inside. I'd followed for a good time without using my headlights. It becomes much harder to remain invisible when so few cars are on the street. Only when she took the 101 onramp did I turn my headlights on.

I'd watched with interest the interaction between her, Cummins's son and the Spangler women. Agent Crane's body had bristled with tension. What was between them? It could be an entanglement I had not foreseen.

"Are you ready to order, sir?" The waitress said from beside the table.

I looked her over. She was in her middle thirties, with dark hair and eyes, a little on the thin side. Her name tag read Gretchen. "I have much appetite, Gretchen. What would you recommend to

quench it?"

She smiled. "What are you hungry for?" she said with a teasing tone.

"Perhaps you? When does your job end this day?"

Her face reddened. "Sorry, I'm not on the menu."

I smiled. "Are you sure about that?"

"Yes. I'm sure."

"Then, I will have bacon and eggs. Over easy on the eggs, wheat toast, extra butter, black coffee and orange juice."

She nodded and hurried away.

I looked toward the window in time to see Agent Crane drive from the parking lot. American women. So many times they never knew what they really wanted. It was good that I was here to show them.

Chapter Thirty
Gail Crane

I LISTENED AS Rick Kaminski gave Dwight a description of Vladik Yakov, one of the crashed plane's passengers.

"He was on the tall side, maybe six foot one. Light hair, almost white."

"Color of eyes?" Dwight said.

"I don't remember. Juan, you get the color of his eyes?"

"No idea, but he had some over-the top cowboy boots. Those had to be Ostrich."

"How about his nose?" Dwight said.

"Nose?" Rick answered. "Yeah, he had one."

I tuned them out. Thought about the mess I'd walked into at Pappy's. Were they still together? How long was Bethany going to stay in Santa Maria? I hoped like hell she'd be on tomorrow morning's flight out to anywhere. On my drive to Global Air I'd finally admitted I was in love with Duke Cummins. It seemed crazy, but truth is truth. Did he love me? I had no idea.

"Agent Crane. Agent Crane."

I looked up. Dwight held a paper toward me.

"This is as good as I can do with what I've been provided."

I looked at the sketch. The man pictured was Slavic, blonde, blue-eyed, maybe in his late forties. Nothing remarkable about him. I'd scan it in to the database, but didn't feel very confident it would get any hits. "Thanks, Dwight."

He turned back to Juan and Rick. "Next one."

I glanced at the clock. That sketch had taken two hours and there were three more to go. Was it all a waste of time?

My mind kept drifting to Duke. I wouldn't give him up without a fight. The word scar caught my ear. I turned to Rick. "What did you say?"

"The pilot, Jacob Stanislaw had a long scar. It started about

here," Rick touched the side of his face just above his cheek,"and ran all the way down to his chin."

"You didn't mention a scar before," I said.

"I just remembered it."

I reached in my purse for my cell phone, pulled up the photo of Stan Jacobs. I held it out toward Rick.

"Yeah that's him, Jacob Stanislaw. He was the pilot when the Lear took off."

I surged to my feet. "Dwight, you don't need me here. I've got to get this positive ID out to NTSB and my boss. Give me a call when you are ready for me to see the other two sketches."

"Sure thing, Gail."

"Guys, thanks for coming in and doing this,

"Sure, Agent Crane," Rick Kaminski said as Juan nodded.

I picked up my purse and almost ran toward the hanger's doors.

Outside, I stopped at the side of another hanger and tried to wrap my mind around what I'd just learned. Stan Jacobs and Jacob Stanislaw were one and the same. How had the pilot from that Lear ended up dead in a motel in Montreal, Canada? Who was the body they'd found in the wreckage? Were any of the three, who we thought they were? Couldn't be. Not if one of them was still alive twenty-four hours later. Who were they? What in the hell was going on? How did Duke fit into all of this, and his dad?

I dialed Harry Shindley's number.

"Yeah."

"Harry, things just got a lot more interesting."

I called Dave Kelicoe next. He was mystified too, and a little peeved since the Lear case suddenly wasn't as cut and dried as it had been looking. Luckily they hadn't released the four bodies. I didn't envy him the feat of trying to ID them. From what I'd heard there wasn't much to work with. I'd offered him the Bureau's resources; he'd accepted and promised to get to me with anything they discovered.

I started toward my car.

"Hey."

I halted at the one word. My hand went to my weapon as I looked in the direction the voice had come from.

"I know something about the guy with no memory?"

The voice came from the shadows beside another hanger. I took a step toward the space.

"Stop right there. You don't need to come any closer," the voice said.

"Who are you?" I said.

"Don't matter for right now. I know who you are though. FBI, that so?" the voice said. "I saw 'em, the guy and an old man. They got in the fight with a rat-faced guy with a scar."

I took a step nearer to the speaker at hearing the word scar.

"You come any closer and I'm outta here."

"You saw Duke Cummings and his father, Everett Cummins, where?" I said.

"If that's the name of the no-memory guy and the old man, then yeah."

"Where did you see them? How many people did you see?"

"I figure it's gotta be worth something to you. You fibbies pay for information all the time."

"How do I know you're not lying? Give me something, and then we'll talk payment."

"Okay, there were four of them. The rat-faced guy had a long scar and he spoke with some kind of accent."

"Accent? Spanish?"

"Hell, I know what Mex sounds like. This was different."

"Why were you there," I asked.

"That's it. I'm not sayin' more. What you gonna do for me? Ya gotta cigarette?"

"I don't smoke."

"Well shit."

"Wait right here." I turned and hurried back to the hanger. Inside Dwight was putting his equipment away. Rick and Juan were nowhere in sight. "Dwight, do you have a cigarette?"

"Since when do you smoke?"

"I don't. I just need one and matches too."

He reached into his shirt pocket, pulled out a pack of cigarettes and handed me one, along with his lighter. "You need some back-up?"

"You have a camera with you?" I said.

"I do."

"Come with me, but stay out of site. When the guy takes the

cigarette, snap his photo and get it to Harry Shindley. I want to know who this person is, a-s-a-p."

Dwight nodded.

I walked back to the shadowed corner of the other hanger. "I have your cigarette."

The man stumbled from the darkness. He wore layers and layers of filthy clothes that reeked of booze, urine and puke. He stopped an arm's length from me, and snatched the cigarette and lighter. I stood in silence as he puffed and inhaled.

"Thanks," he said. "Now what about the money?"

"I'll need an hour to get it. Where can I find you?"

He smiled, showing me surprisingly white teeth. "You come back here. I'll find you." He handed the lighter to me. I took it by the edges with my fingertips.

The man turned and walked away.

Dwight waited for me at my car. "I already sent Harry the photo. He says he'll have the ID in about five minutes, that is if there's one to have."

"Thanks, Dwight." I opened the car door, found an evidence bag in the console and placed the lighter inside. With any luck the guy would be in the system.

"Harry also said, he's sending Tom Singer out for back-up and you're not to do anything until he arrives."

I thought about ignoring Harry's orders, what if the guy took off. Dwight didn't seem in any hurry to leave and I knew he also followed Harry's orders to keep an eye on me. "How did it go with the boy's descriptions?"

"I had to pry it out of them, but I think they'll work. I'll enhance them on the computer and then get them to you."

He backed a step, took a cigarette from his pack, felt around for his lighter with a puzzled look, and then glanced at me. "Sorry." I held up the bag. "I'm hoping for a good print if they can't ID him from the photo." My phone rang. It was Harry. "Hello."

"The guy's name is Roland Franken. He's been busted a few times for public intoxication. His address is a local homeless shelter."

I heard a car approach and looked up. "Tom's here now. We'll have a chat with Mister Franken." I ended the call, tore open the evidence bag and handed Dwight his lighter. "Harry got a positive ID."

"Thanks." He lit his cigarette.

Tom Singer parked next to me and climbed from the car. "Harry authorized a hundred bucks." He patted his jacket pocket.

"More than enough," I said. "Let's go find him."

He must have been watching for me, or maybe he had been watching Dwight and me all along. He stepped from the shadows as Tom and I neared. "You bring me my money?"

"We have it," Tom said, as he pulled a white envelope from his jacket pocket.

The man reached.

"Not so fast," I said. "Talk first."

"What if you don't give it to me?"

I swore beneath my breath. "Give Mister Franken half." I looked at the man. He smiled at me calling him by his last name. "The other half when we are satisfied."

Tom counted out the bills and held them out toward Roland Franken, who took them and stuffed them inside his layer of clothes. "Got another cigarette?"

I looked at Dwight, who tapped one from his pack, lit it from the one he smoked and passed it to the man.

Roland Franken, inhaled, blew smoke and then began. "I crawl in through the fence and sleep over here most times. The old man was arguing with the guy with a funny accent. It's what woke me up. The rat-face guy was with 'im. The old man was protesting this wasn't part of the deal. The rat-faced guy knocked out the old man and drug him to a big black sedan. He shoved him in the back seat. The guy with the accent got in the front and the car drove away fast."

"What about the no-memory guy." I asked.

"He just stood there."

"He did nothing?"

"Like I said. He just stood there."

I felt sick inside. Duke had watched them assault his dad and throw him in a car, and he'd done nothing.

"What else happened?" Tom said.

"The rat-faced guy and the others all got in the airplane and flew away."

"What others?" Tom said.

"The ones that came with the foreign guy, I think there was some kind of last minute change of plans. When the line boys drove off

with the fuel truck, these guys started rushing around. They acted like they were hurrying to take off before the line boys came back."

I held up my phone with the photo of Jacob Stanislaw. "You're sure this is one of the men?"

"Yeah, that's the rat-face guy."

Dwight stepped forward, flipped open his sketch book. "What about them?"

Roland Franken took his time looking at the sketches. "Could be. My memory'd be clearer with the rest of my money."

I nodded toward Tom, who then handed the white envelope to the man.

"Yeah, that's them."

"And Duke, the no-memory man. What happened to him?"

"Don't know. He was still standing there when I left. You finished with me? I got some shoppin' to do." He patted the envelope.

"Yeah, we're all finished," Tom said.

Roland Franken turned and was soon lost in the darkness between the hangars.

"Now what?" Tom said.

"We ID the bodies in the Lear. One thing we know for sure Jacob Stanislaw wasn't one of them."

Tom nodded. "I'll catch you later. " He turned and walked away.

I'd just fastened my seat belt when my cell phone rang. "Agent Crane."

"Gail, it's Morgan."

"Good Morning."

"Could you meet me for a cup of coffee?"

"I've had just about all the stimulation I can handle this morning," I said as I started my car.

"Gail, it's important…about Darcie."

I felt my stomach tense. "Is she okay?"

"She's fine. I just need to talk with you."

"Morgan, what's this all about?"

"I don't want to do it over the phone. I'm at Café Noir. It won't take long."

"Okay, I'm on the way, but I can only give you about ten minutes."

At Café Noir, I spotted Morgan sitting by the window. At the

counter I ordered a vanilla latte. Morgan saw me and stood as I neared. He kissed me on the cheek and settled back in his chair.

"Gail, good to see you; I got a big problem."

His words ran together in his rush to get them out.

"Steady boy, what's going on?"

"Darcie wants me to move in with her."

I felt a surge on impatience. This is what couldn't wait? I resisted an urge to look at my watch. "So, what's wrong with that? Don't you want to?"

"Yes and no. I want to get married. I want to go to Vegas and ask her there. I'm in the process of setting it all up. I've asked Duke to fly us over and I've made all the arrangements. I just need a firm date. You have to go."

"Whoa, hold on. Duke will fly you over to Vegas and you want me to go?"

"Sure. We'll need witnesses and Darcie would want you there. You like Duke don't you? I saw how you looked at him at the funeral."

My stomach cramped. "Things change, he and his dear step-mommy have kindled a new relationship."

"Bethany Spangler. Bull, where did you get that idea?"

"I saw them together this morning, and they were pretty cozy at the memorial weren't they?"

"That's crazy. Come on what's going on here?"

"Hey, forget it Morgan. It's not important." The waitress brought me my latte and I took a long drink. "You're going to ask Darcie to marry you, and you've already got it all arranged in Vegas?"

"Yeah. Darcie doesn't like big weddings." He stopped and a look of panic crossed his face. "She hasn't changed her mind has she?"

"How the hell would I know?"

"I thought women talked about that kind of thing."

"Do Darcie and I seem the type who would chat about weddings?"

Morgan took a long drink from his coffee cup. "Then you won't know what kind of ring she would like either?"

"Maybe you should ask her mother," I said.

He grimaced. "I'd rather not."

"Her parents do know about this?"

"I spoke with Brady, by now he's probably told Samantha."

I grinned. "You're afraid of Darcie's mom."

Morgan flushed.

"You know they say if you want to know what a woman will be like on down the road, you should check out her mother," I said. The color left his face and I almost regretted my teasing words. Almost.

"Samantha's wonderful. It's just taking longer to smooth the road I tore up with the drinking and all," Morgan said.

Okay enough teasing. "Get Darcie a plain gold band and yourself one just like it. Have it engraved with your initials and the date of your wedding."

"That's it?"

"Yes." I wasn't sure if that was what Darcie would want, but it was what I wanted.

Morgan placed his coffee cup on the table and leaned toward me. "Will she say yes? Come on Gail, you know her. Am I crazy?"

He was as sincere as I have ever seen him. Here was a big tough guy, who didn't back off from anybody, reduced to a mountain of doubt, when everybody in Santa Maria knew Darcie was crazy about him. "Darcie loves you."

He stood. "That's good enough. Please don't say anything about all of this. I want it to be a surprise. I know she likes surprises."

I wasn't so sure about that. "I won't say a word."

"You never did say if you'd go with us."

"I'll go. Just let me know when to be at the airport." I glanced at my watch. "I've got to run." I finished my coffee and stood.

"Thanks, Gail."

I shook my head as I walked toward the door. Going to Vegas with Duke, was I crazy?

Chapter Thirty-One
Darcie Devonshire

I GLANCED AT the clock. Almost 3:30. Where was Wes? I had an appointment to talk with mailman Keith Osterman at 4:00. If Wes wasn't here within the next ten minutes I'd go without him. He'd left a message on my cell phone saying he was attending a parent teacher conference. I'd tried to call him, let him know about the meet with Mailman Keith, but he hadn't answered his phone.

Damn. I couldn't wait any longer. I pushed back my chair and stood.

Keith Osterman waited for me at a window table in Starbucks. He still wore his uniform. "Mister Osterman, I'm glad you could talk with me." I settled into a chair across from him.

He took a drink from his coffee cup. "I'm not comfortable about what I'm seeing and feeling on my mail route."

"What have you seen?"

"I've delivered quite a few of those manila envelopes, and each time I see the same reaction, stark fear, and that's before they even open them."

"Have you delivered more than one to the same business?"

"Usually just the one."

I frowned. "Then why are they frightened before they open the envelopes."

He stared across my shoulder, out the window for a moment, before he replied. "Word gets around."

"What have you heard?"

"Sometimes I walk in on conversations, like I did when you and your partner were at Nichol's Pawn Shop. They clam up real fast, but I've heard enough. Someone's shaking them down."

"How many businesses?"

"At least ten, probably all of them."

A man came in the door, glanced our way and I could see Keith

159

tense up. "Do you know him?" I said.

"Don't know. Maybe?"

I reached across patted his hand. "Relax. It's not like I'm in uniform. You're just having coffee with a friend."

His attempt at a smile was pathetic. "You think they don't know who you are? They most likely know the name of every cop and detective in Santa Maria."

"Don't you think that's being a tad paranoid?" I sat back in my chair.

The man collected his coffee and settled in a chair behind us. A fact that made me give a little more credence to the mailman's fears since Starbucks lacked an abundance of customers at this moment. I pushed my chair back. "It was great talking to you, Keith. Tell Grace I said hi. We've got to get together sometime."

He looked shocked I knew the name of his wife, but I had checked him out before I'd agreed to meet with him.

"Sure Darcie, we'll have to do that."

I hadn't told him my first name, so I knew he'd checked Wes and me out also. I didn't look back as I walked toward the door.

In the car I debated, then called Wes.

"Detective Smith," he said.

I told him about my conversation with Keith-the-mailman.

"What now?" Wes said.

"I'm thinking my hair could use a trim."

"And there's a beauty-shop right next door to the pawn shop."

I laughed. "Hair salon, partner. They haven't called them beauty-shops since the fifties."

"Whatever. You want me with you, English?"

A man accompanying his wife for a trim? Didn't happen much now-a-days. Besides I didn't want to made as a cop, maybe the owner would be more open with me. "I'll take this one alone." Wes didn't respond, but I knew what he was thinking, number one rule, partners stuck together. "How about you wait outside?" I said.

"That'll work, but can we do something else first?"

That surprised me. "What?"

"I've got Flores's sister."

Wow, Morgan had been fast. "Any problems?"

"She puked in your boyfriend's truck."

I groaned. I'll hear about that, and not just once. "Does Flores

160

know?"

"Just called him. He's already at the Metro Club."

"I can be there in five minutes," I said.

"See you then." Wes ended the call.

I started the car and backed from the parking spot.

*****

In front of the Metro Club, I spotted Wes' car. It was empty. I parked, climbed out, and walked inside.

In the dim light I could see Wes sitting in a chair on the right. Next to him a slight form slumped in another chair. The same burly guy, as with our past visits, stood behind the bar. We exchanged glares as I moved toward Wes. I grimaced as the soles of my shoes stuck to the floor and released with each step. I'd have to soak them in a gallon of disinfectant or better yet, just burn them.

I stopped beside Wes, but before I could speak the bartender yelled.

"What will you have?"

"Nothing."

He pointed to a sign behind the bar. Two Drink Minimum, I read.

"You've got to be kidding."

He wiped the counter with a rag. "Nope. You sit, you drink."

"Bloody fine. Coffee." I noticed then Wes and the girl each had two full cups of coffee in front of them. "Where's Flores? I want to get the hell out of here."

The bartender brought my two cups of coffee, placed them in front of me. "That'll be ten bucks."

I fished out the money and handed it to him with another glare. "What no napkins?"

He grinned, showing me a mouthful of yellow teeth. "Fifteen dollar minimum for napkins." He turned and sauntered away.

Well, bloody damn hell. There had to be something I...

"Forget it, English. He isn't worth it," Wes said. Anita Flores suddenly slumped to the side and he grabbed for her. "Shit. Flores, get out here, now, or I'm taking your baby sister's doped-up ass to lock-up."

A side door opened and a very round woman came out of it. She barged toward us. All clad in black, except for a white shawl, she reminded me of an Emperor Penguin.

Who the hell was she? I pushed my chair back, surged to my feet,

161

my hand going to my gun. "Stop right there," I said.

The woman ignored me. She pushed between me and the girl, her ample hip batting me aside like a pesky fly.

"Hey, that's assaulting a police officer," Wes said, scrambling to his feet.

"Nita, my Nita. What have they done to you?" I heard her say.

"No. No." Flores came through the door. "She's our mother. She will take Anita home."

"Damn straight," Wes said. "Then we're going to talk."

I watched in amazement as the woman cooed over the nearly comatose girl. With Flores's help, they got Anita to her feet and all three headed toward the door.

"Mother love, there isn't anything stronger," Wes said.

We settled down into our chairs. Five minutes later Flores returned. He glanced at the coffee cups on the table and then looked at the bartender with an approving expression. I added another hash mark in Flores's against column in my mind. Flores didn't sit down, he hovered above us. Wes frowned, looked like he was going to say something, but with a slight shake of my head, I touched his hand. "Who is El Rios?" I said.

Flores took his time answering. I let him have his little moment of power. I'm sure he had damn few of them. Wes shifted in his chair, fidgeted with a coffee cup.

"His name is Esteban Dominguez. He owns a bunch of dry cleaners. Has them from Santa Barbara to Ventura. Clean and Dry. You heard of them?"

I shook my head.

"He gives a lot of money to Scarsdale."

"What do you mean?" Wes said. "Like political contributions?"

Flores shrugged. "If that's what you want to call them."

"Was he a supporter of Devlin St. James too," I asked.

"It started with St. James. He got the zoning changed so Dominguez could open his first store. That was in 2001."

"He dealing out of his stores?" Wes said.

Flores smiled. "El Rios does not deal, if you are meaning drugs. That is old school and he is a very modern guy. But no, nothing happens inside the stores. He keeps Esteban Dominguez and El Rios far apart."

Wes snorted. "Right. Modern. Prostitution's been around since

the Ice Age."

Flores looked insulted. I think he admired Esteban Dominguez. Yeah, a guy who drugs your baby sister and sells her for sex is a great role model. We learned what we'd come for. Another St. James tie in. Gail and Morgan would be interested in what we'd found out. I pushed my chair back, stood. "Let's get out of here, Wes."

Outside, we stopped beside my car.

"Now what?" Wes said.

"Let's divide and conquer. You go back to the office and see what you can find out about Esteban Dominguez and I'll pay a visit to the hair salon and see if I can get any more information on the protection racket that's going on there."

"Okay. You coming to the office afterward?"

"I'll be there. It shouldn't take much longer than an hour."

*****

I stood in front of Cut and Curl. Judging from the acrid smell wafting through the open door someone inside was getting a manicure. I looked at the large posters of hair styles in the window. How could hair defy gravity? And that color of red looked like it should be on a fire engine. Nope, no trim for me. I'd stick with Charles at The Hair Castle. A sign in the window also offered waxing and they were having a special on the bikini line. Again, no thanks. But I could inquire about some highlights.

As I walked in, a buzzer sounded. A young woman with the same flaming hair as the model featured on the poster in the window glanced up, smiled. Another woman, this one closer to middle age was in the middle of assaulting someone's head with a blow dryer. "Be right with you," she said, without looking in my direction.

I walked to a chair, settled into it and picked up this month's gossip magazine, nothing new there; the latest couple's having the latest crisis. I tossed it down and looked around the shop. More posters of neon hair colors on the walls and racks of hair products made up ninety percent of the décor. There were a couple of personal photos on the work stations in front of the two barber chairs. Is that what you still called them if they were in a hair salon?

The woman turned off the hairdryer and reached for a curling iron. She looked in my direction. "How can I help you?"

"I was thinking of getting some highlights."

"You're in luck. The next appointment canceled. Cynthia can do

163

you." A young woman came from the back of the shop.

"Oh, I can't right now." I hurried to say and, "I'm on duty," slipped out.

"You a cop?"

So much for not being made. I nodded.

"Well thank God. It's about time someone looked into…"

"Shut-up, Cynthia," the woman snapped."

"But Gina, you said you can't afford…"

"Cynthia, go in the back and fold some towels." The woman pointed with the curling iron. Then she turned to me. "I'm sorry, we can't help you. I forgot I had a customer getting a perm."

I knew she lied, but I'd learned enough. "Oh? Okay. Maybe I'll go next door and mail a package."

"You do that." She turned back to her customer.

I stood and walked toward the door.

In my car I glanced at my watch. Almost five-thirty, time to call it a day. I'd stop by the department, see what Wes had dug up and then head home.

Chapter Thirty-Two
Duke Cummins

MY NEW LAWYER's business card touted a West Main street address for his office. I pulled into the parking lot in the front of a yellow and white Victorian-style house, found a space and switched off the engine. Two spaces over sat a red and white Mini-Cooper. It had a rental sticker. It looked like Bethany had found herself a car.

I walked in the front door. An oak desk stood in the middle of a hardwood floor, a young woman sat behind it.

"May I help you?"

"Jonathon Cummins to see Nelson Oates, I have an appointment."

"Yes Mister Cummins. Your mother has already arrived. I am so sorry about the loss of your father."

I'd fixated on her use of the word mother, and had almost missed the part about my father. "Thank you." I said.

She stood. Her name tag read Abigail Oates. Nelson's grand-daughter maybe? "This way please." She led me down a short hall, the floor made of the same hardwood, but an added carpet runner of subdued flowers. She stopped at a door and knocked.

"Yes."

She opened the door. "Mister Cummins has arrived."

I walked in behind her. More hardwood and another oak desk sitting on another muted floral rug. A painting of a vineyard dominated one wall and behind the desk was a wall of framed credentials. In front of the desk were two dark, wooden chairs with red upholstery. Bethany Spangler perched in one, one gorgeous leg crossed over the other. She wore a dark green suit, with a skirt that stopped demurely at her knees, but the suit's emerald color made her red hair blaze in the sunlight pouring in through the window. Mother-my-ass.

Nelson Oates did not stand, instead he motioned me forward.

"Jonathon, right on time, I may call you Jonathon?"

"I'd prefer Duke, if you don't mind."

"Of course. Duke it is. Please sit down."

I walked to the chair next to Bethany's.

"Mrs. Cummings and I were speaking of France. Some prefer Paris, but we both agree the beauty of the French countryside outshines the city of lights."

"Maybe," I said. "But neither out-do the sun rising over an escarpment in Africa."

"I'd love to see that someday," Bethany said. "Maybe you can show me?"She leaned toward me, placed her hand on my arm, and I caught a whiff of some spicy perfume.

"Maybe," was my reply.

Nelson Oates cleared his throat and shifted papers on his desk. "Shall we get started?" He looked up at the receptionist. "Hold all calls please."

She nodded, walked out the door and closed it behind her.

The lawyer looked from my face, to Bethany's and back to mine. "Right after his marriage, Everett came to me for help in preparing his will."

Out of the corner of my eye I could see Bethany shift in her chair.

Nelson Oates went on. "That will Everett and I drew up is null and void." He waited and when no one spoke went on. "Six months before his accident Everett changed his will." He picked up a single sheet of paper. "He and Delilah Willoughby brought it into me. Mrs. Willoughby and I both witnessed Everett's signing of it. I'll now read it.

I, Everett William Cummings, being of sound mind and body, declare this as my legal will. It cancels out all wills written before. To my son, Jonathon Wayne Cummins, I leave all of my worldly possessions, except for one dollar which I bequeath to my always absent wife, Bethany."

Relief rushed through me. The Stearnman bi-plane was mine. Beside me I heard Bethany laugh.

"Way to go old man," she whispered.

I glanced at her. She was smiling, but tears tracked down her face.

Nelson Oates cleared his throat again. "Duke, Jones Taylor handles all of your late father's investments." He held out a business

card to me. "You'll want to contact them. As far as the banks, I can help with that once you get copies of Everett's death certificate."

I nodded.

The lawyer leaned toward me. "Aren't you curious about the dollar amount of your father's estate?" I could see he was dying to tell me. He glanced at Bethany and I wondered if he'd been ordered to pay close attention so he could report back to Mrs. Willoughby.

"Well, yes, I guess," I said.

Nelson Oates took a deep breath. "Everett Cummins's estate, including all stocks, bonds, investment s, cash and physical goods comes to a total of three point two million dollars."

I couldn't have heard him right. Over three million dollars? How had my father accumulated that much money? "I'm sorry, did you say three point two million?"

"That's correct."

"But how?"

"Everett always paid attention to when dear step-daddy bought and sold stock, how he invested his money. Everett did the same. It must have paid off."Bethany pushed back her chair and stood. "I'm very happy for you Duke and I'm sure Everett is celebrating too."

I rose to my feet, reached to touch her arm. "Wait. Let's get some lunch. I'd like to talk to you about my father." I could see her hesitation. "Please. It won't take long."

"Well, okay."

I turned back to Nelson Oates. "Thank you, sir."

"You are most welcome young man. If I can be of more assistance, just let me know."

I followed Bethany from the room.

In my car I called Gail on my cell phone. It went right to her voice mail. "It's Duke. Please call me when you get this."

*****

Bethany chose the Red Lobster for lunch. The noon crowd had thinned so we were able to get a quiet booth in the back. Even as the hostess handed us our menus a waitress appeared and asked if we would like something to drink. Before I could respond Bethany did.

"A bottle of champagne, please." She glanced at me. "To celebrate your great news."

The waitress smiled and hurried away.

"Celebrate?" I said. "My father's dead."

She didn't even pretend to be embarrassed. "A father you don't remember. I do, and Everett would approve. You'll have to trust me on this one." Bethany smiled. "I'd like my dollar now."

"What?"

"My dollar inheritance. I'd like it now. God knows I deserve it."

What did she mean, she deserved it? From what I knew she skipped out before the reception was even over and had been partying around Europe. Without a word, I pulled a dollar bill from my billfold and slapped it in front of her. "Paid in full."

Bethany picked up the bill, kissed it and placed it in her purse. "This will certainly make that old witch Willoughby happy."

"Delilah Willoughby seems to really care for Everett," I said.

"Oh, no doubt about that. I think she wanted to be Mrs. Everett Cummins herself."

The waitress returned with the champagne. We sat in silence as she opened it and poured each of us a glass.

"I'll have the snow crab and a baked potato with everything," Bethany said before the waitress asked.

"And you sir?"

"Broiled salmon, a salad with Italian dressing and a cup of clam chowder."

The waitress walked away.

Bethany picked up her champagne. "To Everett. You will be missed."

I picked up my glass. "Will he? By you?"

Her eyes glistened with sudden tears which surprised the hell out of me.

"It isn't polite not to clink glasses," Bethany said with a choked voice.

I touched my glass to hers, took a sip of champagne and watched her down the rest of hers. She picked up the bottle and refilled her glass. What was going on here?

"I loved old Ev, but I should have never married him. It was a fuck you to step-daddy."

"Okay, I think it's about time I heard your side of things."

"Yes it is." Bethany took a deep breath. "I like nice things. Champagne, Gucci purses, Chanel perfume. I also like to gamble a bit. Las Vegas is a lovely town, but not as nice as Monaco."

"Uh huh," I said.

"I met your father when I was twenty-nine. My third marriage had failed and I'd come back home to lick my wounds. We were both night owls and avid readers. Normally I'd have been out on the town until the early morning hours, but there isn't a load of nightlife in Santa Maria."

She sipped champagne. "So I read. St. James has a wonderful library, that's where I first met Ev. He and Step-daddy had been up late, so he'd spent the night, on dear Daddy's insistence, and had come to the library to exchange a book. "Bethany smiled. "We talked for hours. He told me about you, your mother, about her death from breast cancer. I'm very sorry about that by the way."

"Thank you," I said.

"Ev never put me down, made me feel childish or stupid." Bethany refilled her glass with champagne. "I knew he had a crush on me. I thought it was cute and it stroked my bruised ego." She reached to touch my hand. "It would have stopped there, Duke. I swear. If my step-father hadn't gotten involved."

"What do you mean?"

"Step-daddy likes brandy and cigars. When he's had one too many brandies he likes to talk, loves an audience, and sometimes he says things he regrets the next morning."

I nodded, but I felt my stomach tense.

"Your dad was a terrific listener and I know he would never have repeated anything said to him in confidence, but Devlin St. James has a paranoid streak about a foot wide down his back. Always, the next morning after a late night chat, he berated himself for what he'd said, or might have said to Ev." Bethany took another sip of champagne. "That's where I came into the picture. Dear Step-daddy saw Ev had a thing for me. He decided he needed more security where your father was concerned; some revealing photos, some incriminating conversations, just in case Everett Cummins decided to talk to anybody."

"You married my father so you could keep an eye on him, blackmail him if needed?"

She laughed. "Nope, not marry him, just be nice to him, sleep with him, keep him happy."

"Why the hell would you agree to do that? I thought you liked him."

"I did. I adored him."

"Then why…"

"I had no choice." She reached for her glass, but it was empty, reached for the bottle, but it was empty also. "Could we get another?"

I shook my head.

"I told you I liked nice things and gambling. Devlin St. James always covered my bills and they were many. At that time I owed close to a million dollars. Suddenly, Step-daddy wasn't going to pay, not unless I prostituted myself to your father."

I stared at her in silence, watched her cheeks redden.

"Yes, I'm not very proud of it, but I did as required. I was nice to Ev and my bills were all taken care of."

"Then why marry him?"

For a long time Bethany did not answer, then she said softly. "I married him out of spite, to get back at my step-father."

My cell phone rang. It was Gail.

"Received your message," she said when I answered.

"Gail, I can't talk right now. Can I call you back?"

"More champagne, Duke," Bethany asked.

A long moment of silence came from my cell phone and then Gail said. "Whatever," and ended the call.

Shit. I sat back in the booth, stared at the innocent, yet satisfied look on Bethany's face. Why the hell had she done that? She couldn't be interested in me. Women. "You married my father as a fuck you to St. James and then walked out on him even before the wedding reception was over?"

She lowered her head. "That's exactly what I did. I left for Europe that night and never came back, well, not until now."

"Why didn't my father divorce you?"

"I don't know."

"How did you live in Europe?"

"Step-daddy paid."

"Why?"

She smiled. "I black-mailed him, told him I'd go to the media about what he'd made me do."

I laughed. "Nobody would have cared."

"Devlin St. James did. His great name couldn't be sullied."

"St. James still paying you," I said.

Bethany nodded.

"Then why are you back? Did you think my father would leave you a bunch of money?"

"No. I came back for one thing and one thing only, to tell you this; I don't think your father died in a car accident. I think my step-father had him killed."

"Are you insane?"

"I told you he's paranoid; there are things you don't know."

"What things?"

Bethany slid to the end of the booth and stood. "I've already said too much. Talk to your friend, Gail. See if she's told you everything." She looked down at me. "Duke, I'm betting your loss of memory is also tied into all of this."

She turned away, dodged the waitress who had arrived with our lunch, and kept on going.

I looked at the shocked waitress. "Check please."

In my car, I called Gail. Her phone rang on and on. I started to end the call, but she answered. "Duke, I can't talk now."

"Was my father murdered?"

She didn't answer for a long moment, and then, "Why would you ask that?"

"Yes or no Gail."

"It's not my case, you are."

I felt a hot rush of anger. "My father isn't a case."

"Detectives Devonshire and Smith are looking into your father's accident."

"Was it an accident?"

"All the facts aren't in yet."

I knew a stall when I heard one. "Everett Cummins was my father. I should have heard it from you."

"Duke…"

I ended the call.

Detectives and agents, they had their hands tied with regulations, not so with the private sector. I fished in my pocket and found Morgan Garrett's card with his cell number, but before I could call, my phone rang. "Hello."

"Duke, it's Sam Hughes. I've got a problem and I hope you can help. I need someone to fly a shipment into Vegas for an oil company. You'd have to leave in the early morning. Can you do it?"

"I sure can, Mister Hughes. What time can you have the aircraft ready?"

"Seven o'clock."

"I'll be there."

"Thanks Duke." He ended the call.

Now I had something, a bargaining chip. Morgan wanted a trip to Las Vegas. I wanted to know about my father's accident. Let's see if we can trade.

I punched in his number.

"Hello."

"Mister Garrett, it's Duke Cummins. You still want that trip to Las Vegas?"

"I sure do."

"How about we get together and talk about it?"

"How about the Roadhouse at seven o'clock tonight?"

"I'll be there."

Chapter Thirty-Three
Morgan Garrett

DARK TOOK OVER the evening as I parked at the Roadhouse. The usual Friday night crowd had cleared out and I walked right in to find Duke in front of the hostess's kiosk.

"Hi ya Morgan," he said.

"This way Sirs." The hostess was young and gave us quite a salute with her hips as she led the way toward a booth. I slid in, ordered an Amber O'Doul's as I did.

"Make it two," Dude said.

I started to say you don't need to do so because of me, but he probably didn't know I was an alcoholic.

Looking around the room I could see why we'd gotten right in, they were having a slow night and had seated everyone on the same side of the room. One waitress lounged by the rail and watched us as she chomped her gum.

I turned back to Duke. "Have you got things settled? Do you plan to stay in Santa Maria?"

"Things settled? Not hardly, but I'm staying in the area until I do."

"I appreciate you taking Darcie and I to Vegas. She's going to be blown away."

"When are you going to tell her?"

"After we get there."

"How are you going to get her to go?"

"That'll be easy, she loves Vegas."

"And Gail? She's going too?"

"Yeah, I already talked to her. She was a little reluctant, but she agreed. You and her are okay, right?"

"We were, but now I don't know. Our last conversation wasn't good."

Our waitress brought our O'Doul's' and took our orders.

"What happened?" I said.

Duke took a long drink from his bottle. "I asked for some information she couldn't provide." He looked at me. "Thought about asking Darcie, but I'd most likely get the same answer."

My senses went on alert. "That right?"

"And then I thought of you. It doesn't seem you'd have the same rules."

I drank from my bottle. "What rules would that be?"

"I had lunch with Bethany Spangler today, an informative one. She thinks my father's accident, wasn't an accident. You wouldn't know anything about that, would you?"

Oh shit. I stalled. "You asked Gail?"

Duke nodded. "She didn't say it wasn't."

"What makes you think I'd know anything? I…"

"Let's cut the crap, Morgan. You need something from me and I'd like some straight answers."

"This smells like blackmail. I don't like blackmail."

Duke leaned toward me. "I see it as an exchange of favors. Everett Cummins is my father. If someone killed him I have a right to know."

Hell, he was right. He should know. "Your father was dead before his car went over that cliff."

Duke sat back, drank from his bottle. "Thank you."

I grabbed a peanut out of the bucket, cracked the shell and dropped the hulls onto the floor to join the millions already under our feet. One of the reasons I liked this place is the rustic atmosphere. "So when are we leaving for Las Vegas?"

"Tomorrow morning, seven o'clock. I plan to fly back Sunday. Can you make it?"

"We'll be there, all three of us. Hot damn. Can you excuse me for a moment? I've got to make a phone call."

*****

The call was short and sweet. Everything was a go now for my wedding.

I settled back in the booth. God damn. My wedding. I grabbed for my O'Doul's, took a long drink.

"Morgan,I don't think I had anything to do with the crash, but I'm afraid my father was, at least to the extent he knew something was going on? Maybe it got him killed."

174

"It's the only logical answer." I stopped talking with the arrival of the waitress. We sat there in silence as she arranged our steaks. She lingered over Duke's a little longer than necessary. "I think you have a fan there," I said as she wiggled away.

"Hell, I have socks older than that. She needs to radiate those pheromones in another direction."

"Not on me, Darcie's a cop you know; she knows what she has."

"So how's the wedding going to go. Have you got it all set up?"

"That's what the phone call was all about. The wedding, the limo, the license, everything is in motion now, all we have to do is go down and get in the limo." I must have looked stunned because Duke burst out laughing. "What?"

"You know that old saying, be careful what you wish for, 'cause you just might get it."

I grinned. "Well I can't speak for anybody else, but I know what I want, and I plan to get it."

The rest of the meal we talked NASCAR. Duke liked Carl Edwards. We dickered over the check but I won. After all, I had invited him.

Outside we stopped for a moment enjoying the cool fresh night air.

Duke turned to me. "Morgan, I want to know who killed my father. I'll pay whatever the going rate is."

"I'm sure Darcie and Wes will have your answer soon."

"I want to handle it myself," Duke said.

I stared into his face. I got it. I understood payback, and who had more right. "I've got a few ideas. I'm overdue being home, but we'll talk about them in Vegas."

"Sounds good, but for right now I've got someone I have to see."

*****

Driving north on 101, I couldn't shake the thoughts of not knowing who you are or where you came from. No childhood memories, that was a scary thought, but on the other side, I had some memories I could dump without regret. Not Darcie though, never Darcie.

Chapter Thirty-Four
Gail Crane

I STARED AT my phone. Duke was pissed. I wish he hadn't found out about his father's murder like that. That damn bitch, Bethany. What had she said to him? Why the hell were they drinking champagne together? They were going to the reading of Everett Cummins's will. What were they celebrating? Oh yeah, going to Las Vegas was going to be fun. Could I get out of it? Let Duke take Bethany. Shit. I knew that wouldn't work. Maybe I could invite Andre. How long was he going to be in town?

Duke and Bethany together, drinking champagne, laughing and clinking glasses and right after they'd visited the lawyer. It didn't sound like Duke, but what did I really know about him. How could anyone know someone in five days? I didn't think he would be the kind of man who could watch his father be beat up, and be tossed in the back of a car either. But according to Roland Franken, that's exactly what Duke did.

I felt tears threaten and I stood. Damn, how had this happened? Duke's my case. I don't get involved. But I was—big time involved. I should walk away, let Tom Singer handle it. I paced the length of the room. No. I'd finish it one way or the other. I'm a professional. I can handle this. Follow the evidence. If Duke's dirty, then he's dirty. If not, well then we'd see after the dust cleared. One thing I needed to get him out of my head for awhile. I walked back to the sofa and picked up my phone. Andre's business card lay on the end table. I punched in his number.

He answered on the first ring. "Hello."

"It's Gail. Is that invitation to dinner still open?"

"But of course, Gail. I hoped you would call."

"How about Italian? Giuseppe's in Pismo Beach is fantastic."

"I love Italian, but you already know that."

I did? Whatever. "How about seven-thirty? Would you like me to

176

pick you up?"

"No, no. no. I will pick you up. What is your address?"

I gave it to him.

"I will see you then." He ended the call.

I stared down at my phone. What had I done? I felt as excited about this date as I would about a visit to the dentist and a root canal. I looked at the clock. 6:30. I'd better get dressed. What the hell. At least I'd get a good dinner. My cell phone rang. "Hello."

"Gail, it's Morgan. Pack a bag girl we're leaving for Vegas in the morning."

"In the morning?"

"Perfect timing, right? We'll have all day Saturday and head back late Sunday night. You won't even miss a day of work. No way can Darcie bail on me for this. It's damn perfect."

"How...?

"Global Air has an emergency delivery to Las Vegas, and we're all going along. You have to be at the Santa Maria Airport by seven A.M., you can make it right?"

My heart started to pound. I'd get to see Duke, a second later I felt a surge of anger at the leap of joy, but I had promised to be a witness at their wedding.

"I'll be there."

"Thanks Gail."

I ended the call.

Okay a quick flight to Vegas, no more than an hour. Duke would fly the plane. I'd stay in the back with Darcie. It's doable. We can be civil.

*****

Andre poured more zinfandel into both our glasses. Diners occupied every table in Giuseppe's. Ours was close to the pizza oven. The meal had been superb and the waiter had just taken our desert order. Crème Brule for the both of us, a decadent splurge for me, but I was having a good time. Andre had made me laugh almost continuously with his wry observations about those surrounding us. Granted some of my laughs had been tinged with guilt at his cutting comments, but still it felt good to let myself embrace my inner bitch.

I smiled across the table at him. I didn't remember Andre as witty with biting arrogance, but years had passed since we'd seen each other.

177

"So Gail, when did you decide to become a federal agent?"

"I knew I'd go into some kind of law enforcement from the time I watched the first Cagney and Lacy episodes."

His blank expression surprised me. Maybe they hadn't televised that program in Paris. "You know the show about the two women cops."

"Oh, oh yes. Not my favorite." He reached for the bottle. "More wine?"

"My glass is still full."

He laughed. "Why yes it is. See what you do to me. You dazzle my wits."

How cheesy, but the words were a balm to my battered ego. "So how much longer will you be in California?"

"I leave in two days." He reached across the table and touched my hand. "Am I crazy to think you will miss me?"

His fingers were warm on mine, but I still felt the urge to draw mine away. "So where are you off to next?"

He frowned as he moved his hand back to beside his plate. "I do not know, maybe Las Vegas. I hear Sin City can be fun."

Andre in Las Vegas, maybe tomorrow night, we could get together, what would Duke think about that? "When would you be there?"

"I do not know. Perhaps next week."

"Oh."

"You sound disappointed. Why is that?"

"I'm going to be there tomorrow. I thought maybe we could have gotten together."

"I am sorry. If I'd known…."

"That's okay. I just found out myself. It's a spur of the moment thing. I'm going to be a witness at a friend's surprise wedding."

"Surprise and wedding. Not two words you hear often together."

I laughed. "That's for sure. I just hope Morgan knows what he's doing."

Andre drew back from me. "So you are going to Las Vegas tomorrow for this Morgan's wedding?"

"Yes, another friend is flying us, a damn early flight, seven in the morning."

"Where are you staying? Perhaps I can change my plans and meet you there."

I shook my head. "I don't even know. Morgan's made all of the plans."

"Yes. Seven is very early." He finished his wine. "We should get you home and into bed."

The glass of wine I'd just picked up, stopped in mid-lift on its way to my lips. "Excuse me?"

Andre laughed. "Oh Gail, you should see your face. Sometimes my use of your language gets me into much trouble. I did not mean I would join you in your bed." He paused for a long moment. "Unless of course you wish it?"

Did I?

He reached across the table and patted my hand. "It is okay. There have been many years since our last time, yet we would be good together, me and you."

My face flushed. "You think so?"

"Oh, I know so. Maybe at a later date, oui?"

I pushed back my chair, stood. "You are correct about making it an early night."

"Yes. Yes. I will see to the check." Andre stood. It almost seemed he couldn't get us out of Giuseppe's fast enough. Did my lack of interest in going to bed with him have something to do with it? Well to hell with him, and to hell with all men.

*****

In blue-bird-print, flannel pajamas, face scrubbed and teeth brushed, I sat cross-legged in the middle of my bed, my laptop open. It was all of nine-thirty. Andre had given me a chaste kiss on the cheek and scurried back to his car. I'd had a, it's late and I have to be at the airport early, excuse planned, but it hadn't been needed. So much for wanting to go to bed with me.

I read again the notes I'd made after talking to the homeless man outside Global Air. How could it be possible that Duke had just stood there and let them drag his father away? I didn't believe he'd lied to me. My instincts said no, but could they be off? Was I letting my feelings for Duke cloud my judgment? No, the man had to be wrong. He was probably drunk. The Duke I knew could never do that, he'd said as much, but what if he had, and doesn't remember? Was the memory loss a lie too? Was everything a lie? I swiped at a strand of hair that tickled my cheek. The only things I knew for sure were Jonathon Wayne Cummins was Everett Cummins' son, that he'd

arrived in town the night the Lear took off from Santa Maria Airport, and that he'd been found lying next to the crashed plane. Four burned bodies were found inside the jet, but one of them was not the pilot seen leaving from Santa Maria, that man, Jacob Stanislaw, had been found dead in a motel room in Canada. So were the other three bodies Jerome Clark, Vladik Yakov, or Josef Urni? If not, who were they? How had they gotten on that Lear? I suppose the jet could have dropped below radar, landed, and the people switched, but why?

I rubbed at my forehead. What had caused the crash, and why had Everett Cummins been murdered? The drunk at the airport said, Cummins had argued with a man whose description fit Jacob Stanislaw, and then had been dragged off to a dark sedan by another unknown man. Had he been the killer? Did Everett Cummins know something that got him killed?

I paged down the file. The Lear was owned by Devlin St. James. Everett Cummins worked for Devlin St. James. St. James had pulled strings to get Cummins's body released to him and had arranged a very hurried funeral and cremation.

Bethany Spangler, St. James's step-daughter, married Everett Cummins and then left for Europe before the wedding reception had ended. She'd never come back, until two days ago, What was that all about?

St. James. St. James. St. James. I needed to talk to the man and soon.

My doorbell rang. Who would be coming to my place at ten o'clock? Had Andre had a change of heart? Well that was just too damn bad. I headed toward the front door.

I unlocked it, jerked it open. "Andre, I said I had...." Duke stood there.

"Not Andre, but we need to talk."

He wasn't smiling; in fact he looked damned grim. I could see a muscle jump in his jaw and felt a stab of fear. The man facing me I didn't know. Was he the one who'd let his father be taken off to his death?

"It's late. Can't it wait until morning?" I started to shut the door, but he stopped it with his hand.

"No, it can't wait."

"What are you going to do? Force your way in?"

Duke lowered his hand. "Of course not, but Gail I just had dinner

with Morgan. Please, I need to talk to you."

I groaned. Dinner with Morgan Garrett. One guess as to what they'd talked about. What had he told Duke? I couldn't confirm or deny, but I could listen. I stepped back. "Come on in." I led the way to my living room. Duke settled onto the sofa, so I sat on the recliner across from him.

"I know you can't say anymore about my father," Duke said. "That's okay. I know what I needed to know."

So Morgan had told him. "I am sorry Duke. The FBI will take care of it."

He looked away from me. "Yes, it will be taken care of."

I tensed up. "The bureau doesn't care for vigilantes."

"I don't know what you mean."

The hell he didn't. "Duke…"

"I'm still your case, aren't I?"

"Yes, but…"

"Then we can discuss that, can't we?"

"I suppose. What…"

"Bethany feels my memory loss and my father's murder are both tied together." Duke's eyes scrutinized my face.

Bethany. My irritation rose. "What the hell could she know about it?"

"She's St. James's step-daughter. She married my father; she's been around from the beginning."

"Well does she have anything to offer but conjecture? I need facts." I heard the bitchy tone of my voice, but didn't much care. I didn't want to talk about Bethany Spangler. "Maybe it was the champagne talking?" I stood, walked to the fireplace and stared into it. "Why the hell were you drinking champagne anyway? You have something to celebrate? I can't see you toasting your dad's death, but maybe you were, and I don't know you at all."

Duke's face flushed. "Gail, what the hell is your problem? First you give me the brush off at the memorial, then the cold shoulder at Pappy's and now you're being a bitch about me having lunch with my father's widow. "

I whirled around. "God, how can you be so stupid? Bethany Spangler has the hots for you. Why wouldn't she? You're everything she saw in Everett Cummins, but in a younger package."

Duke lunged to his feet. "I'm not here to talk about Bethany. I'm

here to talk about me, us."

"Us? There is no us. You're a case number, nothing more."

"Bullshit. I know what I felt when we kissed."

I clenched my hands into fists. "That was a mistake. I don't even know you. What you're capable of."

Duke frowned. "What does that mean?"

"Who are you Duke? What have you done?"

"I don't know what you mean."

"How do you know you weren't involved with your father's death?" I watched his face pale, his lips tightened and his fingers curled into fists. I stepped back, reached my hand behind me and rested it on the fireplace poker.

"How can you say that to me?"

I could hear the pain in his voice and I cringed. Yes. How could I? "You can't know, not for sure. You have no memory, at least that's what you claim."

"God, Gail, doesn't any of our time together tell you anything? Do you think I could kill my own father." He came toward me.

I held up my empty hand, even as I curled my fingers tighter around the poker with the other. "Stop."

"Could you feel the way you do when I touch you, if you believed I could kill?"

His fingers grazed my cheek and I trembled.

"Duke, I…" His lips closed over mine, smothering the rest of my words.

Sky rockets exploded in my head. This was insane, but damn it felt so right. My hands rose, I curled my fingers in his hair, something I'd wanted to do from the first time I'd seen him sitting in that hospital chair. My lips parted and his tongue slipped inside my mouth. His hands cupped my backside and pulled me closer against him.

Stop. Stop. What are you doing? A small corner of my still rational brain demanded.

I started to step back, but then his hands rose to cup my breasts and instead I grasped his hips and pulled him closer against me.

Duke tore his lips from mine and trailed hot kisses down my neck, into the opening of my pajama top. His hand left my breast and I felt his fingers undoing the middle button. His scorching fingers touched the bare skin of my midriff. I moaned, even as my hands

slipped between us and began to work on the buttons of his shirt.

Then it was open and my fingers glided over his skin, gloried in the softness of his chest hair. Duke gasped when I grazed his nipple with my thumbnail.

"Two can play that game." I heard him murmur and my pajama top fell away. I felt him kiss his way across the upper slope of my breasts, his mouth trailed downward, my body tensed and then with one smooth, shocking movement, Duke pulled my pajama bottoms down, tossed them aside and lifted me into his arms.

"Bedroom?" he gasped.

"Down the hall, first door," I managed to say.

My hands kept busy on his body during the short trip. He laid me on the bed, stepped back for only as long as it took to strip his jeans and boxers away. Then he was with me, hands, teeth, fingers—there was nothing gentle about it. We worked on each other, teasing, touching. Gasps and moans filled my ears. His or mine I couldn't say. My world exploded and for one delicious second I forgot how to breathe.

I collapsed back, the air whooshing from me.

Duke rolled off of me, then reached to pull me close against his side.

My God. What had happened? This wasn't the way I'd imagined it, me in flannel pajamas, angry words instead of sweet promises. For our first time I'd envisioned me in something lacy, sheer and red. Well, at least I'd brushed my teeth. I felt tears burn my eyes. "Duke, I…"

"No." He pulled me atop of him. "No words, Gail. Just feel. Let your body do the talking."

His fingers danced across me again, a fire erupted inside and I pressed my lips against his. There would be time for talking later, much later.

Chapter Thirty-Five
Pieter Orloff

I TOSSED THE newspaper aside and turned to glare at my still silent cell phone. Stupid. Stupid. I should always be able to get in touch with El Rios. None I had worked with had been out of touch, not for a minute. I glanced at my watch. 6:00. The plane would take off from Santa Maria in an hour. This was our chance to take care of Garret. and El Rios did not even know. "Not El Rios," I murmured. "El Stupido."

Perhaps I should see to it? I could be in Las Vegas in but an hour. Yet, I did not know where the little wedding party would be staying. "To hell with this. El Rios will not know either."

Just as I stood my cell phone rang. Caller ID showed me El Rios' name. "Ya."

"What news is so important that you would call my home number?"

"You've not been home all night? I called last evening."

"I turn off this phone when I walk in the door. My family is my family."

"I must be able to…"

"What is you want?"

I felt the blood rush to my head and my hand clenched the cell phone. When this was over El Rios would be buzzard food, and I would see to it myself. "Have you seen to the Garrett problem yet?"

"It is taken care of."

"When? Last night?"

"Why are you asking? I said it is taken care of."

"Does, 'taken care of,' mean something different here than in my land? Taken care of means dead, correct?"

"I don't like to be questioned. Perhaps you are a big man in Russia, but you are now in Santa…"

"Shut the fuck up."

184

"You, you can't talk to me like that." El Rios screamed his outrage. "I will have you gutted and your heart mailed to your madre."

I let him wail on. I could picture the spittle flying from his lips, his face red, eyes bulging. When he stopped to take a breath I interrupted. "We can take care of Morgan Garrett this very day, and perhaps Duke Cummins also."

"Who is this Duke Cummins? Why do you want him dead also?"

"That isn't important, what is, is that I know Garrett will be in Las Vegas in about two hours, he and his woman."

"The puta Darcie Devonshire will be with him?"

"Ya. They are going to be married."

El Rios laughed. "Then she will become a bride and a widow on the same day. What do you know?"

I told him of my conversation with Gail Crane.

"You are sure of this," he asked.

"I am. Do you have someone in Vegas?"

"I do. Many someones."

"You'll see to Duke Cummins also?"

"As a favor to you, I will."

A favor I know I would be called on to return. "Good. Good. Call me when it is over."

"Si."

I ended the call, settled back in my chair. Gail would be upset when her friends were killed. Perhaps dear Andre would telephone and be there to comfort her. My stomach growled. Satisfaction always gave me an appetite. A ham and cheese omelet, that would do nicely. I stood and walked toward the door.

Chapter Thirty-Six
Duke Cummins

FROM THE COCKPIT I heard Gail talking with Darcie. She avoided me, or maybe we avoided each other. This morning hadn't been a good one, to say the least.

When I'd awoke, all alone, I could smell coffee brewing, not what I'd had in mind at all. I'd pulled on my pants and walked into the kitchen, hoping I could convince Gail to maybe have breakfast in bed...a little later. I'd been met with a cold shoulder and a stiff posture. Without looking at me she'd said.

"Coffee's almost ready. I'm going to catch a shower."

My words of greeting died on my lips.

She walked by me, still not meeting my eyes. Had I imagined last night, the passion between us.

"Maybe I could join you in that shower?"

Gail didn't answer, instead she kept on walking. At the doorway she turned, at last looked at me. Her expression gave me no clue as to what went on in her head. "It's getting late. Why don't you go on without me. I'll come in my own car."

"Gail..."

"I mean you're the pilot and all, don't you have things to do before we all arrive?"

"Last night..."

"Oh yes, last night was great—you were great. It's what we both needed to release some tension."

I took a deep breath, let it out slowly before I replied. "That's what it was, tension release?"

She looked away from me. "Well yes. What did you think it was?"

"I'm not in the habit of using women."

Gail smiled, but it didn't reach her eyes. "Well how would I know that, and furthermore, how do you?"

186

I felt like she'd kicked me in the stomach. Last night hadn't changed anything. Gail glanced at the clock. "We don't have time for anymore chit-chat. I've got to get dressed. I suggest you do the same." Without another word I'd turned and walked away.

I stared out the cockpit window. Just how did I get in the cupid business? Well yes, I knew how. Morgan wanted something from me and I needed something from him. What the hell had happened last night—well I knew what happened and it was damn good, but this morning…. "Shit."

"What? Is something wrong?" Rick Kaminski looked at me sharply. He was getting some free flying time as my co-pilot and his newness to the Lear had him nervous.

"No, no, everything is okay. I just was thinking."

"There is sure a lot of nothing out there." Rick leaned forward to look at the desert below.

There were dry barren stretches reaching from mountain range to mountain range, with roads that seem to branch off and go nowhere. I am always amazed when I look at one of God's masterpieces. Rick was experiencing it for the first time and his wonder was understandable. When Morgan had seen Rick in the co-pilot's seat he'd asked him what his plans were. Rick had none, so Morgan had insisted the young man become a part of the party. Rick had protested, but at last gave in.

"We'll be starting our descent soon," I said. As if on cue a voice came through my headset

"Lear 25Tango, descend to and maintain 9,000, turn right to 090 and contact Desert Center on 124.8."

"Roger, 25Tango down to 9, turning to 090." I started my descent to Las Vegas McCarren field. "Rick, tune number two radio to Tower and watch my airspeed. I want 180."

"Yes Sir."

I looked toward the back and announced over the PA system. "We're going down now. Vegas is on the left and we'll be on the ground in a few minutes. Every one buckle up please."

Turning, I put my mind to flying the approach and landing. "Keep your eyes open Rick. There's lots of traffic out there."

Minutes later we were on the ground. I turned the Lear toward the private landing area and brought her to a halt. The ramp at the

executive terminal was full of high dollar jets. It looked like the high rollers were in town. The two guys Sam Hughes had told me about were there. All I had to do was get out and turn the jet over to them. A new experience for me, leaving my plane in someone else's hands, but Sam was the boss.

Gail, Morgan and Darcie had already exited and were waiting for Rick and me.

One look at Morgan's tense pre-occupied face told me the deed had yet to be accomplished. Why had he waited? I thought he planned to pop the question on the flight over. Did he have doubts? When Morgan had joined us in the cockpit Rick had ribbed him some, but that couldn't have been it. Oh well not my business.

I saw Gail was still going overboard with not looking at me, or giving us a chance to talk one-on-one. Fine, let her play that game, but we would talk.

Taxis were lined up as we trailed out of the terminal. Gail went to the nearest one and opened its door. "We girls will take this one. You guys get your own."

"Say what?" Morgan said.

Darcie looked surprised too.

Gail's face flushed. "I need to make a quick stop—personal stuff." She motioned for Darcie to enter. With a shrug, Darcie did. The bags were loaded and the taxi took off.

In our own taxi I turned to Morgan. "You haven't asked her yet?"

"There didn't seem to be a right time. She and Gail chatted all the damn way here." Morgan frowned at me. "What the hell happened between the two of you? From what I gathered you two had a blow-up."

Blow up? Not what I'd call last night, but if that's the way Gail wanted to play it. "A misunderstanding," I said. "We'll work it out." I glanced out the window. "Where are we going?"

"The Luxor. We have rooms side by side." Morgan turned to Rick. "Want you to know I haven't forgotten about your grandfather. I've got a friend doing some checking for me, once I hear from him we'll know what to do next."

Rick nodded. Morgan didn't say anymore and I knew he'd left it to Rick whether or not to fill me in. I was curious as to why Morgan would say something like that with me around, but when

Rick turned to me and told me about his grandfather, the letter, his death and St. James' connection, I got the picture. I didn't know where it fit in with the plane crash and my father's murder, but it did, I was sure of that.

"I'm asking her at dinner," Morgan said. "I'd like you all to be there. They have a great steak house. I'll make the reservations."

"You sure you don't want to do it in private?" I said.

"Yeah, what if she says no," Rick added.

For a second Morgan looked stricken, then his face cleared. "She won't. We love each other."

The driver pulled into the Luxor's entrance.

Vegas hotels are noted for their opulence and splendor. The Luxor with its black pyramid shape was no exception. We were met, coddled and hustled from our cab to our rooms in record time.

I hadn't seen any sign of Gail or Darcie. Had they arrived before us? Which room was Gail's? I had a heart-jerking thought. Maybe we were sharing one. I looked around. The room had an Egyptian theme going on, all brown's and tans. The king size bed looked welcoming. They had a nice little sitting area in front of a large window. A great place for some morning coffee. I walked to the window. We were on the twelfth floor. It would provide a good view of the city lights once night arrived. I looked at my watch. It was nine-thirty in the morning. Morgan had said dinner. That would be about six. What to do between now and then?

The telephone on the table next to the bed rang. "Hello."

"Duke."

It was Morgan.

"I don't know where my head is. Gail says I can't wait until tonight, Darcie'll need stuff. We're all having breakfast. I'll ask Darcie then. Let's say thirty minutes in the Pyramid Café."

So Gail and Darcie were here. So much for us sharing a room. "Sounds fine to me."

"Good." Morgan hung up his phone.

Pyramid Café, thirty minutes, that gave me plenty of time to unpack and settle in.

I picked up a brochure lying on the table. The café was on the casino floor. What were the plans for tonight, a bachelor party, maybe take in a show? I read their write up on some fantasy thing, beautiful, topless women, singing and dancing. It sounded a prime

choice for a bachelor party.

The phone rang again, maybe it was Gail. "Hello."

"Gail says not in the café," Morgan said. "Gail says here. We are ordering in."

"Okay." I knew they were right next door. "Still thirty minutes?"

"Yeah."

"I'll see you then."

*****

In Morgan and Darcie's hotel room, the only one who didn't look like a long tailed cat in a room crowded with rocking chairs was Darcie, although I didn't see how she couldn't pick up on the tension Morgan gave off. In the five minutes I'd stood here, he'd crossed the room and back five times. Gail looked like the grinning Cheshire cat from *Alice In Wonderland,* well except when she let herself look in my direction.

Another ten minutes passed as Darcie went on about the choices we had for the rest of our day and Sunday. "Look here's a guy who sings just like Frank Sinatra. I love old Blue Eyes. You guys up for that?"

I smiled out the window and listened to everyone else's non-committal responses to her question.

Someone knocked on the room door and I turned in time to see Morgan jump at least three inches off the floor. Darcie did give him a strange look as she answered the knock. Rick stood there.

"Sorry I'm late." He looked at me. "Sam Hughes called. Everything's fine with the Lear."

I nodded.

A knock sounded again, and this time it was our breakfasts: bacon, eggs, pancakes, coffee, orange juice and three bottles of champagne.

"On the house, Mister Garrett," the waiter said.

Gail and I exchanged a quick smile, while Darcie stood looking impressed.

"They must think we are some high-rollers," she said.

Morgan grabbed a bottle of champagne. "I'll open this while your start dishing out the food, Darcie."

I almost groaned. He wasn't going to do the old, drop the ring in the bottom of the glass, thing. I knew someone who'd almost

choked to death when she'd swallowed the ring. "No orange juice in my champagne," I said. "Don't care for mimosa." Whoa, another little bit of information released by the cubby holes in my brain.

"Darcie, can you come here?" Morgan's voice sounded like he was scared to death. Uh oh, it must be show time.

Darcie looked up from dishing scrambled eggs onto a plate. "What?"

"Come here please."

She looked around at all of our grinning faces, but remained frozen in place. "What's going on?"

Gale stepped forward and took the plate of eggs from her. "Get over there."

Darcie still didn't move, so Morgan came to her. He dropped to one knee in front of her. Ole blue eyes would have been proud of him.

"Morgan, what the hell are you doing?"

"Shush, don't talk, just listen." He reached for her hand. "Darcie Devonshire, I have loved you a long time. I haven't always been the best I could be, but I have always loved you. I want more than us living together; I want you to marry me. I've ask your father and I checked with Wes, everybody thinks it's a good idea." Morgan took a deep breath. "So, what do you say?"

"What do I say?" Darcie dropped to her knees in front of him. "Yes, you silly ass, yes. I thought you were going to ask me at dinner the other night. When?"

"Tomorrow, I've got it all arranged. We get our license; we go to the chapel, it's all set."

"You've already arranged this?"

"Yeah, the limo comes and takes us all down to the license place, we get the license and head for the chapel. We could have had an Elvis impersonator, but I opted for the straight service. After that he takes us to our wedding dinner. It's all right here in this e-mail they sent. Very romantic, right? It's like an elopement, but with our friends here with us."

Darcie looked at each of us. "Gail, Duke, everyone knew, but me?"

"Well, uh yeah, I wanted it to be a surprise."

"You talked to my mum and da?"

"Your dad, he told your mom."

"And they were okay with them not being at my wedding?"

Darcie's voice had grown quieter with each word and Morgan now looked a little worried.

"Your dad was fine with it. He just wants you to be happy. We will be happy, Darcie. I promise."

Gail jumped into the conversation. "I talked to your mom, Darcie. I promised you'd call her right after you gave Morgan your answer."

Darcie looked at her. "Gave him my answer?"

"If you said yes, then she's going to give the two of you the biggest reception ever, right after you get home."

"But, she -- they won't be here."

Morgan's stricken face told me major doubts were flooding through him. "Darcie, we can wait. I'll cancel it all. We can do the whole big, white wedding, thing."

"I don't have a dress…"

"Taken care of," Gail said. "Dress shop downtown is holding three for you to try."

Darcie blinked." You mean that place we stopped at earlier? Not about getting a negligee?"

Gail smiled. "Yes, but not one for me."

"Woo-hoo," Rick said. "Is it red?"

Our laughter following his remark seemed to release some of the tension.

Morgan stood, helped Darcie to her feet. "I mean it Darcie. We can wait…"

"No," she cut him off. "We've waited long enough. We'll make it legal and have the real celebration when we get home." She held out her hand. "Now put that ring on my finger."

Morgan did.

Darcie held her hand up, catching the sunlight with the diamond in the ring. "It's beautiful."

"It's time for a toast," I said and we spent a few minutes filling and selecting our glasses.

Morgan lifted another one of the bottles and I could see it wasn't champagne, but sparkling apple cider. He poured himself a glass.

I lifted my glass. "To Morgan and Darcie, health and happiness, forever."

We all drank.

"Now let's eat," Rick said. "I'm starving."

Gail reached for a plate. "And then Darcie and I have some major shopping to do."

*****

I strolled past the entrance of the Luxor, walked away from the noise and hubbub of the busy casino. I stopped to watch the busy traffic, shook my head. Everyone rushed around like there was no tomorrow, and I'd bet they'd all come here to relax and have fun. We Americans could learn a lot from the African natives, live easy and take it one day at a time. Now where did that come from? I don't suppose I'll ever get used to these random thoughts that seem to sprout from nowhere. God, will I ever remember my entire past?

The splat sound came from behind me. Concrete chips splattered on my pants leg from the wall a few feet away. I turned toward the street. Damn, someone's shooting. Hell, they're shooting at me, and they're using a silencer.

"Get down Duke."

I heard the call, but instead of hitting the ground I looked back to see who it was.

"Dammit Duke get down, they're shooting at you," Gail shouted.

My reflexes kicked in and I dropped to the pavement.

I heard the sound of a car accelerate away. Still a little confused, I was halfway back up onto my feet by the time Gail rushed up, with Darcie right behind.

"What...?" I said, now standing.

"They were shooting at you, you damn fool, and you just stood there," Darcie said.

"Jesus, Duke." Gail's voice had a quiver as she pulled on my arm. "We have to get back inside. Darcie where's Morgan?"

"Here he comes."

"What the hell's going on?" Morgan demanded.

"Someone tried to take out Duke," Darcie said.

I shook my head. "No, it had to be a random drive by, gang initiation maybe. I was in the wrong place at the wrong time."

"It didn't look random to me," Gail said. "I saw the car there. They didn't open up until you came into view."

"Who would want me dead?" I said.

Darcie looked hard at me. "Good question." She turned to Morgan. "Just who knew we were going to be here in Vegas?"

Morgan shrugged. "Could be anybody. It wasn't a big secret."

"It was to me," Darcie said.

I heard an edge in her voice. Maybe surprise weddings weren't the way to go.

Gail reached to pat Darcie's arm. "Let's get back inside."

"Better yet, let's get back to our room," Morgan said.

*****

"We have to call the police." Gail dug in her tiny purse, pulled out her cell phone.

Morgan touched her arm "We don't want to call the police. We'll never get away from them. We got a marriage to take care of."

"Yeah, but, uh, I'm FBI, remember. We need to call."

"You're our friend also. Please don't."

"I'm sure it's nothing," I said. "Who would want me dead?"

"Maybe the same person who killed you father," Gail snapped.

"Why?"

Gail's tight smile didn't reach her eyes. "Now that's the twenty-four-thousand-dollar, question, isn't it? Got any answers?"

We looked at each other for a long moment, then Gail shook her head and turned to hug Darcie. "After you're married. I'll call then. Okay, let's get back to that shopping extravaganza." She pointed at Morgan. "You think you guys can stay safe until then?"

"The groom and the best man will be just fine. You gals have a great time."

Gail and I exchanged a long look, before she and Darcie turned and walked out of the room.

Chapter Thirty-Seven
Darcie Devonshire

I CLOSED THE door behind me, stood and stared at it as I tried to organize my jumbled thoughts. Getting married. Tomorrow. I looked down at the engagement ring on my finger. Very beautiful, just as I imagined it would look from my tenth year onward.

But a Las Vegas wedding? No Mum and no Da.

They're only words, said in front of a man who doesn't know us, the real fun starts after. It wouldn't be any different at home wearing a frilly, white dress. I blinked back tears. Yes it's different. Da wasn't walking me down the aisle, hell he wasn't even here.

"Darcie? Darcie, you okay?"

I took a deep breath, turned to face her. "That man of mine is full of surprises."

Gail searched my eyes. "You don't have to do this. Morgan said so. His heart's in the right place."

I forced a smile. "No, it's always what I told him I wanted—and it is want I want. We don't need a big wedding. Besides it's always the reception that's the fun part, and we're going to have that." I crossed to the safe where I'd placed my purse and my gun. I should have left the gun at home, but it didn't seem right not to have it with me. "Did you bring your gun with you?"

"What? No, it's in a safe at home. You?"

I nodded. "One thing about a private plane, no cares what you bring aboard it." I fished in my purse and found my cell phone. "Time to call my mum." It rang only twice. Mum must have been waiting for my call.

"Hello."

"Mum…"

"You said yes?"

"Of course I did. I love Morgan."

"I've got the guest list in front of me. How does next Saturday

sound, or is that a tad bit soon?"

"I…"

"A 50's band. I know you love that era. How does salmon and roast lamb sound, and a cake of course, chocolate with raspberry filling, your favorite."

Everything she said was perfect. I felt tears threaten again and I swallowed. "Great, Mum. I wish you and Da were here with me."

Silence was her response, and then Da's voice said. "Hey pumpkin, you alright with getting married in Sin City."

"Sure, Da. It's only saying some words and signing a paper. You know the hard stuff comes after."

"Who is walking you down the aisle?"

I forced a laugh. "There probably won't be an isle. How are Becky and Rainbow doing?"

"You've only been gone a day, but they miss their momma already."

I had to get off the phone before I totally lost it. "Well, I'll be home on Monday, an old married lady. Give Mum a hug from me. Bye, Da." I ended the call before he could respond.

I turned, walked to the window, stared out as I struggled to get my emotions under control. I heard footsteps from behind me and Gail handed me a glass of water. I smiled my thanks and took a long drink. We stood there in silence for a moment and then I walked to dresser and placed the glass on it. "Okay, let's go find me a wedding dress."

*****

I stared at myself in the dressing-room mirror. Yes, the pale green color looked good with my hair. The simple two piece suite was sensible and I could wear it afterward for dinners out, maybe even Sunday services. I heard a tap on the door.

"Try this one," Gail said.

I opened the door and she held out an ivory satin and lace sheathe toward me. "Oh no, way to weddingly. What would I do with it afterward?"

"Try it on, Darcie."

I accepted the dream of a dress. "Fine. To humor you, but I'm not buying it." I closed the door.

The dress slipped over my body. It fit like it had been made for me. The scooped neckline would have shown off grandma's pearls

perfectly, but then I didn't have grandma's pearls with me, or Mum's white bible. My vision in the mirror blurred. "Bloody-damn, no more crying," I scolded my reflection. "I love Morgan. He loves me. That's what's important."

"Let me see," Gail demanded.

I let her in.

"Oh, it's beautiful. You will make a lovely bride. Those satin pumps across the street will look perfect with it."

I looked at the price tag, groaned. "I'm not spending that much money for a dress like this. The green one will work fine."

Gail didn't say anything, just turned and walked out of the dressing room.

I admired myself in the ivory satin for a moment more and then stripped it from my body. I'd almost finished dressing when Gail tapped on the door again.

"I'll take care of the rejects."

I opened the door and handed her the four dresses I'd rejected. "Thanks."

"Give me the green one too. I'll have the sales girl ring it up while you're getting dressed. By the way Morgan's buying."

"What? No way."

"It's already taken care of. Part of the wedding package."

Wedding package? How had he chosen, two from column B, one from column A? I added the green suit to Gail's arms. "I'll be right out."

"No try this on." In her other hand she had a white negligee.

I held it up to the light. "Are you serious? You can see right through it."

"Just try it on. It will get the marriage off to a good start." Gail backed out of the dressing room carrying the cast off items and the green suit.

I stared at the sheer white, concoction. There wasn't a male over thirteen with a pulse that wouldn't love it. I took of my clothes and slipped into the gown. Dear God. I looked like I was wrapped in mist. My face heated. Would I have the nerve to walk from the bathroom, wearing this? I smiled. What the hell. At least the honeymoon would be what I'd dreamed of.

When I came out of the dressing room, Gail already had the suit, bagged and across her arm. She cocked an eyebrow at me. "Well?"

"I'm taking it."

"Good girl."

I noticed then the bottom of the beige satin dress hanging from the bag. "Gail, I said no to that one."
She shook her head. "It's perfect and my gift to you."

"I can't let…"

"Already done." She turned and walked toward the door. "Now let's get those shoes I saw."

*****

Back in the room I called Morgan.

"Hello sweet stuff," he said. "Shopping all done?"

"Yes. What's on the agenda for tonight?"

"We're having a girl's night," Gail called to me. "Let the boys take care of themselves."

"You hear that?" I said to Morgan.

"Yippe, a bachelor party. I know just the place to burn some hours."

"Not too wild I hope, you party animal."

"Not to worry woman. I'll be coming home to you."

I laughed. "Well don't wake me up when you get in."

"What's Gail got planned for you?" Morgan said.

"I've no idea." I turned to Gail. "My man wants to know what you have in store for me."

"Nothing special, just some girl talk and maybe a male stripper or two."

"You hear that?" I said to Morgan.

"Hum, I'm not sure I approve. Maybe we should rethink this last night of singledom."

"What?" I said. "The strippers?"

"No, the girl talk." Morgan laughed.

"Your are so whacko, but that's why I love you."

"See ya later, sweet cheeks." Morgan ended the call.

I faced Gail. "Let's get this party started."

Chapter Thirty-Eight
Morgan Garrett

I'D TAKEN DARCIE at her word and called Duke and Rick. Boys night out, I'd told them and I knew just where I wanted the three of us to go and we were on the way there.

"Hey Rick, this is serious man's business, this drinking," I said.

"Yes sir Mr. Garrett, but I'm not much of a drinker."

"Good for you. One won't hurt most folks. Me, well I can't stop at one. So it's a problem."

"So then why are we doing it?" Rick said.

"I'm going to be a married man tomorrow and this is my last hurrah. I always promised myself that I'd be visiting this bar in Bally's for one last drink as a single man, and we are. I am drinking, just not any booze."

I hustled across the busy Las Vegas Boulevard, with Duke and Rick trailing behind.

"Where is this place, Morgan?" Duke stopped at the bottom of the legs of the Eifel Tower reproduction. "Is it in Paris?"

"No, but we are going through here. Rick about this drinking; you college guys just don't understand the seriousness of the whole ritual. Now you take most guys, they order something exotic they have heard about. like say a Singapore Sling. Now that's no good, too much fruit juice and sugar. A real man wants Scotch and branch water, or Bourbon straight up, stuff like that. So what are you going to have?"

"Uh, well I think I'll have a beer."

"Ha," Duke joined in. "You missed the point of the whole thing son."

We walked into Paris.

I watched Rick take in the City-of-Lights street scene. "There's a

bar there. Is that it?"

"No. We're heading to Bally's. Come on. Let's keep moving," I said.

"Is this your first time in Vegas?" Duke smiled.

"Yes sir." Rick turned away from the crowded bar. He looked up at the ceiling and its simulated sky. "How do they do that?"

"No idea."

I led us down passage that opened into another casino. "Welcome to Bally's." I pointed. "See that hall? That's where we are going."

Duke looked at me questioningly, but took off for the hallway.

About halfway down the hall we stopped and I led the way into a small bar with just a few customers. "This is it," I said.

"How in hell did you ever find this place?" Duke said.

I shrugged. "Gamblers have a different Vegas than the tourists ever see. They come here to gamble and they like their privacy. There are several places like this around town."

Once my eyes adjusted to the dim lighting I could see they had not changed the simple gay nineties décor. The broad mirror behind the bar, lined with bottles and glasses, was the same, as well as the polished dark oak everywhere. The bar still had the curved elbow rail padded and ready to lean on. I walked to it.

Moving onto the stool to my left Duke maneuvered Rick to the stool between us. "Okay Rick, what'll you have?" Duke said. "The first round's on me."

"You want that Singapore Sling, or the Scotch?" I said.

"Uh, no I'll have a lite beer."

"Okay, lite Beer it is, and Barkeep, make mine a club soda with a twist of lime, Duke?"

"Scotch, water, not to heavy on the water,"

Waiting for our drinks we were silent for a moment, then Duke said, "You know Morgan I've been here in Vegas for a wedding before."

I watched as he stared at his drink. "Who got married?"

"I wished I knew. It could've been me—hell no, it wasn't me. I hate this no memories shit."

Our drinks arrived. "Well, here we go guys, drink. *Compai.* Down the hatch." I held my glass up in toast mode and we all took a drink.

"I almost got married last year." Rick shook his head. "I don't

think I loved her but she sure was good in bed."

"What happened?" I said.

"Found out she was good in bed with everyone I knew." Rick laughed.

I shook my head. "Yeah, that happens."

"You know marriage is the cause of most divorces." Duke looked at me with a dead serious expression. "Have you thought about that Morgan?"

"Hey man, this is real. Darcie's the one. I have no doubts. We've been through the mill together. I'm sure."

"Yeah you know the trouble with being the best man? You don't get to prove it." Rick grinned. "I think you're going to have your hands full with Darcie."

"Yeah," I grinned back at him. "You got a girl now?"

"No sir."

"Enough with the sir crap," I said.

Rick saluted. "I don't find many girls hanging around the airport. I did see a beauty with Everett Cummins several times. Found out later that she was his wife."

Duke leaned toward Rick. "And that beauty is my step-mommy, so watch how you talk about her."

"Nothing bad to say, she was a sight better than those mobsters hanging out with Senator St. James." Rick sipped at his beer and turned to face me. "That bunch was up to no good. I'd bet my car they know what happened to my grandpa."

"Could be. I'll know more when I talk with my contact." I pushed back from the bar. "Right now I'm getting married. Let's get out of here and go see the lounge show across the street."

Outside I spied a man wearing a funny pork pie hat. I had seen that same hat as we went in. I steered us directly toward him. As we neared, he turned and moved across the street. Could be nothing, but my senses went on alert, especially after what had happened earlier with Duke.

"Let me tell you about an Ubala wedding," Duke said, as we crossed the street. "First the chief spends the night with the bride. Then the women of the tribe cover her with white ash and stick feathers in some of the more strategic parts of her body. Later, while the couple dances around the fire, the chief tells about his night with the bride."

"Doesn't sound like they have much respect for women," Rick said.

Duke winked at me. "What do you think Morgan, you want an Ubala wedding?"

"Save it for your own. You getting close with Gail?"

"Hell, I don't know. Just when I think we are okay she changes. I think she believes I had something to do with the crash."

I stopped in front of the lounge club's door. "Here we go, let's see the show." I stood back and let Rick and Duke pass me while I scanned the casino looking for pork pie hats.

*****

I looked down at Darcie, she snuffled, not a snore, but soft. I eased from the bed, found my pants and slipped them on. I shouldn't have had that last cup of coffee. The lounge act had been a salute to burlesque. A little bawdy, but good for some belly laughs. When I'd gotten back to the room, Darcie had already been in bed.

I eased into my shoes, sockless and stole my way into the other room. I'd started to sit on the little couch when I heard a sound that seemed to be a scratch at our door. I moved to it and laid my hand on the door handle. It moved ever so slight. For sure not a maid, not at three in the morning. I waited, felt nothing more, but that doorknob hadn't turned on its own.

Darcie says sometimes I lack the patience of a monkey, this was one of those times. I grabbed the door and jerked it open in one quick motion, then jumped into the hall. Well almost. I slammed into a wall of flesh and we both went down in a heap in the hall.

"Shit, shoot the Pendejo." I heard a voice yell. It wasn't the guy I had in a hammer lock, so there were at least two of them. I pushed off, scrambled to my feet and turned. I felt the blow coming before it made contact. I relaxed, fell to the right. It landed on my left arm, nearly paralyzing my elbow. I spun, rushed the nearest body, felt a gun in his waistband as I slammed into him.

The sound of a Glock firing twice vibrated in my ears.

"Nobody move, and I mean nobody. Shit, stop you asshole. Well, damn," Darcie yelled. "Morgan; you okay?"

"Yeah, yeah." I stood, could see a big guy laying on the hotel's carpet, spewing blood from his head. "Did you shoot him?"

"I just tapped him a little. I should maybe have shot the other one though." She motioned with her gun. "He ran that way. Why the bloody hell are you out here starting a fight?"

I looked down the hall and could see a crowd of people running toward us. "Maybe I should take it from here." Darcie looked down, realized her nearly nude condition and ducked back into our room.

*****

Explaining the fiasco took a lot longer than the fiasco itself, but I finally satisfied the Las Vegas detectives, assuring them we would come down and make a statement. Their last words to me were, try to stay out of trouble while you're here. I guess I just look like a trouble maker.

So who the hell were those guys? I hadn't seen the one who hightailed it away, but had heard enough to know he was Latino too. It had to be El Rios. The dude had a long arm. Damn, messing with me the night before my wedding. Not smart. El Rios and I had some talking to do when I got back to Santa Maria.

Chapter Thirty-Nine
Darcie Devonshire

I lay in the bed watching the room lighten. I'd been awake for the past two hours, listening to the fan cycle on and off. I could blame my sleeplessness on the earlier excitement out in the hallway, but I knew that wasn't it.

Morgan mumbled, turned onto his side, nothing I could understand. Was he dreaming of tomorrow—no make that today. Our wedding day. I said the words again in my head. They didn't seem any more real.

I slipped from the bed, walked to the window. In the distance the lights of Las Vegas glimmered. In the sky the stars tried to compete, but it seemed a losing battle. The moon, fat and swollen, hung in the middle of them. I hoped Becky wasn't giving Mom and Da bad time, she was always restless during a full moon.

"Darcie, what is it?"

I looked at Morgan. "It's nothing. Woke up and couldn't get back to sleep."

He pulled the covers aside. "Come back to bed."

I joined him and he pulled me close against his side.

"In a few hours you're going to be Darcie Garrett—Mrs. Morgan Garrett—Mrs. Garrett."

I watched him smile.

"It's going to be weird the first time I hear someone call you that. My mom's Mrs. Garrett."

"Darcie Garrett," I said. "It has a nice sound, but maybe I won't change my name."

"Yeah, we never did talk about that. You don't have to change your name, maybe it can be Darcie Devonshire-Garrett."

I laughed. "Now that's a mouthful. No, it'll be Darcie Garrett. I'd always planned to take my husband's name." I looked over his shoulder. "When the minister says, 'let me introduce you to Mister

and Mrs. Whoever,' it was always my newly acquired name."

"Don't think that'll happen at our wedding, but it can. I can arrange…"

"No Morgan, it's okay. You know what they say, 'man plans, God laughs."

He pulled me close, kissed me. "Let's get a few more hours sleep. It's going to be a busy day."

"Sure." I turned on my side; let him pull me close against the length of him. In a few moments his even breathing filled my ears. I watched the room lighten.

*****

Morgan stretched beside me. "Morning, Beautiful," he whispered into my hair.

"Mornin'." I kicked the covers aside. "I'll take the bathroom first."

"Sure thing. I'll make us some coffee."

I padded to the bathroom, opened the door. I'd hung the ivory and lace sheathe on the shower railing to make sure it remained wrinkle-free, the sight of it hit me like a slap in the face. A choked cry burst from me, then another. I sank to my knees. I can't do it. I can't. I tried to muffle my gasps, reached behind me to close the door and found Morgan's bare leg.

"Darcie. Darcie. What is it? Did you fall? Are you hurt?"

I couldn't get words from my clogged throat. Instead I shook my head and sobbed. Morgan knelt beside me, reached to pull me into his arms and I shook my head with more force and scooted back from him.

"I don't understand," Morgan said.

"I can't do it," I managed to wail.

"Can't do what?"

I waved my hand at the dress. "I can't wear that."

"You can get another dress…"

"No, no, I can't marry you."

I watched Morgan's face grow pale. "You don't want to marry me?"

I grabbed a wad of tissue and wiped at my nose. "Not want, can't."

He sat back from me. "I see."

No he didn't, judging by his tight lips. I reached to touch his

arm. "I thought I could. I didn't think it was important…"

"Marrying me's not important?"

"God, Morgan, will you listen, please." I looked up at the dress. "I want it all."

He still looked devastated and confused.

"I lied to you. I lied to myself. I don't want a Las Vegas wedding. I want to stand in front of a minister, tell the world I love you, with all of our friends in chairs behind us. I want my da to walk me down the aisle. I want my mum to be in the front row, crying, hell Morgan, I even want Becky and Bow to be there." I started to cry again.

He didn't say a word. Dear God, had I bloody blowed it with him? I wiped my eyes and looked up. Morgan was smiling, then he started to laugh.

"Laughing? You're laughing at me?" I tried to get to my feet, failed.

He stood, reached for me.

"Don't you bloody well touch me," I snapped.

Morgan continued to laugh. "Darcie Devonshire, I love you. I don't care how you marry me, just as long as you do."

"What?"

He lifted me, drew me into his arms, then gave me a small shake. "Don't you ever scare me like that again."

I rested my forehead against his chest. "Then it's okay, but all of the money you spent…"

I felt him kiss the top of my head. "You're worth all the money in the world to me, besides I won five hundred playing craps last night. That'll about cover it."

It was my turn to laugh. Someone pounded on our room door and Morgan moved to answer. It was Gail.

"I've come to kidnap the bride. You…"

"Not going to be a bride," I said.

"Darcie, you've been crying." Gail glared at Morgan.

"She's called the wedding off," Morgan said.

Gail looked stunned. "Oh, I'm sorry."

"Don't be a horse's arse, Morgan," I said. "There's going to be a wedding, not just today, or in Las Vegas."

Relief flooded Gail's face. "I see."

"You'll still be my Maid of Honor."

"Of course." Gail blinked hard.

"Oh shit, more tears." Morgan grabbed for his pants and shoes."
I'll let the guys know the change in plans."

Chapter Forty
Morgan Garrett

DUKE AND I walked down the steps leading to the pool area. The guys hadn't seemed so surprised when I told them of the change in plans. I hadn't realized I'd stopped moving until Duke poked me in the back.

"Hey, what's up?" he said.

"Sorry, I was thinking."

"About the canceled nuptials?"

"Duke I have really screwed this up. I made all these plans and it wasn't what Darcie wanted at all. I feel stupid."

"Not stupid buddy it's just the Mars Venus thing. Women can have a different set of needs, you just guessed wrong on this one. Darcie loves you, it'll all work out in the end. We'll go home and you talk to her, get her mother involved. Women love to plan weddings. It'll be okay."

"Yeah?"

His words sounded good, but I wasn't so sure about any of it. Darcie and I talked all the time? Maybe I didn't listen.

My mind continued to struggle with my self-made dilemma. Well one thing Duke for sure was right about, we need to get out of here. I turned to him, "Let's go home to Santa Maria. What do we need to do?"

"The jet's ready. All we need to do is get packed and go."

"Okay, let's tell the ladies."

****

Santa Maria looked good today, a light rain had washed the streets last night and the sun had burned away the coastal fog early. Darcie had left for the police station a couple of hours ago. I watched Becky and Bow chase each other in the backyard and felt a surge of contentment. Things were moving forward. I had received an e-mail from Johnny Scott. His friend in Graves Registration, a general, had

some info for me about St. James and my phone call now worked through the maze of secretaries as I admired the beauty of the central coast.

"Mr. Garrett?" a male voice with a twinge of southern said. "Johnny tells me you are an old friend so I have done some deep digging. This is highly sensitive, and mostly incomplete, but I have something for you."

"Sir I am grateful for you efforts. I have a real problem here and I hope you can help, particularly where it comes to St. James and General Harden Hathaway."

"I will forward copies of most of this, but let me give you a thumb nail sketch of what we have.

"The Army investigators at the time of General Hathaway's disappearance believed Lieutenant St. James was involved, but solid evidence was not available and the witnesses had been transferred or disappeared, making it impossible to continue. Here is what I have.

"Sometime in the fifties a congressional committee headed by Congressman St. James requested the records for this investigation. After that the files were corrupted and much went missing. The cold war arrived and new leaders took over. They lost interest and Old Hard-Case Hathaway was forgotten. St. James had become a senator, so who was going to mess with that. To get it down to the short version, St James got away with it. I have a copy of the letter from Asa Kaminski, the prisoner who claims he saw St. James kill Harden and set fire to the Hooch: this letter was never acted on. They just stuck it in the file. The documents all are date stamped whenever they go in or out. The letter has never been out of the file.

"Prior to the senators leaving the Senate an ethics committee was being convened to look into some of the St. James' investments, but when he chose to not seek re-election the matter was dropped. One note of interest, there is some question about the airplanes the Senator owned and how he was using them. You may find more in here, but if you want my opinion I think you are already on the main track, if you can prove any of it."

"I'm in your debt General. I hope I can return the favor."

"Just nail the bastard. We don't like people killing our heroes."

"Nor do I Sir, nor do I."

I punched off the phone, but before I had a chance to digest all I had been told, Darcie walked into the kitchen. I hadn't even heard

her come in. I glanced out the patio doors. Bow and Becky were still involved with chasing each other around the back yard. Some watch dogs they were. "Hey, Sweet-thing. What are you doing back so soon?"

Without answering she came right to me and pulled me in for a strong hug. "Are you pissed at me? I don't want you to be; I love you."

"I know, Baby. You came home to say that?"

"Wes had to go to court and I'm waiting for him so we can run down some of the gang in the insurance swindle. Are you pissed?"

"No."

"Then kiss me, I have to go back to work."

So I did and the whirlwind went back out the door and left me standing in the kitchen by the phone.

I wondered if Rick would be at work today. I tried his home phone first. It went to the recording so I called Global Air.

"Global Air, Sam Hughes speaking."

"Rick Kaminski please."

"He's out in the hanger with Duke, can I take a message?"

"Sure, this is Morgan Garrett, tell him I'm coming by with some information."

"I will as soon as I see him, Mister Garrett."

"Thanks." I hung up the phone, glanced at the clock. Twelve-thirty. "As they say back at the ranch, we're burning daylight." Out the door I went.

*****

Duke perched on the edge of the cockpit, with one foot on the wing and the other in the leather trimmed opening. I could hear the clinking of a wrench followed by a clang and the sound of something heavy hitting the fabric at the bottom of the floor.

"God dammit."

"Steady boy," I shouted up. "What's going on ?"

Duke, with hair hanging in his face, rose up from the cockpit and looked at me for a minute. "Where's Rick?"

"Beats me, I just got here, but I'm looking for him too."

"Well, shit, I need that skinny kid to reach down and get my wrench…what are you doing here Morgan? You and Darcie change your mind and want to go back to Vegas?" He grinned at me.

"Hell no. I've had all the Vegas I can take. I need to talk to Rick

210

about his grandfather and St. James."

"Yeah? Let me get washed up. Where the hell is Rick?" Duke looked around the hangar, spotting Juan he called, "Hey Juan, have you seen Rick?"

"He's out on the ramp. What you need?"

"Yeah you're skinny enough. Reach down there and get that wrench for me." Duke dropped down to the floor and Juan took his place. In minutes he handed Duke the wrench.

"Maybe you need to lose…"

Duke shook the wrench at him. "Don't even go there."

I laughed. "Let's go find Rick."

Walking with Duke toward the opening in the large hangar door we arrived as Rick came waltzing in. He smelled like jet fuel and carried an oil stained clip board.

"Hey Mr. Garrett, what's up?"

"Rick I want to talk to you about your grandfather. Got a minute?"

"Yes sir. Just let me post these fuel readings to Mr. Swain's account. That old Baron of his burns fuel like it was on fire." Rick ran for the office, calling back over his shoulder. "Good customer though."

*****

We stood in the doorway; the bright sun shone on our backs and warmed the cool ocean breeze. I could tell Rick was nervous by his constant shifting from foot to foot. It had gotten worse as I told him of my conversation with the general from Graves Registration. I finished with, "Rick I'm am sure St. James had something to do with your grandfather's death. I can't prove it right at this moment, but I will, eventually." I heard a car come through the gate.

Duke had remained quiet through my words, now he leaned and looked out the door. " Hey, I think that's Gail."

"I am fairly sure that Senator St. James suppressed the letter your grandfather wrote to the army. It was soon after that your grandfather was killed; it all ties together but proving it is going to be hard." I looked beyond Duke in time to see Gail disappear around the corner of a hangar one building away from where we stood. "Where's she going?"

"I don't know." Duke stepped further out for a better view. "Rick what's over there between the hangars?"

"Nothing. Well, that's where that homeless guy hangs out when the weather gets bad. I think I saw him this morning."

"Homeless guy? What are you saying? They let some bum hang out over there?" Duke had already started in that direction with me right on his heels.

Chapter Forty-One
Darcie Devonshire

I GLANCED AT the office door. Wes should be back any time now. Damn that he had to make a court appearance over a traffic citation he'd written.

I squirmed in my chair, looked at my watch. Time seemed to have stopped. It wouldn't have made any difference if Wes had been here, we weren't to be at Nichol's Pawn Shop for another thirty minutes, but misery loves company. Bloody hell, I hated waiting.

The bridal magazine I'd picked up this morning lay open on the desk. It showed two pages of towering wedding cakes. Did I want one of those monsters? I hadn't wanted a Las Vega wedding, but did I want a wedding that required a cake kin to a skyscraper?

I sat back in my chair, smiled as I relived the phone call I'd made to Mum and Da last night right after I'd apologized to Becky and Rainbow for leaving them behind for two whole days. Da had brought the two basset hounds home in the early afternoon.

Da must have been hovering over the phone, because he answered before the first ring had quit peeling.

"Hello."

"Da."

"You're home. How's it feel to be a Mrs.?"

"I wouldn't know…"

"You didn't get married?"

Behind him I'd heard Mum say, "I told you so."

"Here's your Mom."

I took a deep breath. "I couldn't do it, Mum. I hope you don't have to call a lot of people."

"I don't have to call a single soul, Darcie."

"What?"

"I know my daughter, and a Las Vegas wedding isn't what she wants."

I felt tears threaten. "So you waited?"

"Until I heard it from you that the deed was done."

"I love Morgan, don't doubt that, it's just…"

"You want a true wedding. Every first-time bride does. It's to be your one and only. It needs to be done in the correct manner."

"Mum, not to extravagant."

"Of course not dear, just a few close friends. You'll wear your Grandma Penelope's gown, the same one I wore, and your Grandma Eleanore's pearls. You'll carry the family wedding bible. Who is to be your Maid of Honor? Your father will of course walk you down the aisle."

"It's Gail Crane. I've already asked her. Mum, about the gown. Morgan bought me a beautiful dress…"

"I'm sure it will do nicely for dinners out, but not for your wedding. What's the date, Darcie? We'll need to book the church. Do you have a…"

"No church, Mum. The wedding will be right here in our backyard."

"Backyard? But it's so small. With a gazebo in the front we'll only be able to seat thirty or forty."

I laughed. "That's more than enough. Small remember?"

"We'll see dear. About the cake…"

"Samantha," I heard Da call. "Let the girl catch her breath. You've got plenty of time to plan a wedding."

"Okay. Okay." Mum laughed. "You come for tea on Saturday, Morgan too of course. We'll talk more."

"I'll check our schedules and let you know."

Becky had whined and butted me with her head and I had ended the call.

I glanced at the office door again. Wes where are you? We've got to leave soon. I heard his voice, scanned the room beyond and saw him coming from the break-room with a donut in each hand.

I met him outside the door. "One of those better be for me."

He looked from the donuts into my face and then back again. "Oh, yeah, for sure."

He held the glazed one out toward me, quite a sacrifice, since glazed were his favorite. I took pity on him. "Changed my mind. You eat it."

"You sure?" Wes said, but he already had it going toward his

mouth.

"Come on," I said. "We've got to be at the pawn shop before El Rios' goons arrive."

*****

Wes and I stood out of sight in the back of Nichol's Pawn Shop. In the front Dominick paced behind the counter. We'd already wired him up and the tape recorder was set to go in the back room. It had taken some hard talking and promises to get the man to agree, but we'd gotten him to see the truth of it all, El Rios had to be driven out of Santa Maria, or the shake-downs would never end. I was cynical enough to believe, our sting wouldn't shut El Rios up for good, but we'd get him out of our town.

"He's looking nervous," Wes said.

"It'll be okay. They're most likely all nervous when the collectors come a-calling. All he has to do is get them to say he's paying for protection."

The door opened. I risked a glance around the door. A young woman stood there. She couldn't be who we...no, she held out a jewelry box. Her soft words came through loud and clear on the microphone. They couldn't pay the rent and were getting low on food. I felt a lump rise in my throat.

Dominick Nichol's response was polite, business like, he made the transaction as painless as possible. The young women took her money and with head held high, walked out of the shop.

Wes and I didn't say a word, just looked at each other and shook our heads. Ten minutes passed before the door opened again. Two men swaggered in, one a tall, blonde, white guy with a limp, the other a mountain of a Latino. I knew without a doubt these were the same two Morgan had dealt with before. I flipped on the tape recorder.

"Senores," Dominick said.

"Ya know why we're here." The white guy said.

Dominick frowned. "You want too much. This week business has been slow."

The big Latino leaned across the counter. "But it's been safe, right?"

"How do I know that has anything to do with you?" Dominick said, taking a step back.

215

The two thugs looked at each other. Then the white one smiled. "I guess you'll find out if you don't pay." He reached behind him and pulled a revolver from the back of his jean's waistband.

"You will shoot me if I don't give you money? "

"Nah, of course not. El Rios don't allow that. We'll just shoot up your store a little." He took aim at a vintage Budweiser sign.

"No. No, that belongs to an old man, a good customer. His daughter bought that for him. He'll be in at the first of the month to get it." Dominick stepped in front of the beer sign.

"You want me to take you out instead." The white guy lowered the barrel of the revolver toward Dominick's right knee. "You choose, the sign or your leg."

Wes took a step forward and I grabbed his arm, shook my head.

The Latino guy grabbed the other one's arm. "What the hell are you doing? Where'd you get the gun?"

"I'm tired of being a punching bag. The next time some asshole tries to take me on, he's got a surprise coming."

"We don't play like that. We walk in, we leave with the money, all civilized like."

"Civilized shit. This is all of that damned Russian's fault. I want the old way back." He waved the gun. "El Rios's turned into a pussy. We'd never be doing this shit if Juan Carlos still ran things."

"Don't you listen? We're stepping up. Drugs and girls, that's the old way. This is modern." The big Latino waved his hand around. "The way they do it New York."

"Santa Maria ain't New York." The white guy turned back to Dominick. "You think we're too expensive? How much is your wife and kid worth?"

I stood, took a step toward the door.

"I pay you $250.00 a week, and for that my shop doesn't get damaged and my family is left alone? Is that right?" Dominick said.

I held my breath, my hand on the doorknob.

"Yeah, that's right." Both of the goons said.

Wes drew his gun and kicked the door open. "Santa Maria Police Department. Drop the gun."

I released my in held breath and darted around Wes, my gun pointed at the white guy. "Are you bloody deaf? Drop the gun." The big Latino guy darted a look at the door. "Don't do it. You can't outrun a bullet."

"Shit," the white guy said as he lowered his revolver.

Wes walked around me and took it from his hand. "I bet that's the only thing smart you've done this year."

"Hands behind you," I said, staying in front of them so they could see my gun as Wes cuffed them. I pulled out my cell phone, punched in a number. "We've got them. Come on in."

Five minutes later the door opened and two uniformed officers came in. By then Dominick Nichols had removed his wire. I put it and the tape in an evidence envelope, dated and sealed it. We had them. No way were they walking, now if we could get them to give up El Rios, or at least any others that were working the protection game in Santa Maria. "Take them in." I said.

Wes and I watched them hustle the two thugs out of the door. I turned to Dominick. "We couldn't have done this without you. The businesses on this street owe you big time."

"If it plays out right," Wes said. "Not just the ones on this street."

Dominick Nichols took a deep breath. "I guess we shall see."

*****

I looked up as Wes came through our office door.

"Those two are singing like canaries. We didn't even have to give them the, who talks first gets the deal spiel."

"They give up El Rios?"

"Yes, Esteban Dominguez. Owns a string of dry cleaners. A real upstanding citizen, just like Flores said. The Captain's talking with Santa Barbara now. "

"He'll lawyer up fast."

Wes nodded. "I'm sure Mister Dominguez will know nothing about the nefarious happening here is our little town."

"Well as long as he bloody well leaves us alone. " I rubbed at the back of my neck. "Who'd ever think I'd be glad to have to just deal with gang-bangers."

My cell phone rang and I picked it up. "It's my mum." I put the phone back down.

"You're not answering?"

"She's going to want to talk wedding. I'm not up for it right now."

"You and Morgan got a date?"

"We will. Bloody-hell, we've only been engaged for two days."

Wes laughed. "Well, let us know if we can help. Janey loves

planning weddings. She's had Jackie's planned since our darling daughter was two months old."

I smiled. "I'll pass that one to Mum. I know I'd like Jackie to be my flower girl."

"And I'll pass that on."

"Devonshire. Smith," the Captain yelled. "We've got a drive-by shooting over on Newlove. Go check it out."

Chapter Forty-Two
Gail Crane

DUKE CAME TOWARD me, a single red rose in his hand. I felt my heart pound as I took it from him. "It's beautiful." I whispered.

Our clothes disappeared and our bodies entwined. I felt passion, joy.

Someone pounded on my bedroom door. I tore my lips from his, looked toward the door.

"Gail, Gail, you have to listen to me." It was my boss, Harry Shindley's voice

"No," Duke said. "Ignore him." He placed a kiss upon my neck and I shuddered.

"No, Gail. Do you really know him?"

"I love him," I screamed toward the door.

"But do you know him? Can you love a murderer?" Harry demanded.

I looked into Duke's eyes. "He's not."

"Did you ask him? Did you ask if he killed his father?"

Duke rolled away from me; suddenly clothed he stood looking down. "Do you need to ask me? Don't you know? Could I kill my father?"

I pulled the covers up to my chin, avoided his eyes. "How could you stand there and let them take him away?"

Duke did not answer; instead he walked toward the bedroom door.

"Stop. I have to know. You have to tell me."

His hand on the doorknob, he turned. "What if I don't know? What if I never know? Can you love me, not knowing?"

I wanted to scream yes, but the words could not get by my pressed tight lips. Duke opened the door. Beyond him I saw an airstrip. His Stearman stood there, Bethany leaned against it. Duke reached into his pocket, pulled out a cell phone. He tossed it and it fell on the middle of the bed. "Don't wait too long."

The last thing I saw was Bethany's smug smile as he closed the door.

I stared at the phone. Don't wait for what? The cell phone rang. I stared at it, then grabbed and turned it off. The phone rang again. I fumbled with back, jerked out the batteries, but it still kept ringing.

I jerked awake. My cell phone on the nightstand was ringing. I fumbled for it. "Yes."

"Gail."

It was Harry.

"Yes," I said again.

"Got some news for you. You awake enough to hear it?"

I sat up. "I'm awake."

"The homeless guy at the airport, not so homeless Roland Franken, it's Gavin Reynolds. He's ATF."

"What? How do you know that?"

"Just got a call from his boss. We've been asked not to blow his case."

I felt sick. I'd been telling myself the guy was a drunk. He'd been mistaken. No way had he'd seen Duke just stand there while they carted his da off. But the guy wasn't a drunk. "Why is ATF staking out Santa Maria?"

"Need to know basis, and they don't think we need to know."

"Well the hell with that and he ripped us for a hundred bucks" I kicked the covers aside and stood.

"Now don't go off half-cocked. I'm working on getting it back."

"Shit, Harry. First it's the NSTB, then the Santa Maria police, and now the ATF? How the hell are we supposed to get anything done?."

"We all get along. That's how we do it. We share. We all want the same thing, the answer to this puzzle."

"Answer? To which damn puzzle? Who were the bodies on the Lear? Why does Duke have amnesia, or how does Devlin St. James fit into all of this, and by the way who killed Everett Cummins."

I heard Harry sigh. "One thing at a time, Gail. Slow and steady wins the race."

"Yeah, right."

"When will you be in your office?"

"Uh, I'm not feeling well. I'm taking a sick day."

There was silence on the other end of the line for a long moment.

"You don't sound sick."

"I've got a killer headache, maybe a migraine."

"I see. Well then the best thing you can do for one of those is to stay in bed. That's what you're going to do, right? Stay in bed."

"Oh don't worry, Harry. I'm going to do what's right." I ended the call.

I headed toward the shower. I needed to talk to ATF agent Gavin Reynolds.

*****

On my way to the Santa Maria Airport, I stopped, bought a pack of cigarettes and a disposable lighter. I might as well make it look good. I walked to the same spot I'd spoken with the man before, then pulled out my tablet and pretended to be engrossed with checking email. It didn't take him long to stumble toward me. He looked as decrepit as before and smelled even worse.

"Got a smoke?"

I handed the pack of cigarettes to him and the lighter. He almost jerked them from my hand.

"Next time just give me one." His words were low and angry.

"Look, I'm not trying to blow your cover. I just have a few questions."

"Agent Crane, I've been here over a month. Things are coming together. You screw things up and it's all been for nothing."

Agent Crane was it? He'd do some checking of his own. "I get it." I said. "I've been there. Maybe I can help."

He lit the cigarette and put it in his mouth, but I noticed he didn't inhale. His eyes searched my face. "I haven't heard if I'm to make nice with you or not."

"Well then you wouldn't be going against orders if you did and by the way, I want my hundred dollars back."

Gavin Reynolds smiled. "I don't believe that money was yours."

"Well it's not yours either."

"You offered to pay for information and I gave it."

"I think I deserve more."

"Why? Because you're FBI?" He shrugged. "Nothing more to tell you then what I already did. I was here that night, saw the scuffle. They hustled the old man into a car and drove away."

I took a deep breath. "And the younger guy? He just stood there?"

"Yeah, the one claiming no memory. Don't look so surprised; I keep up with the news."

"Then you know he's been ID'd. Jonathan Cummins. What did he do after they put the older guy in the car?"

"Don't know. I went back to my hole."

"Did the younger guy look like he might have been drugged, or was being detained in some way?"

"He just stood there by himself."

My stomach took a dive. "By himself?"

The ATF agent nodded. "Stood and stared at the Lear, like it was the only thing he could see, didn't even turn when they forced the old guy into the car."

I frowned. That didn't sound right. Wouldn't Duke of least looked? Was he that cold-hearted? "Why is ATF interested in Devlin St. James' Lear jet?"

I thought for a moment he wasn't going to answer, then, "Hell, why not."

Out of the corner of my eye I saw Morgan Garrett and Duke arrive at the side of the hanger. Shit I knew if I drew attention to them Gavin Reynolds would clam up, so I kept quiet and hoped Morgan and Duke would do the same.

The ATF agent went on. "We'd been tracking the Lear. It flew out of Mexico with a load of illegal firearms. It landed here, gained a few passengers, a couple more interesting boxes, and then took off."

I held up my hand. "Wait. Hold it right there. I saw the crashed Lear. There were no guns, or anything else on that jet."

"Yeah, we know."

"Then you made a mistake. Couldn't be the same Lear jet."

He crushed the cigarette beneath his boot heel. "Maybe not the same jet, but for damn sure it was the same tail number, N310DJ." He tipped an imaginary hat. "Have a nice day Agent." Then he turned and disappeared back into the bushes.

"You can come out now," I said without turning toward the two men.

"What the hell." Morgan said. "Guns out of Mexico?" He looked at Duke. "Can two jets have the same tail number?"

"Not legally."

"There were no guns on the crashed Lear," I said. "So where are they?" I looked at Duke, memories of the dream rising to the top of

my brain. I pushed it away.

"Could they have stopped and unloaded them?" Morgan said.

Duke frowned. "Between here and Nojoqui Falls? I don't know. Are there any open fields? Dirt roads?"

Jacob Stanislaw aka Stan Jacobs, had been the pilot for the Lear that left Santa Maria. I repeated the tail number three times to myself, N310DJ—N310DJ—N310DJ. Stanislaw had ended up dead in Montreal, Canada. What else could be in Montreal?

I turned and started to walk away.

"Gail," Duke called. "We need to talk."

"I don't think so."

"What the hell is the problem? The other night….""

I glanced at Morgan. Okay if Duke wanted to play it out here. "The ATF guy said something else. Seems he was here the night the Lear took off. He saw you. He saw what they did to your dad. You did nothing."

Duke looked stunned. "I…"

"You stood there while they put your dad in that car, against his will, and you did nothing."

"So you think--what? That I was in on it?"

I glared at him. "They forced him into that car. It wasn't his idea. You stood there and did nothing. Why?"

"I don't know. I don't remember any of it."

The dream surfaced again. No, I couldn't talk anymore with him, not until some questions were answered. I had to know the truth, and not only about the puzzles of the case. I whipped around.

"Gail, wait."

Without turning I shook my head and quickened my pace.

Chapter Forty-Three
Morgan Garrett

I WATCHED DUKE watch Gail as she almost stomped away. What was the thing with them? They had to talk. Any fool could feel the electricity. I turned away, shaking my head. They'd have to figure it out on their own. Duke still looked stunned by what Gail had told him about his dad. I wasn't buying it. No way would he stand there and let them hustle his father into a car, not when the old man for sure didn't want to go.

That ATF guy, what else had he said to Gail? I'd overheard enough to make the wheels in my head spin…guns being loaded on a Lear jet with the same tail numbers as the crashed one, but no guns on board the wreckage?

Did they make a mistake? The ATF fellow didn't think so. His words had seemed to light a fire under Gail's tail. I turned to Duke. "What you thinking so hard about?"

"Women."

"Women or a woman?"

"I don't get her. How can she think I'd do something like that, just stand there. There has to be more to it."

Duke looked okay, but his voice sounded hollow, like someone who'd been dealt a hard blow. Well, hell he had. "Any drugs in your system when they checked you out at the hospital?"

"They said no." He looked into my face. "Are there drugs that turn someone into a zombie, and not show up in bloodwork?"

"I'm not an expert on drugs. I know the Soviets were experimenting in that field. There were a couple of cases where the facts pointed in that direction, but of course they denied it all. But I heard they were impossible to detect if you didn't know what to look for. Did Gail ask for something in particular?"

"I don't know. She hasn't shared that information with me. I know she didn't seem to buy my amnesia, hell, it looks like she still

isn't buying it." He raked his fingers through his hair. "No, she'd rather believe I'm lying my ass off, that I stood there, let them beat my father, throw him in the back of car. Next thing you know I'll be the one who killed him, no doubt for all of his money."

I didn't have any answers for him right at the moment, so I changed the subject. "About those aircraft that St. James may have, or had. Is there a way for you to check them out?"

"I could check on this through the Aircraft Registry in Oklahoma City.

"What's the Aircraft Registry?"

"It's a function of the FAA. A normal search can be requested through them for a fee. It can take several weeks, but there's a number of private companies that operate in and around Will Rogers Airport that'll make the search for you and give you complete data background on any airplane or aircraft owner in the databank."

"Can you do that?"

"With Sam's directory I can. Let me ask him."

Duke trotted away. In less than five minutes he was back. "They said they'd call back. I left them my cell phone number. Sam's got a job for me, I'm flying out in the morning. Going to Sonoma."

His phone rang.

"I'll put it on speaker. Duke Cummins."

"Hi, I'm Maxine, with Aircraft Search Service; how can we help you today?" I heard a voice say.

"Well Maxine I need to get a record search on all the airplanes owned by Devlin St. James and I suppose Everett Cummins. Can you do that?"

"Oh yes, sir, we can, but I have to know why? These are airplanes owned by someone other than you, right?"

"I'm sorry I didn't explain. I'm with Global Air here in Santa Maria California. We hangar these planes and sometime lease and crew them so we want to be sure we're legal."

"Oh well sure, in that case we can run the search. How do you want to do this? Do you want a phone call summary or do you want a full printed report?"

"Both I think. Also I have a title I need to switch to my name. Can you handle that?"

"Yes sir, just give me the info and I'll start it right away. How do you want this to be billed?"

Duke gave her the billing info and punched the phone off. "So now we wait."

"When do you think you'll get the summery?"

"Most likely sometime in the morning."

My cell phone went off. "Morgan Garrett."

"Morgan I need for you to come to see me." It was Senator Scarsdale and he sounded upset.

"I'm on the way."

*****

Scarsdale's housekeeper let me in. "The senator asks for you to wait for him in the study." I nodded and made my way to it. I had only a moment to wait before the Senator burst through the dark mahogany door.

"Morgan, good to see you; how are things going in Santa Maria? What about Morris Frost? Am I safe there?"

I looked at Scarsdale, his directness and lack of any small talk caught me by surprise, but his tone did not convey any sense of urgency which surprised me. He'd sounded plenty concerned on the phone.

"Frost's got himself out on a limb but I believe I can clear that up. At least the immediate problem, however he doesn't show good sense. I would draw my funds and go somewhere else."

Scarsdale frowned. "He's an old friend, Morgan. I want to give him some more slack before I do that. You say you can clear up the immediate problem, so let's wait and see. What is this immediate problem?"

"An old fashion protection racket."

"And you can take care of this?"

"Yes, Sir. "

"I know you are good Morgan but that sounds heavy duty."

"I'm getting some help from the Santa Maria police; they're aware of the problem and taking steps."

"Alright then, I trust your judgment. There is one other thing. Very sensitive, I can't stress that enough. It concerns Devlin St. James."

"That's a coincidence; there is something I want to ask you about the former senator myself."

"Have you run across something?" Scarsdale tried for nonchalance and failed.

"He's tied to the Lear jet crash."

"Well, of course he is, he owns it."

"There's more."

"Is there evidence Morgan, or just talk?"

"Some of both. I'll up the evidence part by tomorrow night."

Scarsdale sighed. "I have heard a few things this last week I was in Washington. He has called me twice since yesterday. He seems very interested in what you have discovered about Everett Cummins' son. "

I raised an eyebrow. "Is St. James your friend?"

"I thought he could be, but I have come to learn his reputation is more his own imagination and the talk in Washington isn't good."

"Then you have no objection to my looking into his connections?"

"No, but discretion, Morgan; he is still a powerful man." Scarsdale walked across to the window, then turned and looked at me. "Do we need to open this can of worms?"

"Worms have a way of slipping out of the can; it's always better to stomp 'em before they get out. You're clean Senator. Let's keep you that way."

*****

In the car my cell phone rang again. It was Darcie. She filled me in on what had gone down at the pawn shop. "Well hot damn, you got ole El Rios."

"No we have two gangbangers who were trying to fleece Dominick Nichols. El Rios, AKA, Esteban Dominquez knows nothing about said hoodlums."

"And you're sure those are the same two I've had run-in's with before?"

Darcie laughed. "Oh yes, he mentioned you by name."

"They tell you anything more about this Russian?"

"They've never met him, or so they say. Where are you?"

"Santa Barbara. Had a meeting with Scarsdale."

"Where to now?"

"Heading back to Santa Maria. I'll stop at Frost's office and fill him in."

"Morgan, he did come in and give a statement. His description matches the two we have in custody."

"Well good for him," I said. "That'll make Senator Scarsdale

happy. Well then I'll just see you at home."

"Morgan, Mum asked us over for tea on Sunday. Can we make it?"

"You going to talk wedding?"

"I'm sure we are."

"That's fine. Maybe me and your dad can catch a game or something."

"Thanks. I hear Wes calling me. Later." She ended the call.

I glanced at the clock. Still early. It was a well known secret where Devlin St. James called home. Why the hell not?

*****

I parked at the end of a neat white fence, behind a large oak tree. It seemed safe, since the road patterns indicated most traffic out of the gate went the other direction. Like most surveillance work I didn't have a clue as to what I was waiting on, but I waited anyway.

When a black BMW came out, the darkened windows didn't allow me to see the driver, but most servants don't drive BMW's. Might as well find out who the Senator had for company. I was surprised when it became clear the car was heading toward Santa Maria.

*****

The black BMW turned off the 101 onto Main Street. With the increased traffic, I moved up to position myself three cars back. This could get tricky if the BMW driver got suspicious.

I hate heavily tinted windows. I like to watch the driver of the car I'm tailing. If I can see the driver's head movement, I can anticipate their actions, but with this car tinted so dark, I had to wing it.

At Broadway the BMW continued westward, just before it reached Blosser Road, it turned southbound, into a warehouse area. With the thinner traffic I fell further back as a precaution, but I did see the BMW pull into an alley between two corrugated tin buildings.

I slowed, then preceded to do a drive by.

One of the structures looked abandoned with weeds in the drive and parking area. The welding shop next to it was in operation. Doors stood wide open and sparks flew from the welding torch of the worker.

I eased by the alley in time to see a tall slim man exit the BMW. He ducked in the side door of the building.

I stopped just beyond where I could still see the front and the

door then decided to get closer. Across from the warehouse, I found a place behind some old tires and waited. I didn't have to wait long before my guy, with two others came out. They stopped by the door not ten feet from my hiding place behind the tires. One of his companions wore a pork pie hat like the one I had seen in Vegas. Coincidence, I doubted it. The other was dressed in the typical gang-banger uniform, low-rider cargo pants and shirt with its tail hanging out. He looked vaguely familiar.

"So when will El Rios be here?" My guy said and I picked up on the Russian accent with under tones of a Moscovite. Now that was interesting.

"We don't know. When he comes, he comes. He don't tell us."

Slipping my cell phone out, I started taking pictures.

"I wait for no one. When he comes you tell him to call me." The Russian walked toward his BMW and I slipped back around the tires and scurried back to my truck.

"Hey, Po leeze why you hangin' here?"

The words came from a teenaged punk who stood in the middle of the street. His friends were gathered on the sidewalk on the far side of the street, so he spoke loud enough for his buddies to hear his bravado.

"Beat it kid before I run your ass…."Shit. The pork pie hat and his pal in the cargo pants came toward us. They stopped, looked at the big mouthed gang-banger, and then at me. Shit. Discretion being the better part of valor, I put my truck in gear and hauled my butt out of there.

"Okay my Russian friend, I don't know who you are but I have your picture." I smiled with satisfaction as I drove away.

Chapter Forty-Four
Gail Crane

AT THE OFFICE I stared at the computer monitor and then at my cell phone. I could go the long way around and contact the Montreal Service de police de la Ville de Montréal, or I could call Whip directly. I knew from his brother, Whip had made the move to Montreal and was now working in their police department. What the hell, we'd parted on good terms. I reached for my cell phone.

He answered on the third ring. "Hello."

"Whip, it's Gail."

There was a moment of silence and then, "Well, I'll be damned. How are you?"

"I'm good, you?"

"Getting used to the cold, but all-in-all I'm fantastic."

"Who is it, *Cherie*?" I heard a female voice say.

"An old friend. That's Toni, my wife."

Wife? That's something his brother hadn't mentioned. "You got married. I thought you said you'd never step into that trap?"

Whip laughed. "It just had to be the right woman."

And I wasn't her. The words weren't said, but they hung there just the same.

"Gail, so where are you now? Still with the Bureau I'm sure."

"On the central coast of California, Santa Maria. How long have you been married?"

"Three glorious months. Toni and I are expecting Whip junior in about seven more."

"Well congrats on both." A baby too? I felt a pang of jealousy.

"How about you Gail, you find your Mister Right? I can tell you it's a hell of a lot better than Mister Right Now."

I thought about Duke, started to say no, and then changed it to. "Maybe."

"Maybe? What's maybe? If it's right, it's right." Whip laughed. "Listen to me. Who'd have thought it? "

Here was my opening. "There's some complications, actually it's the reason I called."

"What can I do to help? You know you can count on me."

I asked if he knew about the Stan Jacobs' homicide. He did. I explained about the crashed Lear, the tail numbers and the missing guns. I ended with, "Your Stan Jacobs is in fact our Jacob Stanislaw and he was the pilot when the Lear took off from the Santa Maria Airport."

"You're wondering how he ended up dead here; that maybe the Lear with the guns was his transportation?"

"Yes," I said.

"We've got two airports in Montreal. What's the tail number?"

"N310DJ."

"Let me make the calls and I'll get back to you."

"Thanks Whip. I owe you."

"No you don't, Gail. I just want you to be as happy as I am. I always did." He ended the call.

I killed the waiting time by cleaning out my desk. It wasn't a long wait. My phone rang. It was Whip. "Yes."

"Good call Gail. Stan Jacobs was the pilot of a Lear that came into Montréal-Trudeau last week. Tail number's the same and its registered owner is Devlin St. James from Santa Barbara, California."

"Where's the jet now?"

"In his private t-hanger, he leases one here, has for going on ten years."

"Have they looked inside?"

"Had no reason to do so. I've notified my captain, they're sending someone out. I should hear from them within the next hour. I'll call as soon as I do."

"Thanks again, Whip."

I called Harry and gave him a run down on what I'd discovered.

"Damn, Gail. I'm coming to your office. I want to be there when you get the information from Canada."

"Okay." Two minutes after Harry hung up, my cell phone rang again. A quick glance identified the caller as Andre Gasualt. "Hello."

"Gail, I've been thinking about you. How did things go in Las

Vegas?"

"I thought you were leaving town?"

"I am. Tonight is my last. Have dinner with me."

I heard a knock on my door. "Can you hold, Andre?"

"Oui."

Harry walked in. "I can't believe this. First we find out the bodies in the crashed Lear aren't the ones reported getting on. Then Stan Jacobs, AKA Jacob Stanislaw, ends up dead in Montreal, and now there's another Lear jet, with the same tail number as the crashed one, in a Montreal airport. It's full of illegal guns, and all of it leads back to ex-senator Devlin St. James? Gail, you get your ass out there and interview that man."

"I plan to Harry, just as soon as I hear back from Canada. Can you hold for a minute?" I pointed at my cell phone."

"Yeah, yeah, but make it quick."

"Andre, can I call you back? My…"

"Yes. Yes, I understand. Call me when your business is concluded." He hung up the phone on his end.

Harry and I killed the time by rehashing everything we knew for a fact about the crashed Lear. Dave Kelicoe still hadn't received a positive ID for the four burned bodies inside, but they'd given them a closer look and discovered no searing in the lungs, which meant they were dead before the Lear crashed and burned. Who had they been? Even though one was found in the cockpit, he couldn't have been piloting the jet if he were dead, so the real pilot had to have bailed before the crash. That had to be why those kids found the door well away from the Lear. So what had happened to him? My cell phone rang. It was Whip. "Hello. I'm putting you on speaker phone."

"The Lear carried six crates of automatic and semi-automatic weapons," Whip said. "And another three cases of boot-legged movies."

"Shit and double-shit," Harry said.

"Any idea what their final destination was to be?" I said.

"No ongoing flight plan filed. We've got men watching in case someone arrives to claim them."

It looked as if Stan Jacobs was taken out before the deal was completed, stupid on their part, but good luck for us. "I'll let ATF know. They'll be in contact."

"Sure thing. Gail, let's keep in touch. We had some good times

together."

I knew Whip didn't mean work. What would his new wife think about that? I settled for, "You take care of that new baby. If I'm ever in Montreal I'll come by."

"I'd like that. Now I've got to get back to work."

"So long, Whip." I hung up the phone.

"Good times together?" Harry cocked an eyebrow.

"Ancient history." But my face heated. "I think it's time I visited with Devlin St. James."

Harry frowned. "I hate to say it, but the ex-senator has some questions to answer. Shit. I thought he was one of the good ones." Harry walked to the door. "Keep me in loop."

I stood, grabbed for my purse. "Will do."

In my car I saw I had two missed calls. One from Duke, the other from Darcie. I debated calling back. Was I ready to talk to Duke? I shook my head. I still needed the answers about him and his father. I called Darcie instead.

Chapter Forty-Five
Duke Cummins

THE KING AIR is a big old lumbering beast when put up next to the Lear Jet, but I liked flying it because of its stable instrument platform. Put her on the glide slope and she'd hang right in there for almost forever.

Rick walked with me as I pre-flighted for the hop to Sonoma.

"You know Duke once your dad let me do this with him. I want to learn all I can."

"Are you hinting that you want to go along?"

"Naw, I gotta work today, but anytime I can, sure."

"What else did you do with Everett?"

"Not much; he was pretty closed mouth, hardly talked at times, other times he said things that didn't make much sense. Like a couple of days before he disappeared he told me St. James had too many Lear Jets. I thought that odd since he only had the same two he'd had all along."

"Did he say any more about it?"

"Like always, that just came out of the blue." He stared across my shoulder. "I've been wondering if I should tell you this, something Juan said to me last night."

"What?"

"It's most likely nothing, but with my grandfather's murder, I'm not taking anything for granted."

I waited.

"Juan said he found a needle after the Lear took off that night."

"A needle?" My heart started to pound.

"Juan said it was just a busted syringe laying on the ramp."

"What did he do with it?"

"Threw it away, he didn't want that thing making trouble for him, neither of us mess around with that shit."

I didn't say anything.

"Duke, you okay? Do I need to tell Mister Hughes about the needle? It's not the first one we've found, but usually not that close to the runway."

I took a deep breath. Who had they used the needle on; me, my father, or maybe it was both of us? "No, Sam doesn't need to know."

"Thanks Duke. I feel better telling you about it. I'd better get back to the hanger."

I watched him walk away. Should I tell Gail? Let her know that I'd most likely been drugged that night. I frowned. Yeah, sure. There was no proof, no drugs in my system. Maybe if I had the needle, but without it, it's just my word. Juan and Rick could back me up about the needle, but that didn't prove it had been used to inject me with some Russian drug. This was getting me nowhere and I had a job to do.

*****

It was a beautiful day for flying. There were a few puffy clouds below and traffic had been no factor, causing very little radio chatter.

A syringe? I know my father didn't do drugs. So that would mean someone else, on the ramp, dropped it during the struggle with my dad. I had to have been drugged? I just stood there the ATF guy said, drugged would explain that.

"King Air Sugar Five, you have traffic at your two o'clock, low."

The interruption caused me to look around, search for the other aircraft, a Cessna, going into Fresno, not a factor for me. "Roger center, I got him low and slow."

I'd gone to the web, looked at poisons and had learned a lot. I'd discovered the natives in South America use the datura plant and it leaves no residual trace. The natives measure the strength of the drug by frog jumps. Four jumps, three jumps and so on. One jump is a strong dose. Also the Soviets had done experimentation with the datura plant and puffer fish. Russia keeps coming up. I need to talk to Morgan some more.

*****

In and out of Sonoma with no hassles, I was eager to get back to Santa Maria and talk to Morgan.

I helped the line crew put the King Air away and went into the office to call him. Looking in my box I had two messages, one a call from Oklahoma City and the other from Sam Hughes about the

flying schedule.

Nothing from Gail; yeah you expected she was going to call. I called Oklahoma, got their night message so decided to head home.

At the apartment I parked in the carport, then headed for my front door. I'd taken two steps when I heard a loud plop sound from behind me. I spun, tripped, over the parking curb and fell into the grass, hard. Stunned, I lay there for a moment, then sat up slowly and looked around, nothing. I stood, shook myself off and went inside.

Removing my leather jacket, I realized it had a hole in the sleeve up high. A closer look showed it went through to the backside. Holy shit, I knew a bullet hole when I saw one. I'd been shot at. I examined my arm. Nothing there, not even a graze. My fall must have saved me. I sure had an angel perched on my shoulder. Without thought, I grabbed up my cell phone and called Gail. The ringing went on and on. "Gail, pick up the phone. Damn." It went to her voice-mail and I hung up without leaving a message. My next thought was Morgan. "Morgan it's Duke."

"What's up? You sound excited. Did you finally talk to Gail?"

"Someone took a shot at me. If I hadn't fallen…."

"Easy boy, where are you?"

"I'm home. That's where it happened, outside when I got home."

"I've got to tell Darcie and then I'll be right there."

I ended the call, then went and looked out the front window. Nothing going on, everything seemed quiet. Maybe I was mistaken. No, the hole was real. Was he still out there? A chill went up my spine. I stepped back from the window, jerked the drapes shut. How stupid could I be? I'd made a great target standing there. Why didn't I go outside and walk back and forth like those mechanical ducks in an arcade.

I shook my head. Did my dad have a gun in the house? Did I know how to use a gun?

I settled in my chair, watched the front door and waited, even then the sudden pounding scared me out of my skin. Peeping out the window I saw it was Morgan and someone else, I couldn't tell for sure in the dark.

"Duke, open the damn door." Morgan pounded again.

"Come on in Morgan, jeez you scared the hell out of me."

"Are you okay?" Darcie pushed herself into the room and stood right in front of me.

"Uh, yeah, I think so. Somebody shot at me."

"Hell, Duke, you sure? Maybe it was a car backfiring?"

Morgan looked like he wanted to jump somebody.

I showed them my jacket. "I found the hole when I got inside. It's a new jacket and it didn't come with any holes."

Morgan went outside, while Darcie made me repeat the whole thing again.

Morgan came back in, looked at Darcie, "I didn't see anything. Shot could have come from the street. They must think they got him. They shot, he fell."

"Could be." Darcie threw my jacket on the chair. "The question is what do we do now?"

Before I could respond her cell phone rang.

"It's Gail," Darcie said. "I called her on the way over. Hello. Yes, he's alright. Calm down Gail. I'm standing right next to him. No you don't need...okay since you're almost here. See you soon."

Darcie looked at me. "Gail's on her way."

I felt a spurt of excitement. Almost enough to make me forget about being shot at, almost. Gail must care a little for me, or was she just afraid I'd get killed before she got her answers.

"It's good she's going to be here," Morgan said. "It's about time we all sat down and pooled our information."

Darcie gave him a sharp look, but then nodded. A hard knock sounded on the door. I answered. Gail stood there with a white face. She reached and touched my cheek. "I'm fine," I wanted to pull her into my arms. before I could, she stepped around me and into the room.

"What do we know," she demanded.

"Nothing more than I already told you," Darcie said.

Morgan stood in front of the high boy where my father displayed my picture. He pulled out his cell phone. "Does anybody recognize this guy?"

We all leaned toward the small screen.

"Where--where did you get that picture?"

It was Gail who spoke.

I turned toward her.

She stared at the photo.

"I followed him from St. James' place earlier. I was just curious to see who St. James had for a visitor. This fellow went to a

warehouse off Blosser where he met with some gang-bangers. I don't know how he ties into this, but he speaks with a Russian accent."

"Russian? Are you sure it wasn't French?" Gail took the cell phone to get a better look.

"I know a Russian when I hear one." Morgan said. "Why? You recognize him?"

"I…"

"Gail, how do you know this guy?" I said.

"He…"

Her words trailed away. I'd never seen Gail looking so confused."

"I went out with him," she finished

Darcie took Gail's arm and turned her slightly. "What's going on here? Gail, you know this guy? Who is he?"
"I know him as Andre. My college roommate's brother, or that's what I thought."

"Flores talked about a Russian working with El Rios and the gangs." Darcie frowned. "Wes looked into the people connected with St. James. There is a Russian working for him as a consultant, Pieter Orloff." She glanced at Morgan. "Could there be a connection between St. James and the gang-bangers?"

Morgan looked pissed as he said, "Sure looks like it."

I was still dealing with Gail's; I went out with him, part. "Why would you go out with some damn Russian?"

She glared at me. "I told you I thought he was the brother of my roommate. Stay on the main subject." She thrust the phone toward me. "Have you ever seen him before?"

I looked closer at the photo. "Once, maybe. He could be the guy I saw in the hotel. All I really remember is he spoke with a foreign accent, it could have been Russian."

"I ran into him at Pappys," Gail said.

She looked more collected now.

"He said he was Andre Gasualt. He knew a lot of things about Veronica, personal things and he looks like Ronnie's step brother. He asked me out to dinner, to catch up, and I said yes."

"Yeah, that so," I said. "Just what did the two of you talk about?"

Gail shrugged. "I don't remember. About Ronnie, how things were going with her."

"When was this?" Morgan said.

"The night before we went to Vegas."

Morgan leaned toward Gail. "Did you tell him we were going to Vegas?"

Gail's face colored. "I might have."

"Morgan," Darcie said. "If he's the one who took a shot at Duke tonight, then he could be the one who shot at him in Vegas too."

"But why the hell is he shooting at me?"

Morgan glanced in my direction. "You must know something…"

"I don't remember a damn thing about that night." My almost shouted words hung in the sudden silence of the room.

"He thinks you do," Darcie said. "And that's all that's important."

"It might've not been him, but I did see a guy wearing a pork pie hat that night we were out in Vegas," Morgan said.

I looked at him in question.

"Saw the same hat, or one just like it, on a guy talking with the Russian guy this afternoon."

"So Gail tells her boyfriend were going to Las Vegas, and then he get's one of his buddies to try and take me out. But why?" I said.

Gail threw me a sour look. "He's not my boyfriend."

"What about the Lear jet, Duke? What did you learn with the title search?" Morgan looked as if he putting some pieces together, and didn't like what they revealed..

"The crashed Lear jet does belong to St. James, but there's a problem with the dates. There are two different ones on the record as to when he acquired the airplane."

"There is a Lear jet in Canada with the same tail number as the one that crashed," Gail said. "It's full of guns and boot-legged movies."

"How did you find out that?" Darcie said.

"There was a murder in Canada with ties to Santa Maria." She glanced at Morgan. "After talking with the ATF agent, I called a friend of mine. He did some checking. The Lear jet there also belongs to St. James. He has a leased hanger, has had for years."

"Damn, he's up to his senatorial neck in this." Morgan said.

"I was on my way out to see him when you called."

"I want to go with you." I looked directly at Gail. Our eyes locked.

"This is FBI business."

"This is my life. I'm going."

"What about Darcie and Morgan? You just going to leave them here," Gail asked.

"They can let themselves out." I grabbed my jacket with the bullet hole in it and slipped it on.

"I'm heading into the station," Darcie said. "I want to see what I can find out about Pieter Orloff."

"Can you drop me off at the house first," Morgan asked. "I need to check in with Senator Scarsdale."

In a matter of minutes we were all out the door and I was locking it behind me.

Chapter Forty-Six
Pieter Orloff

"DA, GOT HIM." I watched Duke fall to the ground. When he did not move, I pushed the accelerator. After I turned the first corner I slowed. No sense drawing undue attention. Back on Broadway, I drove onto the large parking lot of a super market and called St. James.

"Where are you? The FBI or someone is checking on the titles on my airplanes. God dammit, what have you done?" St. James shouted without any preliminaries.

"Calm down and tell me what's going on."

"A title search company in Oklahoma called me to say they'd done a background on my Lear jets. They said it was a courtesy call. What have you been doing to get this all stirred up?"

"Senator, I am on my way to you, remain calm. We will talk when I get there."

"There's something else, the police have discovered the Lear in Montreal. Why the hell is it still there? It should be on its way to Afghanistan."

"A slight miscalculation. Just keep calm."

"God damn, Orloff. I can't go to jail. My family name…how could I face any…"

I hung up on the old fool. He is like all these Americans, no back bone. Perhaps he was another loose end I needed to see too.

I drove out of the parking lot and headed for Santa Ynez and Devlin St. James.

Driving in the gate I could see the house. Flood lights lit the yard and grounds, but not a light showed anywhere inside the rambling, three-story monstrosity. Curious. Why would the old man go to bed when he knew I was coming? Perhaps he'd passed out, even though I hadn't detected any slurring in his screamed words.

I drove around to the garages and parked. How am I to calm him

this time? Do I even wish to? He is so driven by his precious reputation. Deny. Deny; I had no idea there were two Lears with the same tail number. I don't know how it ended up in Montreal full of contraband. It must have been Everett Cummins's doings, play dumb, that is always the best way. The old fool is a politician, he should already know this. It is time I reminded him just what is at stake.

I saw the headlights come up the drive just as I started to get out of the car. How had they gotten in? I'd seen the gate swing close behind me.

The car parked in the circular drive in front of the door. Gail Crane climbed from behind the wheel. The sight of her made me smile. I looked forward to our next date. I'd like to see her face when she discovered I was not Andre.

Someone exited the passenger-side door. They walked into the light and the smile fled my lips. No. It isn't possible, the Cummins son I had let live to long. Mistakes get you killed. I can count on my hand those I have made, but he is one. Arrogance, my trainer had accused more than once. Perhaps in that she was right. I'd found it satisfactory at the time, thumbing my nose at the NTSB. I should have killed him. How can it be that he lives? I saw him fall. Anger filled my head. I wavered, stumbled at its intensity. He has more lives than a cat. Well *nyet*, no more. This is his last day; right here—right now. I am a fool no more. I moved into the shadows away from the outside lights and made my way toward the pool-house.

Chapter Forty-Seven
Gail Crane

I GLANCED AT Duke. He hadn't said a word since we'd gotten into the car. What was he thinking? I'd been scared to death when Darcie told me someone had taken a shot at him. First Las Vegas and now this. I'd let him convince me the incident in Vegas was a fluke, he'd hadn't been the chosen target, just a guy in the wrong place at the wrong time. Tonight branded that a lie. Duke knew, or had seen something, and Devlin St. James, or Pieter Orloff were behind the attempts on his life, maybe both. I pushed down harder on the accelerator. I planned to know why, tonight.

Out of the corner of my eye I saw Duke look at me. "What?" I said.

"That night I came to your place, the night we got together, you'd been out to dinner with this Orloff."

It was a statement, not a question, so I didn't say anything. Where was this going?

"So, he'd primed the well and I got the water?"

What the hell? I threw Duke a hard look. "What does that mean?"

"You were out with him, he got you all hot and bothered and I showed up and cashed in."

His words were laced with bitterness, but before I could respond he went on.

"Not that I'm complaining, you were plenty good. When I see old Andre-Orloff, I'll have to thank him.

For a moment I couldn't speak. I gripped the steering wheel tighter, so I wouldn't shove my fist into his sneering mouth. Who the hell did he think he was? I felt tears threaten and my anger grew. "I don't owe you an explanation. What I do is my own business."

"Don't you mean, who?"

I jerked the wheel to the right and the driver in the car next to me laid on the horn in response. My face heated. "Not the right time for this conversation." I said and then before I could stop myself

added, "How's Bethany?" Duke didn't answer, so I chanced a glance at him. He stared straight ahead, tight-lipped. His body language screamed tension. Good God. What were we doing to each other? I took a deep breath. "I agree we need to talk, but can we do it tomorrow? Right now I need to concentrate on St. James.

His answer was a long time in coming. "Okay, Gail. We'll play it your way. You know where St. James lives?"

We were at the Santa Maria town limits. I pressed the navigate button on the GPS. "I programmed it in."

The rest of the drive to Santa Ynez was made in cold silence.

*****

"Your destination is ahead on your right." The voice from the GPS announced.

I turned into a wide driveway. A half-mile down it, we were blocked by a tall iron gate. I stared at it from the idling car. There was a call box mounted on a stone column. I didn't want to announce myself, but it looked like there weren't many choices open to me. I punched in the call button, waited, when no response came, I pushed the button again. Still nothing. How the hell were we going to get in?

"Get back on the main road," Duke said. "I'm betting there's a back way in."

"What?"

"Look." He pointed. Beyond the gate another dirt road joined the paved one.

I backed up. On the main road I turned right. A half mile down I saw another road, this one packed dirt. Its opening was blocked by a wooden gate between the two rolls of barbed-wire fencing. No Trespassing signs decorated posts on each side of it. Duke jumped out and opened the gate wide. He waited until the car was through, then closed in and rejoined me.

The road was rutted and narrow. We'd bumped along the half-mile it took for it to join the paved road just beyond the locked gate. "That's pretty stupid," I said. "A big imposing gate, and then this one just a half-mile further down."

"It's all for looks," Duke said. "Pretty damn shallow."

I wondered if that about summed up the esteemed Senator Devlin St. James. All for show and pretty damned shallow.

We rounded a corner and saw the house awash in a haze of light. It was three stories, white, and still somehow garish. I pulled up,

parked next to the entrance. I glanced at Duke. "When we get inside, please let me do the questioning."

He stared at me for a long moment before saying. "Okay, Gail, as long as you ask the right questions."

"I know what to ask. Just give me some time to get to them."

Duke nodded and we climbed from the car.

At the door I rang the doorbell. We waited. I rang the bell again. Still no answer. St. James must have staff. Had he given them all the night off? If so, why? I felt a prick of unease, something wasn't right, but were my feelings enough for probable cause? This was an ex-senator, still with a lot of clout. The wrong move could end my career.

"They're not answering," Duke said.

I glared at him; bit back my bitchy, oh really.

"He knew we were coming. He's ducking us. One way or the other, I'm going in," he said. Duke reached for the door knob.

"Just wait a damn minute. That's breaking and entering. I'm FBI, remember?"

Duke smiled, but there was nothing happy about it. "I'm not. Why don't you wait in the car, or better yet why don't you leave?"

"Damn-it, Duke…"

"I came for answers. I'm not leaving without them. But you don't have to get in trouble along with me."

I pounded on the door. Listened. "Did you hear that? I could swear it sounded like a moan, almost a cry for help."

"Yeah, I heard it."

I exchanged a look with him, nodded, and Duke turned the knob. I didn't expect the door to be unlocked, but it was. My stomach tightened and I pulled my gun from its holster. "Let me go first."

Duke isn't stupid, with a nod, he stepped aside.

The door opened onto a large entry hall. All inside was dark. A crystal chandelier hung from a high ceiling. To the left a staircase curved upward. "Hello. Senator. It's Agent Crane, with the FBI."

No answer.

On the right I saw light switches. I flipped the first one. The chandelier came to life. I called out again. "Hello. Is anyone home?"

Upstairs a door slammed. Duke and I both jumped. We turned toward the stairs. "Let me go first."

Duke pointed at my gun. "You don't have an extra one of those,

do you?"

I shook my head. "Stay behind me."

At the second floor landing, I heard the sharp crack of a banging door again. It came from the right. I could see another light switch on the wall. "Senator. Mister St. James," I called. No answer. I flipped the switch. By the light's glow I could see the source of the noise, an open window. Wind-whipped shutters slapped the wall. "Wait here," I said.

I moved along the hallway, opened doors. Found bedrooms and bathrooms, all un-occupied. None disturbed. I walked back to Duke. "Let's go up."

The third floor landing opened onto a huge sitting area; all dark wood, and pale leather seating. A Turkish carpet was an island of color in the center. At far end of the room I could see another hallway. The sense of brooding in the air, sent a chill along my spine. Loathe to speak, I motioned with my gun toward the hallway. Duke nodded.

Two doors opened off the hallway, the first a huge master suite, again all dark wood, with splashes of exotic color. No one occupied the room, or its adjoining bathroom.

"Doesn't look like anyone's home," Duke said.

I shrugged. "One door left."

This one opened into a study -- it wasn't empty. The first thing I could see was a figure slumped across an oak desk. A large window filled most of the wall behind the desk. Beige drapes hung there, closed to the night. An abstract pattern decorated the section of drape behind the still man.

"Dear God," Duke said, as he pushed by me.

"Don't touch a thing."

He stopped at the side of the desk. "Is this St. James?"

From the myriad news reports and front page photos in the papers, I knew it was. I also knew the abstract pattern on the drape would be brain matter. St. James had eaten a bullet. The stupid bastard. I swallowed before I replied, "Yes."

"There's a letter." Duke leaned forward, read aloud. "*To all my friends. I never intended to go out this way. To take your own life is a coward's path. I've many faults, but I've never considered myself a coward. How did this happen? How did I let it happen? It all seemed so simple, then one lie led to another, one sin to another, until this --*

my one last, and most grievous transgression.

I'm glad my father and mother are not alive to see me fall. Let me be clear, I've always strived to honor the name of St. James. My desire to keep my name unsullied is what sent my feet upon this path, that event so long ago, it should never have been so blown out of proportion. The girl was nothing, a piece of offal, half dead anyway. She begged me to take her, all for a single hunk of bread. If only the General would have looked the other way, if only that low-class filth, Kaminski, had not seen me and stolen Hathaway's helmet, things would have played out so different.

After the Hathaway incident, it all seemed so easy. People needed things from me, offered me power, position, I accepted. I did no harm, guns to those who had the means. They would have gone elsewhere to acquire them, if not from me. I made clear it was never Americans who were to be killed, and the stolen movies, the counterfeit medications—entertainment for rebels far from home and much needed medicine too.

Until Orloff, Pieter Orloff, the arrogant ass, he took things too far. Yes, I wanted Kaminski's blackmail to cease, but I never condoned murder, that was Orloff. And then after too much brandy, I think I told dear old Everett about Kaminski. I don't know for sure. Everett was my only true friend. I shared many things with him, including my step-daughter Bethany. Everett would have never betrayed me, but Orloff decided differently, even then I never condoned Everett's murder. I agreed to let Everett think that Bethany would die if he ever spoke any of my confidences. He promised to stay quiet. If only Duke had not shown up that night. He saw too much. Orloff ordered Duke's death. Everett went wild. I made Orloff agree to only drug the boy, make him forget what he'd seen that night. I had no idea the drug Orloff administered would give Duke amnesia.

And it hurts me even now to know that still Orloff was not satisfied. He hunted Everett down, killed him, and ran his car over that cliff, Orloff's first mistake. His second, the killing of Jacob in Montreal before he'd seen to the cargo on the Lear.

Now it is all coming back to rest at my door. I cannot be arrested, jailed, sent to prison. My spirit would never endure, so I take this one step to the beyond – my -- one last sin. May God have mercy upon

me. Senator Devlin St. James.

"Orloff killed my father."

"Asa Kaminski and Jacob Stanislaw too."

"Good summation, Agent Crane." The whispered words lifted the hair on the nape of my neck, at the same time I felt a gun barrel poke the middle of my back. "Give me your weapon and step into the room."

I did both.

"Call to your occupied friend."

I knew Orloff spoke the words. "Duke."

Chapter Forty-Eight
Duke Cummins

I LOOKED AT the slumped form of St. James, blood pooled around his head. There was no sense checking to see if he was alive. Where was the gun? I saw it on the floor beside the chair's leg. I read the letter again. St. James had answered a lot of my questions, but not how I'd ended up beside the crashed Lear.

"Duke," Gail said. There was something in her tone, fear mixed with anger. I jerked my head up.

Gail had walked deeper into the study, the man from Morgan's photo stood behind her.

"Jonathon Wayne Cummins, we meet again, but then, you wouldn't remember that." The man smiled.

I took a step forward.

"I wouldn't do that," Orloff said.

I went still, motioned at the letter. "Why?"

"I can't speak for the old fool, but for me it's business. None of it personal. I liked your father. If only you hadn't arrived."

"Me?"

"Everything had gone as planned. The other jet ready for takeoff, the one with guns receiving its fuel…"

"The other jet?" Gail interrupted.

"Don't play stupid, Gail. You know there were two Lears. I heard you telling your boss about the jet in Montreal."

"Why did you kill Stanislaw?" she said.

I heard his sigh.

"A silly mistake. He wanted more money. I asked if the Lear had been seen to. He said yes, then I killed him. His seen to and mine, of course, were not the same."

"Why two Lears," Gail asked. "Why would St. James get involved with something like that?"

"Greed. Power," Orloff said. "After the first job, there was no

249

turning back. We had him." He looked at me. "Your father helped get the illegal jet."

I'd been afraid of that and winced at his words. "My father was a good man."

"I didn't say he wasn't. He loved St. James. He loved Bethany, and he loved you. Too much love can kill you, or should I say, get you killed. After the Lear crashed, I called your father, told him about my mistake with the drug. I assured him there was an antidote and we agreed to meet." Orloff smiled. "Of course there is no antidote. I believe Everett knew this, but he came anyway. For your piece of mind, I killed him quickly and I did not enjoy it."

Heat flooded my face and I took another step forward.

"Don't be stupid, boy." Orloff glared at St. James' body. "All would have been fine. The Buick did not go as far down the cliff as I wished, but the tide would have seen to it, if Morgan Garrett and the bitch cop had not intruded. I told the old man hiring Garrett was a mistake."

"Why crash the jet?" Gail said.

"St. James' panic," Orloff said with disgust. "All would have been fine. One jet would disappear into Afghanistan; the other would be lost in a crash. Gone would be any hint of impropriety, any scent of scandal."

"And him?" She pointed at me.

"Why the drug, the change of clothes and being left beside the crashed Lear?" He smiled. "The drug was to calm his father's fears. Everett did not know it would do more than steal the boy's memories of the night. The rest a joke. You Americans, so smug, so self-righteous, the NTSB, so packed with fools. The clothes were from the pilot who bailed from the crashed jet. I picked him up as planned, but loose ends must be dealt with. He is in Los Padres Forest, dead and naked. His clothes I put on the boy."

Orloff seemed inclined to continue, not a good sign. Confessing to all he'd done, even boasting, we were obviously loose ends too.

Gail pressed on."And the bodies on the Lear?"

"Of no importance. You stop; offer fifty dollars for two hours work. They come with you."

"And me?" she said. "Why the Andre masquerade?"

He laughed. "Oh, Gail, you were a delightful interlude. I'd planned for our night to continue, but then you told me about the

planned trip to Las Vegas. I had to let El Rios know. My new partner wanted Morgan Garrett taken out. His meddling had become an inconvenience."

Her face filled with color. "Is Andre still alive?"

"Hiking in the Himalayas, the last I heard. His death wasn't needed. I told you Gail, I don't kill for pleasure, it's business."

Gail looked at me, and I saw the intent in her eyes a second before she acted. Her elbow went back hard into Orloff's gut. I heard the air rush through his lips. As Gail twisted away from him. I launched myself over the desk. A gunshot filled my ears as I connected with his body. We both went down. On top of him, I could see he still gripped the gun. I grabbed for his wrist, slammed it against the floor. A sharp pain exploded along the side of my head. My vision grayed at the edges. We rolled.

My back came up against something hard, then Orloff was astride me, his fingers digging into my throat. I brought my knee up, right into his balls. He screamed, grabbed for them. I rolled to the side, could see I was by the desk.

"I'll kill you for that," he yelled and lunged toward me.

I saw it then, St. James' gun. I rolled. Grabbed for it, but Orloff was on me before I could fire. His hands closed around mine. He twisted my wrist. Slowly the barrel turned toward me. I pushed back. My finger rested on the trigger, but I couldn't get the barrel pointed toward him. From somewhere inside of me, the answer came, I brought my head forward, slammed it into his. Pain rocketed through my skull, but his grip loosened. The gun barrel dropped and I shot, again and again.

His body collapsed and I shoved it away. Thunder vibrated in my ears as I gasped air into my lungs.

Orloff sprawled next to me, blood flowed from numerous holes. One bullet had entered through his chin. Gail. Where was Gail? My head spun. No way could I stand. I crawled around the desk. She lay on the floor, halfway between the desk and the door. Dear God, no. I crawled to her. She lay on her side. Beneath her right breast a red stain spread, like a Rorschach blob. All I could see in the blob was sick despair. I touched her shoulder. "Gail."

She moaned.

With trembling hands I felt for my cell phone, and found nothing. My panicked eyes scanned the room, stopped on a cell phone, mine?

I could have cared less. I forced myself to my feet, and with head spinning stumbled toward it. I dropped to my knees beside it, blinked my eyes, willed away the gray at the edges of my vision. No, you will not pass out. It took three tries for me to grab the phone, my head and my hands seemed disconnected. I punched in 9-1-1.

"911, what is your emergency?"

"Gun shot victims. I need help," I managed to get out.

"Sir? Sir, are you hurt?"

"Yes." The room tilted around me and I fell onto my side.

"Sir, stay with me. Help is on the way."

Stay with her? Where the hell did she think I was going? But then I had to call Darcie and Morgan. I hung up on 911. I hope that was allowed. Dear God, what was Darcie's number? My fogged brain registered the phone I held was mine. I pushed the button for Morgan.

"Garrett here."

"Morgan, St. James…dead…Gail shot.

Where are you?

"St.James'."

"We're on the way."

I crawled back to Gail's side, grasped her hand and waited.

*****

I heard the wail of multiple sirens, then feet pounded up the stairs. It seemed Morgan, Darcie, the paramedics and the Santa Barbara Sheriff's Department had all arrived at the same time. I tried to call out, be of some help, but my words sounded a whisper even to me.

Morgan came through the door first. "In here," he called.

A swarm of others followed, or maybe it just seemed that way.

Darcie dropped beside me. "What happened?"

"We came here. Gail thought things didn't look right. We found St. James. Orloff found us."

"You've been a busy boy," Morgan said.

The paramedics began working on Gail; blood pressure, heart, they shone a light into her eyes. One ripped her blouse apart. Throughout all of it she remained silent and my heart tried to pound out of my chest again. They brought a collapsible stretcher in.

"Let's get her out of here."

A young paramedic came to me. "How are you?"

"Head hurts a little."

He gave me a quick check over. "Slight concussion."

"He fit to answer some questions." The words came from a burly man wearing a sheriff's uniform. He stood behind Darcie.

They were taking Gail through the door. "I'm going with her." I tried to stand, would have fallen if Morgan hadn't grabbed me.

"Whoah, big guy," Morgan said.

"We've got three shooting victims here," the Sheriff said. "Two dead and one wounded. You need to answer some questions."

"I'll answer," I said. "Right after I know Gail's alright."

"Lee," Darcie said. "Can it wait until we get to the hospital? Duke's not going anywhere."

The Sheriff looked from me to her. I'd give him about another ten seconds to make up his mind, and then I was following Gail.

"I won't let him out of my sight," Darcie said. "And he needs some medical care himself."

"Okay, to the hospital only. I'll be there within the hour to take your statement."

"Thank you," I said, as Morgan led me toward the study door.

*****

I paced the waiting room. Gail was in emergency surgery. The bullet had broken a rib, which had punctured her lung. She'd lost a lot of blood. Beside a headache and a few bruises, I was fine. Sheriff Lee Talbot had come to the waiting room. I'd given him my statement. I think it carried weight that Gail was FBI and Darcie a Santa Maria detective with whom he'd worked before. He'd left after only fifteen minutes, with my promise I'd come in tomorrow for a follow-up session.

Darcie and Morgan sat, watched me and held hands. After three attempts, they'd given up on getting me to join them.

Gail couldn't die. She just couldn't.

The surgeon came into the room. Morgan and Darcie stood, came to stand on each side of me.

"She's out of surgery. We removed the bullet, stabilized the lung. I'm optimistic. They've moved her to recovery. She's awake and responding well."

"Can I see her?" I said.

"Are you Duke?"

I nodded.

253

"She's asked for you." The surgeon turned away. Darcie gave my hand a quick squeeze, and then I followed him.

Gail lay in bed, hooked up to a bunch of machines. The sight made my stomach do a dive.

"Come on in," she said. "It looks a lot worse than it feels."

I walked to her, settled in the chair beside the bed.

"You okay?"

I reached to take her hand. It felt small and chilly inside of mine.

"I'll live."

"Orloff?"

"Dead."

She nodded and then yawned. "Whoah, this is some powerful stuff they've got running into my veins."

"You sleep if you want to. I'm not going anywhere."

Gail smiled. "I love you Jonathon Wayne Cummins."

She said it so softly I wasn't sure I'd heard right. "What did you say?"

Her eyes closed.

"Gail?"

A nurse came in. "She needs to sleep now. Why don't you come back in an hour?"

Hell no, I wanted to shout. She just said she loved me, but I let her hustle me out instead.

Back in the waiting room, I hugged Gail's words close. "She's sleeping. I've been kicked out for an hour."

"Great," Morgan said. "Let's grab some coffee, maybe a bit to eat."

I started to say I wasn't hungry, but then my loud stomach rumble said I'd be lying. I followed Darcie and Morgan to the cafeteria-style eating area. I glanced at the clock more than once as I selected a tuna fish sandwich, chips and a cup of coffee.

At the table I listened as Darcie and Morgan rehashed the events the Lear jet crash had set in motion. Between each swallow, I glanced at the clock whose damned hands seemed frozen in place.

"Called Rick, told him about St. James' letter," Morgan said. "He thanked me."

"What about the helmet," Darcie asked.

"He's going to see if he can find Hathaway's family, offer it to them."

They talked more about El Rios and Santa Maria. I was only about half listening. Darcie had started talking about Vegas when I blurted, "Gail said she loved me. Well, at least I think she said it. Then she went to sleep and the nurse kicked me out."

They both went silent and stared at me. Then Darcie pushed back her chair. "Come on. It's close enough to an hour."

It had actually been only thirty-five minutes.

"If she's awake you go in," Darcie said. "If she's still asleep, then you wait."

I looked into Gail's room. She sat up in bed, staring toward the window.

"Hey, sleeping beauty," I said.

She waved me toward her. "Sorry about dozing off on you. That stuff they gave me really messed with my head. I didn't say anything stupid, did I?"

I captured her hand with mine, looked down into her face. Had it been the drugs talking? She didn't seem to remember telling me she loved me. "Everything you said made perfect sense."

"When Orloff had us," Gail said. "It scared me to death. I've been in tough spots before, but this was different."

I nodded, settled in the chair beside the bed. "A first for me, at least I think it is."

Her fingers tightened around mine. "Do you want to know why it was different?"

I found I could do nothing but nod.

"You," Gail said. "The thought of you getting killed, nearly killed me before Orloff could." She laughed, but it came out shaky. "I meant what I said, Duke."

"What?" I pushed the word through my dry lips.

"I love you."

Her words were the keystone, and the tension inside of me crumbled. "And I love you, Agent Gail Crane of the FBI." I leaned forward and kissed her.

"I'm damned glad that's settled," Morgan said from the doorway. He and Darcie sauntered in.

Darcie continued straight to Gail's bedside. "You've got six months to be back on your feet. You still want to be my Maid of Honor, right?"

"I do," Gail said.

Morgan laughed. "Those are going to be my words and I've waited long enough to be able to say them."

"Six months?" I said. "Then you set the wedding date?"

Darcie nodded. "Six months from this day. We settled on it while waiting for Gail to come out of surgery. Now I just have to tell Mum and Da."

"And you," Morgan punched my arm. "You'll be my Best Man."

I felt a surge of pleasure. "Be proud to be." I gave Gail's hand a squeeze. "Six months. We'll both be there."

Six Months Later
Morgan Garrett

I WAITED FOR DARCIE to be walked up the aisle formed by rows of chairs in our back yard. I've lost count of the times someone has tried to kill me, but I'd never felt my legs shake like they did right now. The bright sun warmed the top of my head as I stared across the blur of faces. I didn't know half of these people, but the ones I cared most about were here and that's all that was important to me.

My gaze returned to the back patio doors. Still no Darcie. The organ music droned on. Duke stood beside me, Gail next to him, a space in between for my love to fill.

Good God, come on. It wouldn't be fitting for me to collapse in front of all of these witnesses. Then the music tempo changed and an expectant murmur rumbled through the guests. The patio doors opened, and Janey came out, escorted by Wes. They marched down the aisle. In front of me, they parted and Janey moved to stand beside Gail.

Jackie came through the doors next. In each hand she held a leash. Rainbow and Becky walked beside her. Against much resistance from her Mom, I knew the wedding rings were tied around the basset hounds' necks with ribbons. Darcie had won the battle on that one.

I held my breath as the three of them moved toward me. Janey stepped forward, took Becky's leash, while at the same time Wes moved to accept Rainbow's. I released my in held breath and then almost gasped again as the music changed to Mendelssohn's Wedding March. Darcie's mom had prevailed on that one. I swiveled my head to the patio doors. Darcie came out on her father's arm. She wore a frothy concoction of ivory lace and satin. I heard a release of delighted sighs from the guests. I couldn't take my gaze from her as she walked down the aisle toward me. You talk about tunnel vision,

nothing else existed.

Her father stopped beside me, patted her hand, then lifted it from his arms, and held it toward me. My fingers shook as I laced them with hers. My God, it was happening. It really was. Darcie smiled into my eyes, and we turned to face the minister.

The rest of the ceremony became a blur. The marriage vows were the traditional ones, all except the obey part, why bother to vow something that you wouldn't do, at least on Darcie's part. I did beam with pride as Becky and Rainbow stood stock still as the ribbons around their necks were untied and the wedding rings released into Janey and Wes' hands. From there they went to Duke and Gail, all a flawless execution. Then somehow Darcie was slipping a ring upon my finger, and I was slipping one on hers. I smiled into her face.

"I now pronounce you man and wife. You may kiss the bride."

I leaned in, took her lips with mine, then whispered for her ears only. "About damned time."

The minister placed a hand on our shoulders, turned us around. "May I introduce you to Mr. and Mrs. Morgan Garrett."

Almost as one the guests rose to their feet, clapping. Beside us, Rainbow and Becky joined in with their distinctive a-r-o-o-s. I pulled my bride tighter against me. Until death do us part, that was more than alright with me.

ABOUT THE AUTHORS

Barbara M. Hodges lives on the central coast of California with her husband Jeff, two basset hounds, Ophelia and Hamlet, as well as a sassy ginger striped feline, Wallace.

Barbara is a big NASCAR fan as well as a decorative painter.

Website: barbaramhodges.com
Blog: http://barbhodges.blogspot.com/
Facebook: http://www.facebook.com/barbara.m.hodges

Randolph Tower is the writer of adventure and action thrillers and is retired from the United States Air Force. With more than 20,000 hours of flying time he is a lover of all things aviation. Mr. Tower lives on the central coast of California and enjoys the many golfing opportunities in that area.

Website: http://sites.google.com/site/randolphtower
Blog: http://randolphtoweronwritong.blogspot.com